FATE OF Magick

BELLA RAYNE

outskirts press

The Fate of Magick
All Rights Reserved.
Copyright © 2020 Bella Rayne
v3.0

This is a work of fiction. The events and characters described herein are imaginary and are not intended to refer to specific places or living persons. The opinions expressed in this manuscript are solely the opinions of the author and do not represent the opinions or thoughts of the publisher. The author has represented and warranted full ownership and/or legal right to publish all the materials in this book.

This book may not be reproduced, transmitted, or stored in whole or in part by any means, including graphic, electronic, or mechanical without the express written consent of the publisher except in the case of brief quotations embodied in critical articles and reviews.

Outskirts Press, Inc.
http://www.outskirtspress.com

ISBN: 978-1-9772-2169-8

Library of Congress Control Number: 2019918798

Cover Photo © 2020 Bella Rayne and gettysimages.com. All rights reserved - used with permission.

Outskirts Press and the "OP" logo are trademarks belonging to Outskirts Press, Inc.

PRINTED IN THE UNITED STATES OF AMERICA

*To my sons, you have my eternal love.
Thank you for all the love and support.*

Bella, thank you for allowing me to express my creativity and imagination through you into every story!

To all the fantastic people who helped me get my first book, Darkest Betrayals, around social media, I love you and appreciate your help. To the ones who helped me to see I could be so much more, thank you. Being cherished by you means more than you will ever know.

1

Dabney West is my name. I could never decide whether I wanted to be in dresses or jeans. The long red curls that hung down my back did not fit my personality. I had cute angel kisses painted all over my face. From the time I was small, I was drawn to the woods. My family didn't care for outings, so I went with my best friend and her family. They would take me boating, camping, or we would hang out at the park. I could feel a deep connection with the earth and the trees around. Sometimes I could see little fairies in the woods. I did not feel like I belonged anywhere but out in nature. Being out in the deepest part of a forest or park was an invitation to go within.

I was a strangely beautiful girl whose dreams were filled with all thing's goth. The darkness within me felt like home. I fantasized about the day when my body would be covered in tattoos. At times I considered coloring my red hair totally black. My parents named me after my mom's friend who saved her life when she was a teenager. Strange name for a girl, I will admit. The name never rang true with me, but I learned to live with it. I found out one day that I was adopted. Why they adopted me, I do not know. They acted more like an extended family with no real interest in who I was becoming.

I seem to thrive in the dark or the shadows; it felt comfortable for me to hideaway. Anytime I let my light shine, I was shut down, so it became easy for me to tuck away my true potential. Being the center of attention was excruciating, so I kept to myself. I would say that I am a loner and self-reliant. A bit of an enigma and a force to be reckoned with!

I was having weird dreams and feeling a connection to a place I did not know. For a moment it seemed like something strange was waking up within me. My neighbor was helping me with yoga and meditation. I was picking up on something I didn't understand. James called it intuition. I felt like I was being followed and watched. I don't know by who, but it was eerie.

I got a letter of acceptance from a college across the country. Because of my family's finances, I would qualify for all sorts of loans. That night we had a huge blowup over me moving away for college. They wanted me to get a full-time job instead. I stormed out of the house filled with rage. I was almost eighteen, and I knew they could not stop me from making something of my life. That night I stayed away longer than normal, when I returned home, what I found altered my life forever.

When I walked into the house, the television was still playing. This was unusual because my folks never waited up for me. The silence in the air was all-telling. There was a sickening smell that hung thickly in the air that I could not describe. Every hair on my body was on high alert. I walked into the living room and came around my mom's chair. I felt the unease and bile rising in my throat. My parents were in their chairs, eyes wide open. The look of shock on their faces hurt my head. It was a gruesome sight to behold. Their throats had been ripped out and scattered in front of them. They looked like they had been attacked with precision by a rabid animal. The high-pitched scream that exited my body still haunts me to this day.

I felt like I was in a tunnel and time had slowed down. I looked around and could see blood everywhere. How I missed the blood before, I do not know. The mix of copper, iron, and bodily fluids was the smell I could not describe when I first came in. There was this intense pheromone smell that I couldn't get out of my nostrils. The police questioned me that night. Mary's parents corroborated my alibi, making it airtight. I was never questioned again in my parents' gruesome murder. To this day, their deaths are unsolved and listed as a cold case, sitting on a shelf collecting dust at the local precinct.

Being almost eighteen kept me out of foster care. My folks left me everything in their will. I was surprised by this. There was enough time for me to decide what I was going to do with my life. The desire to go to college was not there anymore. Whatever I was going to do with my life had to be done with meaning. Even though Dan and Sandy weren't the best, I decided to honor them by living my life to the fullest. It took a year for the probate to go through, and then I took the money and left Savannah. Leaving James behind was going to take its toll on me. Next to Mary, he was the closest family I had, and he was my solid foundation of strength and support.

The move was something I had to do for myself. I found a job at a chemical plant and within five years I worked my way from the bottom up. My next promotion would be vice president of the company. I made good money, and the only thing I seemed to be lacking in was love. Everything changed the moment I saw him.

Rex showed up with one of his friends that worked in my department. He was macho and big. Covered in tattoos and rode a Harley. He was six foot five and was around two hundred and sixty pounds of pure muscle. He was blond and tan. The dimple in his chin gave me butterflies in my belly, possibly because he looked a lot like Kirk Douglas when he was younger. I don't know where my attraction for big men came from, considering Dan was a pipsqueak of a man.

It didn't take long before we were spending every day together. It was love at first sight. He was everything I wasn't. The opposites attract thing worked for a while. He loved riding motorcycles and hanging out with his friends drinking. I didn't realize at first that there was no real relationship connection. I didn't notice because I never needed it before. Growing up with Dan and Sandy, I had to be everything to myself or I would drown in the lack of affection and attention I wasn't receiving.

Rex and I were great in bed, and he was the first man I ever loved. I was established in my job, and he was where he wanted to be. Little did I know that there were going to be a few things changing in my life.

When I moved to my new town, I immediately went looking for the closest park or wooded area. Grounding myself and going within was what I craved the most. I found myself in the forest in a place called the Heart of the Godz. A strange name, RIGHT? There was a myth about this place, but I never took the time to read the plaque. I would rather spend my time exploring. The Heart seemed to spread out for miles. Each time I went, I found myself on a new trailhead leading deeper into The Heart, bringing one adventure after another on my days off. The trees were so old and outrageously large that I would say they were ancient. I could always hear water, but its source was hidden. The foliage was bigger and brighter and unfamiliar to me.

The most delicious smell of sweet warm pine always seemed to surround me when I would take specific pathways. When Rex and I fell in love and got married, I had to lessen my time in the forest, because he didn't like to go. I was always a bit happier when he had to work the weekends because that meant I could go off on an adventure of my own in the Heart of the Godz. After a while we drifted away from each other. Rex was either working on the oil rigs or working out. I wanted to be in the forest or working my way to the top. There wasn't any time for the two of us to build something incredible together. It wasn't anyone's fault. It wasn't meant to be.

It had been a month since I visited The Heart. My next day off, I went for a hike and I was totally stoked to get out in nature and see what The Heart had in store for me. I took a beautiful three-mile hike to a destination that held a deep canyon waterfall surrounded with bright-red bushes. I knew it was time to head back before it got too late. I came around a rock not too far from my SUV when I noticed some peculiar behavior. It took a moment for my brain to register what it was seeing. My company was dumping toxic waste into some deep caverns on the outskirts of The Heart. I was sickened, to say the least. I took pictures and a video.

I oversaw the toxic removal at my company. How could this be happening? I was shaken to my core. Who from my company gave the orders to do this and why? Would I be held accountable? I felt sick to my stomach and a severe headache was beginning to surface. I could not think straight as I heard the core of The Heart screaming at me to do something.

Unfortunately, the truck drivers saw me and reported me to the big boss, Mr. Dean. When I showed up to work on Monday, I was called into his office. I was offered ten million dollars to keep my mouth shut and to give them the photos and video I had taken. They gave me a week to decide what I wanted to do. It was terrifying because I was being watched that whole time.

When I went in to work the following Monday, I was pulled into the office once again. I told them that I could not accept their money, although ten million dollars would have been sweet. I was fired on the spot for unethical conduct. They were trying to frame me for dumping the toxic waste. What they didn't know was that I made copies of everything when they were not looking.

Saying goodbye to the friends I had made at the company was bittersweet. Most of them would not talk to me because someone had started a rumor about why I was fired. This made it that much easier to say goodbye. I took the information with me and made several copies and hid them. I made sure certain people would get them if something happened to me. They didn't expect me to do that. I felt like it was my insurance policy should they ever try to come after me. Knowing that I had this security blanket helped me to feel protected.

Rex and I were finalizing our divorce. I didn't belong in this town anymore. I made the decision to move a few hours away to a new city and a fresh start where no one knew me. I found a beautiful condo surrounded by people and I bought it. I missed Rex and wished things had worked out between us. The divorce left me broken and alone, especially after all I had been dealing with from my last job. I took some time to pull myself together.

For some reason, when I left, they gave me a year's salary severance package, and with the divorce settlement coming in, it gave me some time to figure out what I wanted to do with my life now. After purchasing the condo, I knew it was time to reconsider my career choices. It was time to look at the hobbies in my life I enjoyed. The one thing that stuck out most in my mind was writing. I dabbled in school and loved to journal. I didn't always want to be a writer. I never saw myself as being an author or even thought I would publish a book. Through pen, paper, ink, and many hours spent out on my balcony came the story of a lifetime.

2

When I finished my first novel, I was terrified. The prospect of putting myself out there was terrifying, especially after all the things I went through with my old company. It was as if something terrible would happen if the world read my book. I cannot tell you why I was afraid. It was a deep knowing that I could not shake. I kept telling myself that it was time for me to shine. My next stop was to introduce myself to Twitter, and as a loner, this was agonizing for me. It was time I met some like-minded people. I wasn't sure how the Twitter world would receive me.

When you write about the paranormal, it seems to bring out the worst in some people. It is not just the paranormal, but the unknown I enjoy! One day I would love to write about aliens or beings from other planets and galaxies. I just seem to be drawn to them.

It did not take long to get familiar with people on Twitter. I have come to know so many mysterious, funny people. It is so much fun when we share silly GIFs with each other. There is a truth that resides there that is painstakingly beautiful. We just want to be accepted for who we are and somehow, we find that on Twitter. We have all been able to find our tribes of people that help us to feel like home. It is incredible to watch all the love that flows around interweaving itself through tweets and gifs. Beautiful people being open and free as a hummingbird going from one flower to another. They always seem to make me smile. Sometimes I laugh so hard I cry, and others I just cry. There is so much love and support to be found. How is it that complete strangers all over the world want to know what kind of food we like or the type of books we love?

I met Matt, an incredible man of mystery. He makes me feel so welcome and appreciated. I know they say that you should be careful on Twitter and who you talk to, but he seemed to be a beautiful soul. I didn't know if he would like to be called that, but that was how I felt. We lived galaxies away from each other, it seemed, and yet he was right here in my space. Talk about time collapsing! There was so much of him that I did not know, and maybe it was better to keep it that way. Perhaps it was all just a fantasy!

I was on Twitter for a couple of months when I started noticing that some of my followers' pages resembled other pages. Were they the same person? Or similar tastes? I got close to a few people and enjoyed the daily interaction. Lately one by one even though we were still following each other, they didn't seem to be logging on. It was like they had disappeared.

I've been receiving weird DMs from a few of my followers. They were asking me questions that seemed out of character even for them. Things were getting personal, and those that I would talk to for help were unreachable. I didn't know where to look for them. Whatever was going on, I was hooked! Maybe I would talk to some of the people we shared groups with.

My plans went to hell quickly when a mysterious package showed up at my house. The box was from one of my indie authors that has followed me on Twitter. How did they get my address? Spooky! I decided to let the box sit for a while. I needed some advice and the only one I knew who could give that to me was Matt. I decided to send him a DM and see what he thought.

After waiting for an hour, I heard back from Matt and he felt it was probably some book giveaway I forgot about. I was still apprehensive about opening the box because it was bigger than usual and more substantial. I grabbed a knife and sliced down the center of the box to release the tape that was holding back what was contained within. I cautiously opened one flap and then the other. A big chunk of plastic bubble wrap was holding the product in place and the plastic was held down by a paperweight. The book was held tightly in place, so I had to be careful taking it out of the box. I didn't remember asking for this book or winning a giveaway, but I must have.

I picked up the book and investigated the front and back and slowly opened the front cover. The author had signed the inside of the book. I could see a hot-pink sticky note on the next page. Cautiously I turned the page over to reveal the sticky note underneath. In pencil was written, "Beware, they know who you are on Twitter."

There was no signature or anything else. What did they mean? I was intrigued when I should have been scared for my life. I decided to look through the rest of the book in case there were other clues left for me. As I got to the middle of the book, individual letters were circled for several pages in pencil. I decided to write them down to see what the message was.

The letters (t h e r e) were circled on the first page scattered from top to bottom; (a r e) on the second page was only in the second paragraph; (p r o t e c t o r s) on the third page was in the last paragraph; (a m i d s t) on the fourth page was in a zigzag pattern; (t w i t t e r) on the fifth page was in a straight line from top to bottom.

I kept looking and there were no other messages that I could see. What a strange message to leave to someone. I wonder who the protectors were, and why would I need them? I mean I know the message said beware, but beware of who? If there were protectors, how long had they been watching me? I'd had a lot of trouble with my old job. What I didn't tell you is there had been several attempts made on my life since I turned down the money. I had been attacked physically and in other ways right before I moved away. I never told anyone because I wasn't thinking with a clear mind at that time. Going into hiding didn't even cross my mind. When I decided to write the book, I used a pen name, for my own comfort. I wonder if my old job had found me again?

I'd had a long day, and it was time to sit down with a glass of blackberry wine on the patio. My patio is a perfect place to watch the sunset every night. I ordered some Chinese food, which is my favorite: dumplings, wontons, egg rolls, ham fried rice, beef and broccoli, and chicken chow mein. I decided to bring the book outside with me and think about it. I was deep in thought when I heard a knock at the door. I swear I cleared six feet off my chair. Walking to the front door slowly with my heart pounding in my chest, I was grateful to have a peephole to look through. It was the Chinese delivery guy, who has been to my house once a week since I moved in. I opened the door with a big smile.

"Hey, Reggie, how are you doing tonight?"

"I am exhausted! The parking lot was full and so I had to park down the block."

"I know, it has been crazy out there lately for parking. Everyone is in town for the big boat show. Next time, call me when you leave the restaurant and I will meet you out front."

"That is okay, Dabney. The exercise does me good, and it is my job. Don't forget to open your fortune cookies. I brought you four. I know how much you like them."

I handed the money over to him and said goodbye. I don't know how, but he was my regular delivery guy. I walked into the kitchen and put the takeout bag on the counter. I gathered some napkins and chopsticks. Grabbing the containers of food, I headed out to the balcony. I loved the picnic table and umbrella I had out there. It wouldn't be dark for a bit, so there was no need for me to turn on the outside lights just yet.

Rex always hated Chinese takeout. As a single woman, I decided it was time for me to start enjoying Chinese food again. I could order it anytime I wanted to. I hadn't heard from Rex since the divorce. I was glad that we got the clean break that we did. We were together for five years, and it was weird that there was no connection there anymore. Well, enough reminiscing!

I grabbed my chopsticks and decided to dig into the beef and broccoli and ham fried rice. I poured myself another glass of wine. I decided to eat one of the fortune cookies with my food. I cracked it open and pulled out the small rectangular piece of paper slowly. It said, "When darkness has surrounded, watch for the message."

What the heck could that mean? Today was the strangest day, I swear. The chicken chow Mein and dumplings were calling me, so I set my message down. I'd always had a healthy metabolism and at five foot ten, I was a lean powerhouse. I worked out daily. It helped with my mental health and allowed me to decompress. I was enjoying the shape of my curves. Some might say I am sexy. With long red hair and electric green eyes, I looked a bit like a goddess faerie. I had long legs and a perfectly proportioned torso. I wouldn't say I had huge breasts, but they weren't small either.

There was this woman at the gym who I became quick friends with. We hung out together and enjoyed each other's company. Usually we would go out to the Jalisco restaurant down the road and have peach margaritas and an entrée of some kind. One night, she asked me over to her place. I had only been there one time before to drop off some mail of hers that got placed in my mailbox. You see, we lived in the same condo building. Ginger lived three condos down from mine. She moved in a week after I did. We started off with homemade margaritas and conversation. That was when she told me she was bisexual.

"Dabney, have you ever been with a woman?"

"No, I have not. No woman has ever asked me to be with her like that. I think I would be flattered if a beautiful sexy woman asked me to have sex with her."

"Do you mind?" she asked as she slid closer to me on the couch.

"Is that what you are asking me, Ginger?"

She never answered my question with words. She slid in real close and kissed me on the mouth and lingered there. Her soft lips and mouth tasted of peaches. She sat back. She seemed to be waiting for something. I wanted her to kiss me again. I leaned forward and kissed her back, except this time our tongues became entangled and did the subtle erotic dance that woke up my entire body to full electric. She ran her fingers through my hair and kissed my neck. She softly grazed my skin and trailed her finger gently down my abdomen. There was not much between me and her.

    I was wearing a lightweight tank top and Daisy Duke shorts. I could feel my nipples harden against the flimsy bra I had selected to wear with this tank top. She sat up and watched me as she slid her hand down inside my shorts. I could hardly breathe. I was so close to climaxing I felt like I was coming undone. I watched her watching me. I felt brazen, erotic, and mysterious. I felt alive. I felt myself run my tongue across my top lip slowly and seductively. I watched her blink as I knew this had turned her on. She decided to get me back by slowly rubbing her finger across the sensitive flesh between my thighs. Ginger took her hand out and my body ached for it to be back where it was. OMG! I was so turned on, but something was not right—what the hell!

    "Dabney, Dabney," I could hear being yelled at me.

    I snapped out of it. Who was yelling at me from down on the ground in my backyard?

    "Dabney," he yelled again.

    I looked down and it was the groundskeeper for all the condos. What did he think he was doing in my back yard?

    "What's up, Duke?"

    "Sorry about this, Dabney, but there has been a water leak today. I wanted to let you know that the plumbers would be here tomorrow to fix it. I tried knocking on your door several times. No one answered, and I know how much you like watching the sunset."

    "I appreciate that, Duke. Thanks!"

    By the time I got done daydreaming about Ginger and talking to Duke, my food was cold. The sun had set, and it was getting dark. I decided to go in and get my lightweight sweater with The Pumpkin King on the back. I loved the evening temperatures; they were perfect. I turned the lights off in the condo and decided to sit out in the dark. Plus, the light draws bugs, and who needs those when you are trying to sleep?

I loved watching the moon and the stars. Living in town didn't always make it easy to see them. It was as dark as midnight now. I could hear the neighbors playing their music. I didn't mind because they usually had it turned off by eleven p.m. I loved the song they were playing by Joel Vergel—"Samba e Amor." They were such a romantic couple. This song touched a part of my soul that I could not explain. I often thought of this song while chatting with Matt. I guess it couldn't hurt to think about him in such ways. Out of the corner of my eye, I was catching a weird glowing green light on my table. I looked over and my book had glow in the dark writing on the front cover. I picked it up, not sure if I wanted to know what message it had for me now. I was stumped even more when I saw Matt's Twitter handle written on the book with a thumbs up and a smiley face. WTF did that mean? So, let's see the messages so far were:

1-Beware, they know who you are on Twitter.
2-There are protectors amidst Twitter.
3-Matt's Twitter handle thumbs up and a smiley face.

I wonder if any of this had to do with some of my followers not showing up on Twitter? What did Reggie the Chinese takeout delivery guy have to do with this? I was too tired to figure this out. I yawned and realized it was time for bed. Maybe I would dream of Ginger tonight, or Matt might show up. I guess he could look however I imagined him, considering his looks were a mystery.

I crawled into bed sometime after eleven. I felt melancholy tonight. I turned off the light and opened my bedroom window. A cool breeze with the smell of rain rolled in and over me. I rolled onto my side and felt the tears welling up, and the release came when they rolled down my cheeks. It wasn't that I was lonely. I was enjoying being single. I missed having someone to share my bed with. I reckon daydreaming about Ginger earlier brought that up, and then Matt's name on the book didn't help at all. Really there was nothing there for Ginger and myself because she told me the night after our romantic encounter that she was moving back home and was getting married. I didn't rightly know what I felt about it, but I wasn't happy. Then there was Matt, whom I always seemed to reach out to. If I was honest with myself, Matt was just a fantasy. Was I so desperate that I would fall in love with someone who was probably imaginary? Lady Antebellum's song "Need You Now" was playing through my mind. What if Matt was some tattooed Harley rider like Rex? Hell, what if he didn't like tall redheads? There was no profile picture listed for me on Twitter because I was writing under a pen name and I wanted my privacy. I realized I would have to come out of my shell, but I was not ready for my identity to be known. For the moment, I would let the exhaustion carry me to sleep.

I dreamed of faraway places, of other galaxies and cosmos, and of written ancient languages I didn't understand. There were ancient symbols and lettering that I resonated with, but they did not look human. At one point I felt like something was being downloaded into me. I dreamed of a place with three moons and animals that were foreign to earth. At one point I felt like I was being guided somewhere when to my right a beautiful being stepped out of the shadows.

"I am Aseret Nwad, your guardian and more. I have watched over you your whole life. I know you are confused, Dabney. When the time is right, all will be known. You will understand who and what you are. Until then, be safe and watch your back. You will have those come into your life who are protectors. Others will step in who are not of your earth. BE CAREFUL and STAY STRONG!"

The being called Aseret Nwad wasn't speaking with its mouth. I was hearing this conversation happening in my mind. Before I could ask any questions, the guardian was gone. I was ripped out of my sleep with goosebumps all over my body. Well, that was an incredible message. What the hell do I do with that? I looked over and noticed that the notifications beacon was flashing on my phone. I was surprised I could see it, considering I always put it in my top drawer while it is on the battery charger. I was awake for now, so I was going to see who was reaching out. Checking all my emails, I noticed there were a few messages from some people I just followed on Twitter. The one I really wanted to open was the one from Matt. I enjoyed talking to him. He made me feel good about myself. I would open the other direct messages first.

> @ 999reaper Hey gorgeous, what are you wearing?

I have found with messages like this, it is best to delete them.

> @ 543exitman What's cooking toots?

Delete

> @ 333mysterymachina I bet you taste good.

Good grief, don't these men know how to talk to women? Delete!

> @ 769Sexy~hotness Hey hottie, want to meet up sometime? It is me, Liz!

Delete

> @ exotic8mysterious Hey sunshine! ☺

> @ Author3perks3me3up I was hoping to hear from you today, Matt. I wanted to talk to you about some things, but I need to process them first. How have you been?

> @ exotic8mysterious I would love to talk to you some more. I am getting ready to head to work. Just email me when you are ready, and we can coordinate something.

> @ Author3perks3me3up I will do that thanks, Matt.

I decided I'd better log out of Twitter and crash for a bit longer. As I laid my head down on the pillow, I knew I would go right out. I was drifting into that in-between place when I heard the sliding glass door on my balcony slowly open. I felt my pulse quicken and my breath catch in my throat. Did I forget to lock the sliding glass door? Who would be coming into my house? The floorboards in the dining room creaked. I knew someone was in my house. Before I could think straight that person was already in my room.

"If I were you, I would be quiet and listen. If you try to run, I will kill you," the intruder said in a deep raspy voice.

I sat fully up in bed, hoping to catch my bearings. I was running scenarios over in my mind, figuring out what my next move would be when I felt him slide in behind me and press something sharp into my neck. I didn't want to show him I was scared, so I slowed my breathing down and relaxed. He was a big man. I knew I did not stand a chance trying to run from him. He would overpower me before I took one step.

"What do you want?" I asked softly.

He sniffed my hair. I could tell he was aroused, from his erection pressing hard against my back. He had his left arm wrapped around me, pinning me down and his right hand held the knife to my neck. He pushed me forward with his chest and slowly ran his tongue up my back and the back of my ears.

"I knew you would taste good," he said in a hungered voice fevered with evil intent. "I could smell you a mile away."

His left hand reached out and started playing with my breast and pinching my nipple hard. I was barely keeping myself under control. I didn't want to feed his fever any more than I had to. He let his hand slowly crawl down my belly, and he grabbed my crotch.

"I am going to enjoy this more than I thought I would," he said as somebody started pounding on my front door. "Who the hell is that? Get rid of them. I am not done with you yet," he spewed at me as he shoved me forward.

His large hands sent me flying off the bed. Landing on my knees caused my nightgown to shift high on my hips. I was grateful I was wearing underwear. I could hear him making strange sounds behind me. I got to my feet and walked to the front door slowly and meticulously. My legs were wobbly, and the whole situation was threatening to crash down upon my senses. I sure hoped that whoever is at the front door could help me. I looked through the peephole and turned my deadbolt open.

"Can I help you?" I said to the man that I don't know by name, but I recognized him from Condo Three.

"Hi, I am Mark Mathias from Condo Three. I want you to know I called 9-1-1 and reported seeing a man climbing up onto your balcony. I hope everything is okay?" he asked as he noticed the fear in my eyes and the blood running down my neck. He grabbed me by the arm and yanked me through the door. He pushed me up against the wall and pulled out a gun. "I am going back in. I want you to stay right here."

It seemed like an eternity before the police officers showed up. Mark came back out informing me that my home was clear and whoever had been there was gone. I was relieved, but I was shaking so bad I knew that I was going into a massive panic attack. There was no trace of him anywhere, no DNA, no hair, nothing. I tried to explain to the officer that he had a chemical, almost sterile smell to him. I found out that he had jimmied the lock on my balcony door. What I couldn't figure out was how he got on my balcony. There were no ladders or trees for him to climb. It was a full story drop to the ground.

The cut on my neck was deep but not life-threatening. The paramedic put a couple of butterfly bandages on it and recommended that I go to the ER now or my doctor in the morning. I heard the officer questioning Mark about how he knew I was in trouble.

"I went out on my balcony to get some fresh air and saw movement out of the corner of my eye. I looked over and saw someone working the lock and getting the door open. I went in and put a shirt on, grabbed my gun and called 9-1-1, and headed this direction," he said while he stared at me. "Are you sure you don't need to go to the ER?" He asked as he grabbed the blanket off the back of the couch and slid it around my shoulders.

"No, I am okay," I said to him in a shaky voice. "I am keeping this panic attack at bay," I said as I slowly slid down on to the couch. I had no more strength in my legs. I truly felt like I was going to pass out. Wouldn't that be unfortunate to pass out in front of the hot neighbor? They all left except Mark.

"If you want, I can stay here with you for the rest of the evening so you can get some sleep."

"Normally I would say no, but that would be so kind of you, Mark."

"How about we sit here and talk for a bit, and if you feel like sleeping you can either do it here on the couch or in your bed?"

"I was wondering how you would feel about us going to your place instead. I feel like I need a place to regroup, and right now I cannot get what happened out of my head."

"If you feel comfortable with that. What is your name, by the way? We have never been properly introduced."

"I am so sorry. My name is Dabney Vaughn!"

"If you think you would be comfortable at my place, Dabney, then I would love to have you come over. Do you want to grab some clothes or slip into something more comfortable?" he asked in a gentle tone.

"I will go put a bag together and I will change my clothes. I will be right back. I am going to take a quick shower to get the smell of him off me. I know that it is not really there, but more of an energetic feeling," I said as I walked away, not waiting for a reply.

I walked straight into the bathroom and started the shower. I turned the dial hot. I had this chill that I could not calm. It had nothing to do with temperature, but for some reason, hot water sounded good running down my body. I stripped my clothes off, not caring about the neighbor standing in the living room waiting for me. I just let the water run down my body. I did my centering exercises, and that was when the sobs took over. I was safe and I had survived. I sunk to the bottom of the shower and let the tears flow. I knew it was the best medicine I had available to me at that moment. I let the tears flow for what seemed an eternity. I must have been in there longer than I thought because I heard a light knock on the door.

"Dabney, are you okay? You have been in the shower for a long time. I want to make sure you are all right."

I wiped the tears away and stood up. I stepped out of the shower and reached to grab the towel off the sink. It was then that I realized I forgot to bring towels into the bathroom.

"I am okay, Mark. I will be out in a moment. I am going to get dressed."

"I will go wait for you in the living room. I am sorry I disturbed you."

What I wanted to do was reach out to Matt, but I knew he wouldn't be back on again until much later. One of these days, I had to talk that man into giving me his phone number. It was not like we were in a relationship or anything, but we did enjoy talking to each other. I got dressed and packed my bag of essential oils, lotions, crystals, and stones. I packed my favorite sweater and turned the light off. As I walked out of my room and headed down the hallway, I could hear Mark on the phone.

"She is doing all right. She took a shower, and I am taking her to my place. We need to do a better job keeping her safe. Can you imagine what would have happened to her if I had not been out on my balcony? I hear her coming. I will call you later," he said as he hung up the phone and turned to me.

"Who was that?"

"That was Detective Flye! Are you ready to go?"

"Yes, I am ready. Do you have any wine at your place, or should I bring mine?"

"I have dark ale beer. No wine. I don't care for it. Go ahead and bring yours."

We headed over to his place which was one condo before Gingers. I was grateful it was close. He had a meticulous home for a man. I suppose that sounded sexist. The strange thing was that his condo didn't look lived in. All the furniture was brand new but not sat in. There was an organization and cleanliness to his home that seemed fake. Maybe he had one hell of a housecleaner. He noticed me looking around.

"I work out of state and I am rarely home. The condo is just a place for me to touch base while I am in town. Go ahead and put your stuff down on the couch and I will show you around, so you know your way. It is very similar to yours, but I have had some work done and changed some things around."

I set my bag down on the couch and felt instantly at home. Why did Mark seem familiar? I followed him around and figured out where things were. He took me into the kitchen and poured me a glass of wine. He grabbed a beer and guided me back into the cozy living room. He turned on the fireplace, not for heat but for effect. He lowered the lights and let me have the whole couch to myself. He sat in his recliner and kicked his shoes off.

"Tell me about yourself, Dabney," he said as he lounged back in the recliner.

I could tell he was trying to make me feel as comfortable as possible. "Well, you know my name. I bought this condo after my divorce. I am a new author. He was going to hurt me. He told me he knew I would taste good," I whispered as the tears ran down my face. I realized then that my body was releasing all the pent-up fear I had from not only being assaulted when I was fifteen but everything that had happened with my job. I let the tears flow out of me. I was being purged of the old.

He didn't say anything; he just let me talk. I told him everything that happened and how it made me feel. He let me cry. I felt the couch give some.

"Dabney, I cannot take it anymore. Can I hold you?"

"Yes," I said as I leaned into him.

He held me for the longest time. He let me cry until there were no more tears. I sat up and away from him.

"Thank you, Mark. Thank you for saving me. Thank you for paying attention and helping me. Thank you for listening to me and letting me cry. We don't know each other, and yet you have been so supportive of me tonight."

"I am glad I could help. I have an idea. Anytime I cannot sleep I plug in a *Thin Man* movie. They are black and white and soothing for me. Do you want to give it a try, Dabney?"

I nodded my head yes. I laid back on the couch and snuggled into the warm cozy blanket. I allowed its comfort to surround me. He turned the movie on, and I enjoyed it. What I didn't tell him is that I also watch the *Thin Man* movies and I love them. I drank my wine and before I knew it, I was dozing off. I don't know how long I had dozed off for when Aseret Nwad appeared in my dreams again.

There will come a time Dabney when you will have to make a choice. Pay attention to all your surroundings. When the time is right you will be downloaded with the information you require to awaken fully. There are those trying to manipulate you into thinking their ways are the only way. I will slip information in at the time of the download, so you have the whole picture. I am not supposed to interfere but I feel it my duty to give you everything so you can make the decision that is right for you. The one who attacked you tonight is not of your realm. He eats flesh and you barely escaped his wrath. The one who rescued you is more than he seems. You will soon know who he is and why he is in your life. Trust your instincts, Dabney, and be discerning. Be observant and always pay attention. Soon you will know who you can trust and who you can't.

"Dabney, wake up," I heard as I was being shaken awake.

I opened my eyes and brought Mark down to my lips. It was slow, sexy, and delicious. He pulled away from me quickly.

"Whoa, Dabney. I cannot do that with you. I have been sanctioned to protect you. By the way, incredible kiss."

"What do you mean, you have been sanctioned? And by whom?"

"That is not something that I can tell you at this time but hopefully soon."

"I probably wouldn't understand tonight anyway. Why did you wake me up?"

"You had a fitful dream. I wanted to make sure you weren't dreaming about what happened earlier."

"She said you are more than you seem and that I will know why you are in my life."

"Who said that?"

"Aseret Nwad. She is some form of a guardian or magickal being. I met her earlier tonight. I have received a lot of weird messages. I don't know what to make of any of it."

"I am glad you were not dreaming of what happened tonight. We have got to figure out a way to keep you safe. Do you have any idea who this man was?"

"No, but something he said makes me think of a Twitter DM that I got tonight. The DM said *I bet you taste good* and he said *I knew you would taste good.* How could he find me? And is it the same person or just coincidence?"

"I don't believe in coincidences, Dabney. Why didn't you tell the officers this when they were here?"

"I just remembered it. I was pretty shaken up when they were here. I have had time to calm down."

"Well, we need to let them know as soon as possible. Do you still have the DMs, or did you delete them?"

"I deleted them, but there should still be a record in my email notifications. Aseret Nwad also said that the man who attacked me was not from this realm and that he is a flesh-eater. I am not even sure how I am supposed to process this information. I am going to have a drink of my wine and crash. I am on the edge of delirium."

"Good night, Dabney."

I woke up the next morning to Mark making breakfast. I did not think I could eat, but my stomach started to growl. So many different delicious aromas floating around in the air. French toast, eggs, coffee, bacon, sausage, and homemade maple syrup.

I went to the bathroom and took a shower. I got dressed in my yoga clothes. I sat on the living room floor and began my morning meditations to connect and center myself. I was deep in meditation when I heard Mark walk in. When he realized what I was doing, I heard him turn around and head back to the kitchen. I finished what I was doing and took a deep breath. I walked into the kitchen and sat at the counter next to Mark. He had already dished me up a plate and poured me coffee.

"This looks delicious, Mark, thanks."

"It is my pleasure. You don't have to eat it all. I wasn't sure what you liked, so I gave you everything."

"I can see that," I said as I giggled. "I don't normally eat too heavy of a breakfast, but I will have some of each. After we are done, I need to get back to my condo and do some cleansing work on the energy inside. I want to clean up and figure out what else I need to do."

"If you want, I will come with you. I think you should also call Detective Flye today and tell him about the Twitter DM. You need to be careful, Dabney, about what type of information you give out to people on there. You don't know these people, and some of them can be dangerous."

"I am just starting to understand that, Mark. I will head over to my place by myself. I will give you my phone number and we can keep in contact. Thanks for last night and the breakfast."

I gathered my stuff up and headed back to my place. I wanted to get everything cleaned. I needed to work on my new book. Maybe it would take my mind off of everything. As I walked up to my front door, I noticed that there was a strange aura around the door casing and trim. I could see symbols lightly written all over the door frame and the door itself. I felt welcomed into my home and I felt safe. The same aura was all over the balcony on the outside to the inside and all over the windows. Every doorway contained the same. Somebody had come into my home and done this. Why wasn't I afraid at that prospect? I turned to walk into the kitchen when I noticed her. She was filmy and pearlescent. She had energy wings that held her in place. Her hair was the color of the rainbow but with more colors than I have ever imagined. She was lean and trim and upon her torso she had jeweled chains attached at her belly button and her breasts. She was quite lovely. She proceeded to talk to me in my mind.

I am Dominya. I have protected your home and your being. Your mode of travel has been protected as well. My daughter, I have long awaited your return. When I gave you up to save you when you were just a baby, it broke my heart. You were put into a home where your light would inevitably be snuffed. I hated that for you, but it was better than your death as an infant. You have powers beyond belief. When the time comes for the download, I will add in your abilities and your ancient training so you will be prepared for your battle. You are not of this world, which is why you never felt like you fit in. By reading your book, I can see that you remember some of our ways without having to download you. No, that is not your imagination. What you write about is real. There will come a day soon when all will be revealed to you. There are those you can trust and those you cannot. You must make the decision based on your heart and love. We need you, my dear. Our world depends on your success. If you make the wrong choice, we will be doomed to a life of slavery.

This being came closer to me and touched my face. I couldn't help but feel at home with her.

When the time comes, Dabney, when it is all said and done you will be given a choice of whether you come home with your family or stay here. I must go now. I have been gone too long and they will know that I have left. We aren't allowed to help you with this decision. I want you to know you aren't alone, but you are the only one who can save us. I love you, my dear girl.

As she shimmered away, she blew me a kiss. Well, that was incredibly confusing and life-altering in the same moment. It is funny, all these people saying they cannot help me, yet they are. I wonder if they know what each other is doing. I had no clue what this would mean for me. In the meantime, everything I thought I knew became distorted. What was real and what wasn't?

3

It had been a few weeks since the attack. I had not heard back from Matt since before the break-in. I told him what happened but never heard back from him. Mark was becoming even more of an enigma in my life. I had not heard anything back from Detective Flye since that night. It felt like everything was being swept under the rug. The man, or whatever he was, had not tried anything since that night. Everything has seemed to settle down and this last month had gone by quickly. I hadn't heard anything from my guardian or from the woman who claimed to be my mother.

I seemed to be floundering since the attack. I could not write and the commentary in my head took up precious moments in my day. A month had gone by since I stayed the night at Mark's place. We did not talk after that. He went out of his way to ignore me. I could not get my head in the game. The question of who I was would not leave my thoughts. I felt no different other than knowing certain things and that was it. I was isolating myself and I was afraid to go out. Today was the day that ended that. No more was I going to put my life on hold for anything or anyone. If someone was out to get me, then by God let them come.

I headed out, more cautious and curious than before. I was in full observational mode as I drove through town. A month was too long to be away from the gym. It was hard going there without Ginger being there. Life was going on, and it was time I caught up and lived mine. After the gym, I went to the grocery store and stocked up on some staples and some goodies. Having my groceries delivered for a month was nice, but it was good for me to be social again. I took the groceries home and put them away. I sat down at the kitchen counter and found myself bored. I decided I would take myself out to dinner tonight. It was time for me to reclaim my favorite restaurant.

I decided to eat at the bar. I ordered my regular peach margarita. The chips and salsa were delicious. I took my phone with me and checked my Twitter, hoping that Matt would reach out. No DMs, which I suppose was a good thing, but it hurt that Matt was so out of touch with me. I hoped everything was okay with him. My entrée tonight was something new for me—pollo fundido, grilled chicken with cheese wrapped in a tortilla smothered in a cream sauce. I had them add sautéed onions and green peppers as well. It smelled delicious and divine. I took a picture of my food and I tweeted it. I felt like I was safe enough to do that. I didn't realize my GPS was on and when I posted from my phone, it gave my location.

My Twitter notifications started sounding off right and left. Wow, people must be fascinated in what I had to eat tonight. It was, after all, the best meal I'd had in a long time. I decided to check them out which gave me plenty of time to have another margarita. It was a good thing I lived so close to this place. I could walk home and come back later for my car. I was shocked to see fifty-plus notifications in a span of five minutes. What surprised me more was the three DMs. I wasn't sure I wanted to click on them, but curiosity won this time.

> @ exotic8mysterious What the hell do you think you are doing posting where you are eating tonight?

Wow, the nerve of this guy, thinking he can reprimand me. I am an adult, after all—who the hell does he think he is?

> @ Author3perks3me3up What's up Matt?

@ exotic8mysterious I asked you a question. You know it is not safe for you to be giving out your information like that. Do you realize it posted your GPS?

@ Author3perks3me3up I didn't think you cared, Matt. I haven't heard from you in quite a while. I suppose I wanted to show everyone that I was enjoying myself for the first time in a month. What could it hurt anyway?

@ exotic8mysterious Your location is easy to find. Plus, it has the restaurant's logo all over the pictures you posted. After what happened to you a month ago, how can you be so sloppy?

@ Author3perks3me3up That guy already knows where I live. Look, I don't want to talk about this with you. I haven't heard from you in a month and now you are trying to be protective. Leave me alone, Matt. Don't DM me again.

@ exotic8mysterious I haven't been in contact with you because I have been out of the area for work. I was in silent mode for the top secret mission I was on. I am sorry you don't want me to DM you anymore but if you should need to talk or you are in trouble, please reach out to me.

> @ Author3perks3me3up I will do that, Matt. Night!

This whole conversation made me sick to my stomach. The walk home should do me some good. It was only two blocks to my condo. I headed out the door and started walking. The scent of lilacs in the air made the evening lovely. You could hear crickets and a slight rustling of the leaves on the trees from the light breeze. I felt my back pocket vibrate from a notification coming through on my cell phone. I wondered who that could be. It looked like I have two DMs.

> @ 666Boneznblood Do you remember me? I bet you still taste as good as you did that night!

I damn near dropped my phone on the asphalt as I was about to cross the street to the condo parking lot.

> @ Author3perks3me3up Who is this and what do you want?

> @ 666Boneznblood Don't play coy with me, girly. I know you remember me grabbing your crotch and pinching your nipples. I bet you can still smell where I licked your back. Maybe you even enjoy where my erection was tapping you on the back. I sure enjoyed the smell and taste of you. I think it is time for round two, don't you?

All I could think of doing was texting Mark. He was the closest to this situation.

"Mark, that person has gotten in touch with me again. I am crossing the condo parking lot now can you meet me out front?"

I rushed as fast as I could in hopes that Mark would reach out and meet me.

> @ 666Boneznblood Tsk, Tsk! Your attempts will not reach their destination. I have electronically blocked your calls and texts. When I get a hold of you, I am going to eat you in more ways than you could ever imagine. I will feast upon your bones and blood. Your flesh will be mine. What I do to you before that happens will redefine how you see your life before I take that life from you. You are mine, and when I am done with you, I will paint the room with your essence.

OMG! Who was this maniac? I started to run in hopes of making it to my condo before he reached me. I smelled him before I sensed him. He had this sickening, sterile smell to him that burned the inside of my nose and lungs. I was rushing to get to my threshold that was protected.

"Yes, run. It only makes me want you more. Do you really think you are going to get away from me?"

Before I could answer, he sent me flying across the sidewalk. I hit my head on the curb. I saw something coming at me and then I blacked out. I don't know how long I was out or where I was. The sounds in the room I was in did not sound familiar.

"I see you are awake. What do you think of your kill room?"

I looked around trying not to show him my fear. I felt quite a chill on my skin. I looked down and realized why. I was completely naked, and I was hung with my arms and legs spread and attached to something with what felt like zip ties. "Where are we?" I said in the fiercest voice I could muster.

"You are in the basement part of your condo. It looks like it has never been used. Perfect place for me to take my time with you, and no one will hear you when you scream."

"How did you find me?"

"I know where you live; don't be daft! I have been doing other things and taking care of other problems for the boss. When you posted where you were, I knew it was meant to be."

"I don't understand why you have chosen me. I don't know who you are."

"The boss chose you. Let's say I carry out contracts for him. You have been on my list for a while, but I couldn't find you after you moved. He ordered you to be killed. He doesn't really know what I am. He thinks I am a human who enjoys killing. I like the taste of flesh; it is my nature. He doesn't care how I complete my contract, only that it is done."

"Who is your boss?"

"Why it is your old boss, Mr. Dean. He has become concerned since you have taken up writing that you might become a problem for him. He wants you removed before you become one. He was ready to leave you alone until you showed up on Twitter and you were advertising your book."

"I used a pen name and have not provided an author pic. How could he know it was me?"

"We have been keeping an eye on your friends. Your little love buddy Ginger spilled everything to us. She didn't know who we were, so we didn't have to hurt her. Now it is time to get started. Where do we start?"

"You don't have to do this. I won't say anything, and I haven't said anything to anyone. Please don't do this. Please!"

"I like you, but your begging will do you no good, Dabney. I have already tasted you and I cannot go back," he said as he walked toward me.

He was a handsome man-beast, but he was creepy. So ruggedly handsome, and his etched features were mind-blowing. He was covered in strange tattoos I had never seen before. They reminded me of the ancient language in my dreams. He was strong and was built like a tank. He had jet-black hair and ruby-colored eyes. He stood six foot five and was pure lean muscle. I tried not to stare too much because he was standing in front of me naked. His arousal was heavy and thick. OMG, what was I in for?

"Let's flip you around, and we will start at the back."

He seemed to enjoy wrapping his hands in my hair and yanking my head back. He took his time running his hands all over me. I was covered in goosebumps, and my whole body was on high alert. I could feel the primal instincts flaring within me. "Please don't do this."

He didn't seem to hear me. The sounds in his chest were becoming more feral by the minute. His fingers seemed to transform, and they became longer, and his nails were sharper. He just seemed to be caressing me. Nothing more than that. Maybe I misunderstood him, and he was trying to scare me. This was my last thought before a scream tore out of me so loud and so brutal that it hurt my own ears to hear it. It felt like he had pierced my back and slid a hook in of some kind. I felt something warm and wet running down my legs. It didn't take long before I realized my bladder had emptied.

"You scream all you want to. I told you, no one is going to hear you."

He walked away and I could hear him fumbling through a toolbox. He must have found what he wanted, because he was walking back toward me. He bent down on his knees and was at my butt level. He put his hands on both of my thighs and thrust his tongue into my crevice, swirling his tongue all around teasing with every flick. He licked up and down and made disgusting slurping sounds. His tongue slithered inside of me. He was doing things to me that I didn't know could happen. I could feel myself starting to shiver and shake. Just as he released his tongue, he dug his nails or claws into my right thigh and ripped backward. The pain was unreal. I felt like I was going to pass out, but then the pain was gone. He was slowly licking at the wound and it was healing it over.

He ran his claws up and down my legs, torso, buttocks, and

back, ripping and shredding and then healing them. Each time the screams intensified. He seemed to lose interest in my back when he flipped me around to face him. I held the strength in my heart that I knew I carried. I could not let this monster see me cry or know how terrified I really was.

"You are strong. I figured you would have passed out by now. When you pass out, it makes it more interesting. Do you see this?" he says pointing at his steam engine of an erection. "I am going to show you what if feels like."

I could feel myself gulp. This monster was hung like a horse. I had only been with a couple of men in my life, but neither was this big. I looked up at him and our eyes met. He moved forward and thrust his fingers inside of me, taking his time with each thrust.

"Nope, not wet enough. I will have to do something about that."

"If you think I am going to be turned on by you, you bastard, you have another thing coming. Don't you dare touch me with that monstrosity."

"I have my ways of getting people wet. Those ways can be gentle or brutal. Which do you prefer? We can either use your own juices or your blood."

"How do you expect me to be turned on by YOU? Especially since you have talked about murdering me and enjoying it since you found me."

"Well, you better find a way to get wet, or I am going to make you bleed."

"Then you better make me bleed you son of a bitch because I have no intention of being turned on by YOU." I could feel something stirring in me that I could not explain. On one level, it felt like my body was betraying me. On another, I felt consumed with rage. I had such horrific ideas go through my mind; it was more torturous than what he was doing. Something in me wanted to come out and play with him. I wanted to destroy him over and over until there was nothing left. How could I think such things?

He stood there looking at my defiance. He rolled his neck side to side, looking me over, and before I could figure out what he was doing, he slid his razor-sharp nail across my pubic bone. I could feel something warm and wet running down the cleft between my thighs. He reached down and soaked his finger with my blood and brought it to my lips. He rubbed it across my bottom lip and proceeded to lick it off me. I could hear my blood hitting the floor and I was starting to feel faint. He did not seem to care as he plunged his long soft velvety tongue into my mouth. It was like he was seeking a sweet delectable morsel with every taste. I swear that fucker went all the way down my throat. How was I even breathing at this point?

He started nibbling and biting my skin. I felt him draw blood a few times. He made it a point to make eye contact with me while he was licking my blood from his fingers. He had this eerie growl of pleasure that would sound each time my blood surged past his lips. I was on the brink of passing out. I could feel my eyes roll into the back of my head as I went under.

Dabney hang on! Help is on the way. Call him by his name. Startle him out of his current state. This is not his natural state, and he is being used and controlled. Call him Daegorth, flesh-eater from the Heart Tribe. Hurry, dear girl, before he implants inside of you.

I felt myself lean forward and whisper in his ear. "Daegorth, flesh-eater from the Heart Tribe."

He shoved me back hard against the wall. "What did you say, you little witch?"

"Daegorth, flesh-eater from the Heart Tribe," I conveyed through gritted teeth.

"Where did you hear that?" he said as he belted me across the face.

I felt my head jerk hard to the side and smack the concrete wall behind me. That was it. I was a goner for sure. I felt something vital inside of me snap. As I came back to consciousness, I could hear him pacing back and forth, questioning someone on the phone about how I would know his name. My right ear perked up as I could hear voices and footsteps headed my way. I looked up as he turned to look at me.

"I will find you again. Next time there will be no mercy. You are mine and no one can take that away from me," he spewed at me as he opened a weird blue energy hole in the concrete wall and stepped through. His destination looked familiar.

I felt like I was in shock. I didn't know who was coming for me, but I was relieved that they were there. I seemed to slide in and out of consciousness as they worked on my body. He healed it every time; why were they tugging and pulling at my body? Why did I feel like I was being tortured all over again?

"I think we have her all stitched up. Let's take her down slowly and lay her on the stretcher. Get those IV's inserted and get that blood flowing. Spread those warm blankets over her. She is in shock."

I could hear somehow in my unconscious state. "What is happening? Why does my body feel like it has been cut a thousand times with a claw hammer?" I could hear myself saying to space around me.

"Hello, dear. I am Matilda. My friends call me Tilly. Right now, let's get you to our safe house. We have a doctor on staff that can take care of all these wounds."

"What wounds? He healed them after he created them."

"He must have made more when you were unconscious. Rest, Dabney. We will talk later when you have been able to recover," I heard her say as I felt something being zapped into my neck. I slid under once again. It was for the best, I am sure. At least if I died, I wouldn't know it.

4

I didn't get to talk to Tilly until a week later. What I would come to find out would unsettle me for quite some time. I felt depressed and I could not seem to shake this funk I found myself in. I wasn't sure where I was. It seemed like a heavily protected facility. She came to visit me one day in my locked room, or what I called my cell. I was not free to come and go as I please. Even after a week there were people checking on me every couple of hours. I could hear the medical staff talking about me on the other side of the wall. Since my traumatic experience, my hearing had amplified by three times its normal range.

I could hear someone unlocking my door. As the door crept open, I was trying to think of a way to escape. Now wasn't the time; I was still so damaged.

"How are you today, Dabney? Do you remember me? I am Tilly from the other day. Are you ready to talk to us?"

I sat up in my bed and wrapped my arms around my knees. I felt like a little girl who was in trouble. "Yes, I remember you and I am doing okay. I am ready to talk if you have time."

"Do you know who the man was that attacked you?"

"He is the man who broke into my apartment a month or so ago. He found me again the night he hurt me. How did you know where I was?"

"When Matt saw you post stuff on Twitter, he immediately alerted his bosses. When you texted Mark, he was across town and called this in. You see, both men work for us. They infiltrated your life so they could protect you. The night you stayed at Mark's, he put a tracking chip in your cell phone. When you weren't in your apartment that night, we were able to follow the tracking device, and it led us to the stairwell leading into your basement. Your cell phone must have fallen out of your pocket. We found it there and progressed deeper into the basement. When he stepped away from you is when we decided to move things forward and help you out."

"How much did you see?"

"We barely got there as he was diving through some portal-looking thing. You have a lot of wounds on your body, Dabney, and they are not healing. We have a healing machine that we have put you in several times, but it is not healing you as well as it should. His saliva has created some type of flesh-eating bacteria inside of you. Even though it is not eating flesh anymore, it is not allowing what has been hurt to heal either. There was no evidence of sexual assault. Maybe we can find out who he is by testing some of your wounds for DNA."

"I doubt you will find out who he is. He is not human."

"What do you mean, he is not human?"

"He said he was going to feast on my flesh. That he loved the taste of it, which led me to believe he isn't from our world."

I didn't feel like explaining to them about my guardian and my supposed mother and their messages.

"Well, that would explain the bacteria we found all over your body. I am afraid a lot of your scars will not heal properly. You may need cosmetic surgery to fix them. I want to talk to you about who you think might be after you."

"He said he worked for Mr. Dean, my old boss."

"Why would your old boss hire someone to brutalize and murder you?"

"I found out the company I worked for was dumping toxic waste near a place they call the Heart of the Godz Forest. When I wouldn't accept the bribe, they fired me. For a while, they tried to set me up to take the fall. I kept them at bay by letting them know about the files I have prepared to send out to various people should anything happen to me. The monster said he was sent to get rid of me for his client. The client was going to leave me alone but then found out I was writing, and he felt intimidated by the fact that I might write something about them. I never signed any non-disclosure papers, so I can tell people what I saw. What I want to know is why it has taken me so long to heal?"

"Dabney, we have basically told you why you were not healing. What we didn't tell you is, he flayed you open from your back to front. By the wounds on your sides, he was just getting ready to rip you apart. If he had gone any deeper on your abdomen, he would have gutted you alive. He is quite skilled at what he does."

"Tilly, that isn't possible. I would feel him do things and then he would lick the wounds and they would feel better."

"There was something in his saliva that would take the pain away. He never healed you, Dabney. He just used his natural numbing agent to brutalize you even more. To be honest, dear girl, we don't know if the scars will ever heal. They should be healing more than they are. You are lucky to be alive. When we got to you, you were almost bled out. Do you know what made him stop?"

"Yes. I called him by his name. It seemed to piss him off that I knew it."

"How did you know his name, Dabney? What is it?"

"At one point I passed out. Then this voice came to me and told me to hold on because help was on its way. They told me to call him Daegorth, flesh-eater from the Heart Tribe. As soon as I did, something changed in him. He hit me hard and then made a phone call to someone. As he was pacing, I could hear all of you coming, and then he went through that portal. Strangely, the destination looked familiar to me. Although I cannot seem to remember how I know it, he did say he would be back for me and this time there would be no mercy. With everything that you just explained about the numbing agent he used, that would explain his last comment. Next time he won't use any."

"That clarifies why you don't think he is of this world. What I don't understand is how your boss has found someone like him. It looks like we are going into protection mode with you. I am sorry, Dabney, but your old life ended that night in the basement. You can do a will that leaves everything to your new identity, and we will provide legal services to sell everything you have and put it into a bank account."

"Whoa, wait a minute. Are you telling me I can no longer be me? What about my writing career? What about my condo? I love that place—well, I did. What about my friends? You cannot just rip me out of my life as if I don't exist anymore, Tilly."

"Well, it is that or he succeeds next time and your boss gets away with everything. Which would you prefer?"

"Alright, tell me how this would work."

"We need all the information you have about your old company dumping toxic waste. We will send in our attorney to help you make up a will. You can assign one of our team to be your executor, so they have power of attorney to sell all your stuff. They will be acting on your behalf. No one makes a move without your consent. You still maintain your power in all this, Dabney. You will be given a new identity. You will probably move around a lot for a little bit. You can either color your hair or wear wigs. We are sending you back to where you used to live. You will coordinate with the Bureau there. Any questions?"

"Can I go back and get a few of my things?"

"No, you cannot. I imagine he is watching your place. They all must believe you were killed that night. We will be working up your new identity in the next several hours. The attorney will be in after that identity is set up. You must dump your cell phone and all your contacts. We will add something to your author page about your death. Matt could do that, considering you were friends on Twitter. You will have to decide who you want to work with more—Mark Mathias or Matt Hilden. Ginger is no longer a part of the Bureau, so she won't be helpful."

"Ginger? Are you telling me she was working with all of you? Did you know that is how they found me? She told them about me. How long have you all been stalking me? Why were you watching me?"

"Ginger was let go because she allowed herself to get personally involved with you. We haven't been stalking you, Dabney. We have been watching your company for a long time. One of our oldest clients reported something going on in the Heart of the Godz Forest. We began looking into it, and that's when we found the discrepancies involving you. We weren't sure if you were the actual problem or in trouble and running. Ginger figured out that you were innocent. Before we fired her, she let us know that someone had gotten to her and that she had told them things about you. That is why we were in protection mode with you. Unfortunately, we were not expecting this Daegorth character."

I know deep down Ginger had no choice because Daegorth was so daunting. It still hurt knowing that she was in my life to spy on me. "Okay, how will you let people know I was murdered?"

"It will be in tomorrow's newspapers and all over the internet before the evening news. We have agents working everywhere. Matt will place the information on Twitter. Several of your followers work for the Bureau. We will get them to plaster it all over Twitter and to talk about their loss. You are never to get on Twitter with your new identity, Dabney. It is just too risky. If Daegorth really is from another place and he has access to portals, your path must remain invisible to him. I will get everything started for you. You look like you could use some alone time. When I get back, we will talk about how this all works."

I couldn't help but be disturbed by the state of my life right now. I felt strange inside my body. I guess that was to be expected after the trauma I experienced. I tried to look at my body, but every wound was covered by a waterproof bandage. I could feel all the stitches tugging and pulling my body back into place. It was for the best. I didn't think I could handle seeing and knowing what he did to me that night.

After meditating, I decided to take a nap. I was feeling more tired by the minute. Something seemed wrong inside of me. With all the damage, I imagine my body and mind were going through a transformation.

I knew that once my head hit the pillow, I would be out. Just as I was slipping into the in-between place, I felt the urge to throw up. My stomach hurt so bad. It felt like my stomach was boiling. Before another thought could form, a pain in my lower bowels hit me so hard, I felt like passing out. Making my way to the toilet seemed a feat not achievable but somehow, I made it there. I sat down in hopes that whatever was hurting me would soon pass. I was hit repeatedly with excruciating cramps. The sweat was running down my face and the middle of my back. It was accumulating quickly under my breasts. Maybe it was just everything that had happened, and it was my body's way of getting rid of the emotional trauma I suffered. The more intense the pain got, the stronger my hearing became. As the last pain shot through me and relief came, it was almost too much. I felt like I was in shock. What happened next is hard to explain.

I felt something move out of me and I felt better. It had no smell at all. When I wiped there was nothing there to clean but a little mucous. Interesting, but okay. I stood up and bent over to pull up my bottoms when something gushed out of my vagina. Once again, no smell, but a dark blood mass. It looks like shower number two for the day. As I stepped into the cold shower, my stomach hurt again, but not low. It was more in my stomach. A wave of nausea came over me as I reached down to wash the blood off my upper thighs. I took a deep breath and let it out slowly. That is when my jaws began to clench, and my mouth started producing extra saliva. Before I knew it, I was bent over vomiting this weird-colored mass, but it had no smell. I staggered out of the shower and headed for the mirror. Something seemed to shift when I vomited. I looked into the mirror and there was blood coming out of my ears, nose, and eyes. My cheekbones looked different. Dizziness was starting to consume my reality. The last thing I did was pull the emergency rope before I crumpled to the floor, smashing my face on the ground.

I could hear rushed urgency around me even in my state of unconsciousness. I could hear people talking loud and clear as if I was awake. It was not muffled like listening in a long tunnel, but bright and sharp. They seemed to be overwhelmed by whatever I expelled. Who was Tilly calling?

"We have a situation here, dammit. We have to find out if they know anything about this Daegorth, flesh-eater from the Heart Tribe."

"We cannot afford to bring them into this, Tilly. I know they left some stuff behind before; use that on her. If that doesn't work, we will proceed from there."

Who was Tilly talking to? I could hear what the other person was saying on the line. How? I could feel myself starting to come back to consciousness. I awoke with moans and groans on my lips.

"What happened here, Dabney?"

"All of that came out of every orifice and then I passed out. That is all I can tell you, other than it was excruciating. I don't hurt like I did, but I feel different inside. A transformation has started taking place on a cellular level. I cannot explain to you how I know that; I just do!"

"We need to get you to medical. Once there, we can determine what has happened. Our equipment is more advanced than anything in the world. We have a unit where we can place you and it will tell us everything that is going on in your body. When we figure out what this so-called transformation is; then we can determine how to help you better. Please be patient with us, Dabney. We have never seen anyone at your level before."

"What do you mean my level, Tilly?"

"There was another case that we have investigated that was like yours. We were not lucky enough to get to her before she died. When we reached her, she was—are you sure you want to hear this?"

"YES!"

"She was gutted, skinned, and what was left was a bloody mess. You survived that, Dabney, but we don't know what damage on a cellular level he inflicted on you."

I could feel myself getting sick all over again. Not the same way, but ill because of what she had suffered at his hands.

"Tilly, who were you talking to on the phone earlier in my cell?"

"How did you know I was talking on the phone with someone? You were unconscious."

"Ever since the attack, my hearing abilities have become amplified. I don't just hear physical words but what others are thinking. I feel like my senses are on high alert and more heightened. My sense of smell is out of this world."

"I will let the medical team know what you are experiencing. Shall we go see what they have to say?"

It wasn't a long journey to the medical unit. They made me lie flat on the gurney. They didn't want to take any chances with my body. From what I could gather from hearing them talk when they didn't know I was listening, the stuff that came out of me was like massive blood clots or something similar.

"Tilly, can I ask you a question about our discussion earlier? Why do I have to go back to my old town?"

She stopped the gurney and placed her hand upon mine. She looked me directly in the eyes. "Do you remember me telling you about the clients who know of your company dumping toxic waste? Well, they want to meet with you and protect you as much as possible. They want you to become part of their group."

"That is weird. Why would they want to help me or protect me? They don't even know me."

"The land that the Heart of the Godz Forest sits on is owned by them. They know of everyone who comes and goes. They feel like you understand the land and what it contains. They have cameras everywhere, so they have watched you over the years."

"If that is true, then why can't they go to the police with their allegations and their tapes?"

"I cannot explain that to you right now. One day, maybe. Until then, let us focus on getting you better."

The next several days consisted of them running tests and trying different modalities to heal me. What they didn't consider was my ability to heal myself, although that skill was not working as efficiently on the wounds that Daegorth inflicted on my body. My wounds seeped all day long. During this time, I was bombarded with making a will and setting up a trust for my new identity. I picked Mark to be my executor, and we met regularly until all my stuff was sold or given away. All my computers were gutted and donated. It was hard to see my face in the newspaper with information about how I was brutally murdered. I watched it on the news until I couldn't take it anymore. It was hard to see Rex come forward and talk about his loss. Even though his sentiments were sweet it irritated me that it took my death for him to speak his truth.

I finally met Matt one day. The sick part about it was that I already knew him. It was Reggie the Chinese food takeout guy. All I could do was shake my head in disbelief. Who else running around in my life was a Bureau plant?

Matt showed me his Twitter page and how he was vigilant about reporting my murder. He showed me this because he wanted me to see how much people cared. They also showed me my Twitter page and how many demented DMs had come forth since the reporting of my death. None of them looked like Daegorth.

It took a month to recuperate from the incident in my bathroom. It was time to go to medical and get my last bit of blood work done and to be put into the diagnosing/healing machine one last time. If I was in excellent health, then I could start moving on, which meant they would be finding me a safe house to live in until I reached my destination. I wasn't sure how I felt about driving back to where I once called home with Rex.

This time around I was able to walk into medical on my own two feet. I stepped quickly out of my loose clothing and got into the machine. There was a huge part of me that was ready to get out of this sterile place. On the other hand, I was terrified at what waited for me out there.

"Don't move a muscle, Dabney," Dr. Roxanne said in a loving voice.

I was motionless as the machine scanned every inch of me. It only took five minutes. As I lay there waiting for the device to go through its healing session, I could feel changes taking place deep inside of me. I heard someone gasp outside of the tube. People were bustling around the room in a frenzy. What the hell was going on with these people? I closed my eyes and tuned them out. I allowed the healing process to finish. What came next was fantastical. The door to the machine slid open. I was naked in front of everyone who decided to show up. They were all there.

"What is going on, and why are you all staring at me?" I demanded.

Matt handed me a mirror. Tilly gave me my clothes. Mark just stood there staring at me in awe. When I looked in the mirror, I was shocked to see my body. I could see everywhere Daegorth ripped me apart. Instead of scars, which was what I expected, there were thick, dark almost black rainbow-colored lines all over my body. I knew that I was no unicorn. WTF!

"Look at your face and hair, Dabney."

I investigated my reflection in the mirror. Instead of red, my hair was now as dark as a raven. When the light reflected off it, you could see all the colors of the rainbow. My eyes were now a violet spectrum color. My skin was no longer light-colored and freckled. All my freckles were gone, and I had a caramel color to my skin. How was this even possible?

I walked over to the full-length mirror and studied myself from top to bottom. I turned around, and using the mirror that Matt gave me, I inspected my back. Once again, I was able to see all the damage Daegorth had done to my body. The lines were dark rainbow colors, almost black. I could feel myself shaking inside and the sobs took me over. This was the first time I could look at my precious body. Even though the scars were the colors of the rainbow, I was still consumed by the brutality that Daegorth inflicted upon me.

"Dabney put your clothes on. We will leave you to your grief. I will be in my office when you are ready to come see me."

"Thanks, Tilly," I said as I held my clothes close to my body in comfort.

I could see Matt and Mark in deep conversation. I wasn't in the mood to perk up my hearing to listen to them. I was sure I would hear about it later. In the meantime, I needed to go for a lengthy walk.

I headed out to the track surrounding the building. I felt like I was in prison due to all the security and razor wire around and on the fences. The first question that popped into my head was *Am I becoming a superhuman? Does this mean I have to be a superhero? Who can handle that kind of pressure put on them?* I didn't want to tell Tilly, but I kept seeing little portals everywhere. Would they think I was off my rocker? Was I? It was time for the commentary to stop.

I decided to sit down on the grass next to the track. Sitting with my legs in the lotus position, I closed my eyes. I went deeper within, centering myself. The deeper I went, the louder the humming on the inside became. Then the words started to form. I could hear the grass growing and baby birds in their shells about to crack through into this world. I could hear and feel the surrounding energy. Some sounded like a buzz. Others came through as a hum. Many came through as snapping sounds. The hair on my body stood on end.

I could hear my heartbeat and the blood rushing through my veins and arteries. I could smell rain in the air and the manufacturing plant ten miles down the road as if it were right in front of me. I could feel Gaia alive below and around me. I could hear water in the water pipes and electricity flowing through the walls and into the sockets.

It was time I zoned everything else out and paid attention to what was going on inside of me. My mind wanted to take me back to the night with Daegorth. I kept fighting it, but it insisted. Maybe it was time to revisit what happened. I could feel how scared I was. Being exposed in front of him like that was humiliating. I felt so vulnerable and raw. I didn't just feel physically naked. On every level that I existed; I was naked before him. With each rip and tear, I felt myself fracture even more. That didn't mean I was weak, or that there was something wrong with me. I fractured into a different type of strength and knowing.

There was something being reborn that I didn't understand at the time. I was beginning to see what happened to me that night. I had felt a change coming since I was a child. It was like this was fated to happen. I could never explain it, so I stopped trying, and before long I forgot about that change. Something sparked inside of me the night that I was brutalized. Today was a new beginning for me. I mean who develops thick black rainbow-colored scars? Who changes their hair and eye color during a healing session? It was so much more than that.

It was time to head back inside. I had some questions for the medical staff, and I needed the answers now. I wanted to know what came out of my body a month ago. Everyone seemed to be ignoring the subject.

Walking back to the lab seemed to take forever. I was lost in deep reflection. The corridors and hallways were so sterile in this place and a huge trigger. Daegorth smelled like this place. Why? How could he be who he was and do the things he did to people and smell sterile? He didn't smell like chlorine but a deeper type of clean.

Just as I was passing my living quarters a small portal opened to my left. I was curious and walked over to it. I looked inside and allowed myself to feel the energy coming from it. I wanted to see if I could determine if the energy was hostile or not. I stepped a bit closer when I was sucked in and deposited outside the medical lab. I sat there stunned for the longest time—or so I thought.

"Where the hell did that thing come from, Dabney?"

I looked up and Dr. Roxanne was standing in front of me. Concern and worry were written all over her face.

"I don't know, Doc. One showed up by my living quarters. I decided to investigate and got too close, and here I am."

"We have to tell Tilly about this."

I agreed with her. The portal showing up was a scary ordeal, considering that Daegorth opened one and disappeared. Now, one was opening here in front of me. What could it all mean?

"I want to talk to you, Doc. No one seemed interested in the stuff I released from my body. I want to know what it was."

"Let's go down to my office and I will call Tilly to meet us. You are right; we have been avoiding the subject. We were not sure how much you wanted to know. It was not fair of us to keep that from you."

I followed her in silence. She guided me to my usual chair. I sat and waited for Tilly to arrive. I could sense everything going on inside of the Doc. She was not happy about being questioned about the goo. I could hear not one but three people coming down the hall. No big deal if they all came in. I wasn't threatened by any of them. They all seemed worried. The knock at Doc's door was sharp to my ears.

"Come in, Tilly."

Tilly, Mark, and Matt all walked into the office. I listened to the energy around Matt. There was someone directly behind him that was cloaked.

"What is going on, Dr. Roxanne?" Tilly asked, concerned.

"I was walking back to medical when Dabney was dropped at my feet from a portal. She has asked that I discuss the goo with her."

"What portal, Dabney?"

"Before I answer your question, why don't you explain who is cloaked behind Matt?"

Tilly, Mark, Matt, and Doc all looked at each other. "What are you talking about, Dabney?"

"There is a cloaked being standing behind Matt. I can sense their presence."

They all turned to look behind Matt when the cloak disappeared, and a masculine being appeared. I cannot explain what he looked like, because he was still cloaking that part of himself.

"Ramsey, what are you doing here? You look different since the last time we met."

"Tilly, it is time for her to make the journey. Dabney has to come back to the forest and show us where the toxic waste is being dumped."

"Wait a minute. I thought you guys had video proof of the dumping site?"

"Dabney, my dear. We have a video only of certain parts of the forest. We know it is being dumped somewhere in the Heart of the Godz. We do not know where that location is, because it is being hidden from us. We need your help to save the forest. Please tell me you are ready to start your journey."

"We are not sure she is ready for this yet, Ramsey. You heard us question her about the portal. Do you know anything about that, Ramsey?"

"I do not know of this portal you speak of, Tilly. Maybe Dabney can explain."

"I have seen portals all around here. I was not interested in checking them out until today. I got too close, and it sucked me in. I landed at the medical lab in front of Doc. That is all I know."

"Why didn't you tell us you have been seeing them all over the compound?"

"I did not want you all to think I had lost my mind. Besides, I didn't know if I was hallucinating them or not. I came here to find out about the goo my body released about a month ago. No one seems interested in telling me what it was. Do you all think that I don't care?"

"Dabney, it is not that at all. We have been running tests and letting you heal."

"So, what have you found out, Doc?"

"Please, all of you, take a seat. The goo from your body consisted of saliva cells and DNA from an unknown ancient species. Whatever was in his saliva when he licked you formed into those clots. We are not sure what they are, but it was full of ancient DNA. Do you know why your lower body would have rejected the mass?"

"I found out when I was younger that it was impossible for me to get pregnant. When the voice came to me, it told me to hurry before he implanted inside of me. That is all I know."

"I was not aware, Dabney, that you were attacked. Why was I kept out of the loop on this, Tilly?"

"Ramsey, we didn't think it had anything to do with you. We kept silent about it to protect her. Do you know anything about this monster that flayed her alive?"

"What do you mean, flayed her alive?"

"I was told after the first time he attacked me that he was a flesh-eater. The second time around, he flayed me alive. I was found hanging on for dear life. He made me think that he was healing me each time after he would rip me open. That was not the case at all. There was a numbing agent in his saliva. I had no clue that I was bleeding out. The voice told me to call him by his name and that would stop him."

"This is important, Dabney. What name?" Ramsey said ebbing in and out of view.

"Daegorth, flesh-eater from the Heart Tribe."

"That is impossible," Ramsey stated as he turned around, lost in thought.

"Is this impossible, Ramsey?" I said as I dropped my clothes to the floor.

The look on his face was utter disbelief when he saw the black rainbow lines all over my body. If I had to describe how I looked, I would say that some hack did an autopsy on me alive.

"It is not that I didn't believe you, dear girl. This has become even more critical than I first thought. We need you back to the forest as soon as you can get there. I would take you through one of these portals, but I cannot travel through them. When will she be ready, Tilly?"

"Don't you think you should supply us with some answers first?"

"I have none to give you. Believe me when I say that what happened to you should be impossible. I need to get back to the forest and figure some things out. Please, we must hurry!"

"What do you say, Dabney? Are you ready to make this trip?"

I looked at all of them. None of them seemed to have any answers for me. I could tell Ramsey was not telling me the whole truth and that he wasn't as puzzled as he was putting on. I knew it was time for me to leave here. There would be no benefit to my staying any longer. I would have to find out the answers on my own. I knew something about Daegorth. I felt as if I knew him. We had a deeper connection that I didn't understand that went beyond the brutalization I suffered at his hands. I could not reach that knowing. At least, not right now. I never thought I would go back to the town where all of this began, but circumstances were leading me back in that direction. I was not sure this journey would be good for me.

"I am ready, Tilly. I have my trust information, vehicle, cell phone, and a list of safe houses. I can leave this afternoon. I am ready to leave right now."

"You don't have to leave right now. I would not stop you, however, if that is what you want to do. It is time you take control back over your life. I am sure the Doc has some supplements for you to take with you to keep you strong. You will be missed, Dabney. When all of this is over, I would like to offer you a job here at the Bureau."

"Let me get this worked out and I will get back to you. I should be able to get in a couple hundred miles today. Is there a safe house or hotel that I can stay at on the way?"

"There is one about two hundred and seventy miles away. It is a small hotel that we own for occasions such as this. They will feed you and make sure you are safe. The woman who owns it I believe you know. She is Liz, @ 769Sexy~hotness on your old Twitter page. You will be safe there for the night. Your next stop will be a few miles out from the forest. We have a trailer park that one of our agents takes care of. When you leave, I will give you an itinerary with all the important information you will require. Go get your clothes packed. Chrysie went clothes shopping for you yesterday. I believe she put your clothes in your room while you were out."

Walking out of that office was the hardest thing I had to do. On the other hand, it was liberating. I packed up my cute new clothes. It was comforting to see she bought me jeans and long-sleeved shirts.

With my bags packed, I was ready to head back to Tilly's office. I hoped the Doc was there waiting with my supplements and meds. I was prepared to say goodbye to this place for good. I stopped at my door and turned around, taking in every inch of the place that I had called home for over a month. I was excited and yet terrified to leave this space of comfort. Turning back around, I hit the light switch and shut the door. As the door came to rest against the threshold, I heard a voice in my old room.

We will meet again. You are mine! Next time I will have the time to implant in you. You got away easy last time, witch!

I ran to Tilly's office. My heart was pounding so hard I couldn't catch my breath. I blasted through her door with sobs convulsing out of my body as I slumped to the floor. They all gathered around me, concerned.

"He is after me. He spoke to me as I was leaving my room. I have got to get out of here. Doc, you might want to add some anxiety medication to that regimen of pills you are sending with me. Do you have all of my paperwork taken care of?"

"No worries, Dabney. We have had you on anxiety medication from the beginning. Your body needed time to heal. I have your meds right here and prescriptions with your new identity, Starlene Jasper, on them. I hope the best for you. This will be the last time we speak. I have given you the names of doctors all the way back to your hometown."

"Thank you, Doc. I appreciate that," I said as I hugged her goodbye.

"All your paperwork is ready to go. Are you sure you want to leave, considering what just happened?"

"Yes, It is time for me to reclaim my power. My old boss is going down. Daegorth would keep coming for me even if the hit was called off. I want to help the forest out before he succeeds in murdering me. I have left a note in my room where you can find a copy of all the information about my company. Should he find me and kill me before I reach my destination, then those files can be used to end this. I love you all and thank you for everything. I have got to go. I want to stop before it gets dark."

I walked through the door of the Bureau feeling lighter on my feet. I had a new set of senses or gifts. Those would be my protectors. The car they gave me wasn't the greatest. Once I got back home, I would find me something better, like a 1970s Dodge Charger. Getting in the driver's seat felt great. I buckled my seat belt, started the car, and set the radio. I put the car in drive and never looked back.

It felt great to have the music playing loud and the wind blowing through my hair. Junk food sounded good right now. Pulling into a gas station reminded me of my last road trip with Rex. I needed to top the gas tank off. No point getting stranded somewhere along the freeway out of fuel. Once my tank was full, it was time to hit the restroom and get some treats. I enjoyed the thrill of going up and down aisles searching for little trinkets that would become mine. I found some fun things to buy. What did I want to eat? Chocolate licorice, root beer, water, tea, jerky, blackberry pie, popcorn, chocolate, marshmallows, and barbeque potato chips. I walked out of the store feeling satisfied with myself.

The sky was filled with clouds. On the horizon a storm was brewing. It was time to get on the road and settled into my hotel before this storm touched down. I had about seventy-five miles to go before reaching Raedico Inn! I sure hoped there was a Chinese restaurant close to the hotel.

I pulled into the inn just as the rain started to come down. The storm decided to follow me. It felt ominous. The town was more significant than I expected. I was hoping they delivered food to the inn. Stepping up to the counter to check-in felt strange.

"How can I help you, hon?" I heard from a sexy smoky voice.

"Are you Liz? Tilly made a reservation for me."

"You must be Star! It is so lovely to meet you. Tilly has you booked for as long as you need to stay. Sometimes that first step is the hardest one and it can wear you out. If you are going to check out, please let us know by eleven."

"I appreciate that, Liz. Are there any Chinese restaurants around here that deliver?"

"There is one about two blocks down. It is delicious. They will deliver to the front counter. We don't allow any delivery services to the rooms. We offer safety to our clients. We cannot provide that if strangers are coming and going as they please. All restaurant information for the area is on the table by your bed. Give them a call and when they deliver, I will let you know," Liz said as she handed me the key for room three.

I grabbed my bags out of the car and walked to my hotel room. Number three was a good number for me. I never expected the room to look how it did. There were two queen-size beds, a microwave, a coffee maker, and a bathroom with a shower and tub. The décor reminded me of the 1970s, with avocado-green coloring. The rooms were clean and pleasant smelling and no harsh leftover cigarette smell. This room reminded me of the times we would go visit Mary's grandparents' house. I felt so at home there.

I sat down by the bed and looked at the menu. Everything I could want was there. I called them up and ordered my meal. They said it would take forty-five minutes—a perfect amount of time to find some wine. On the list of delivery places, there was a liquor store right down the road. When I called them, they were happy to deliver to the hotel. That would give me plenty of time to take a bath.

I grabbed my comfy clothes and everything I would need for the bath. I set my phone for thirty minutes so I would have plenty of time before Liz called to tell me my stuff had been delivered. The tub was everything I needed and more. I was not happy when the alarm went off, but I knew I had to get out and get dressed. Liz should be calling anytime.

It seemed like an eternity since I stepped out of the bath. Liz should have called by now to tell me the food was ready. I had better check in with Tilly and let her know I arrived. Calling her was bittersweet.

"Hey Tilly, it is Dabney, I mean Star. I wanted to let you know I made it to Liz's place. You aren't picking up, so I am leaving you a message. I plan on going to bed early. Talk with you tomorrow." I hung up as a knock sounded on my door.

I could hear a heartbeat, breathing, excitement, above-board energy, and a sweet smell. What I did not pick up was anything menacing. I knew who was at the door. My question was--why?

I opened the door slowly to receive my guest. She was a beautiful blonde with long legs, brown eyes, and dimples at both cheeks.

"I got busy down in the office and couldn't call you to let you know your food was here. Someone delivered some wine as well. Is that yours?"

"I ordered the wine along with the food. Would you like a glass, Liz?"

"I am off duty for the night, so that would be great. I brought some glasses with me. I was hoping you would ask me to join you for a drink," she said as she produced two plastic cups from behind her back.

"Sneaky, Liz, sneaky." We both busted out laughing. "I have enough food here to feed an army. Would you like to stay?"

"You don't have to do that, Star. Are you sure?"

"Absolutely. Should we sit down and watch a movie while we eat?"

"I have one in mind. It started a few moments ago."

She flipped the television on and found the perfect movie: *The Maltese Falcon*, starring Humphrey Bogart and Mary Astor!

We sat back in our chairs, ate Chinese food, drank wine, and watched a movie.

"Do you mind if I sit on one of the beds and you the other, Star? These table chairs are uncomfortable, and my neck is getting sore from the lack of support."

"I was about to suggest the same thing, but I didn't want you to think I was hitting on you. My body needs a little comfort right now, and that mattress is calling me home."

"I wouldn't mind if you hit on me, Star. You are right, the mattress sounds good. I am going to lie on my belly and watch the rest of the show."

So, we each took a bed and like teenage girls, we watched television with our feet in the air and our arms crossed tucked under our chins. I quickly dozed off. The nightmare began as it always does with me down in the basement chained up. I was chained to a device that had the ability to swivel back and forth. That made more sense. I couldn't understand how he flipped me around if I was chained to the concrete wall itself. I could feel my body responding now to the threat in my nightmare. Goosebumps consumed my whole body and my bladder threatened to release. I could hear myself screaming at each attack of savagery being inflicted on my body. The entire experience was so brutal that I either lost consciousness or went within myself to forget. I could feel myself sobbing for what I had lost. The tears were not in my dreams but being released in the present moment. I was being shaken awake.

"Star, wake up. Honey, why are you crying?"

I sat up on the bed. Liz was trying to console me. I looked at her and she looked at me.

"Come here; let me give you a hug. You look like you could use one right now."

In slow motion, I felt myself drift into her arms. They wound around me with love and tenderness. I cried my eyes out. I sat up to thank her. She placed her finger upon my lips to quiet me.

"Whatever happened, I do not need to know the details. We are not allowed to know. It keeps all parties safer that way. I want you to know I am here for you right now. If you want to cry some more, my shoulder is open for you to lean upon. Right now, I want to kiss you, no strings attached, just a kiss. Would you be all right with that?"

What was it about me that I was sexually attracting women to me? I nodded yes. She took my face in her hands and she looked deeply into my eyes. She slowly brought my mouth to hers. She kissed my lips softly and gently. She beckoned my mouth to open as hers consumed mine. The kiss was long and drawn out in the most pleasurable way possible. She released me and we lay down next to each other.

"Let me hold you for tonight. Let me heal the hurt within you."

We spooned each other and fell asleep until my alarm went off at six forty-five in the morning. Sometime in the night I switched to holding Liz. I lay on my back and waited for the alarm to sound again.

"What time is it, Star?"

"It is almost seven."

"I have got to be going. Work for me starts at seven-thirty. I hope you decide to stick around for a bit. I would like to take you out to dinner tonight. I won't be in the office today. I have other places I must be. You should be safe exploring the town, Star."

I was happy to hear that she wouldn't be in the office today. I had already decided to check out early, head to my hometown, and get settled into my new living arrangements. When she mentioned buying me dinner, there was a sexual energy that was pinging off her. This was a distraction I did not currently want or need. To be honest, it wasn't something I could handle right now. It was time I dealt with my feelings about Ginger.

Packing my clothes up, I realized I had not heard back from Tilly. This was unusual for her. I decided to call her again when I heard a knock at my door. I would know Tilly's energy anywhere.

I opened the door, excited to see her.

"We need to talk, Star. We have had some more information come our way after you left yesterday. It is not something that we can discuss with you. It has come to our attention that should you speak about the Bureau; you could jeopardize all that we have worked for."

I knew I hadn't done anything wrong. Why was Tilly talking to me like this? Did she come here to kill me?

"What I would like to suggest is that we do a form of hypnosis on you so that we can replace what you know about us with other memories. We won't take anything vital away, just what you know about the Bureau. It is imperative you keep your memories about Daegorth, otherwise you will not be safe. What you will remember about us is that you were safe, and where you are headed. You will know where to go but not remember how you know it. When the time comes, you will remember everyone and everything. What do you think, Star?"

"I do understand why you have to do this. It saddens me that I will not remember all of you and the time I spent with you. Will I remember Liz?"

"No! You won't remember staying here or meeting her. It has to be this way to keep what she is to us safe."

"I am almost all packed up. Let's do this before I change my mind."

5

I checked out of my room thirty minutes later. I felt empty and lost. Pulling out of the parking lot, I said goodbye, not knowing why. The drive to my destination was one filled with music and freedom, with the air blowing through my hair the whole way. My damn car did not have its air conditioner recharged. It didn't take long before I reached my destination. It wasn't a bad trailer park to speak of. The single-wide, seventy-foot trailer house would have to do until I could find somewhere else to live. I opened the place up and walked inside. It was shut up tight and dark. There was an odor that I could not put my finger on, other than it had a guys' locker room smell to it. I turned on the stereo and walked back outside to get my things. A man walked by me and I realized I forgot to shut the front door. I turned around and went back inside.

This time around I started investigating, and I noticed there was a strange energy on the couch. The smell of male body odor was so thick and heavy in the air it was distracting. I don't know why I didn't open the curtains or turn on the lights to let more light in, but I didn't. There was junk everywhere. I have rented this place why does it look like there are people living here? I don't remember who I rented this place from or how much it cost. I do know that I have a key that let me in, and this is my new place to live.

I walked slowly down the hallway and to the left was the first bedroom. There was an intimidating energy up against the exterior wall by the window. Mind you, there were no sounds as if someone is here other than the male body odor. I walked apprehensively down to the second bedroom and there was no energy there. I could see the master bedroom at the end of the hall, and it felt daunting. Something in the energy of the trailer made me look back toward the living room. I turned my whole body to see what it was when I heard a match strike at the other end of the trailer. I started to walk back toward the living room with my senses on high alert and goosebumps all over my body. I could feel my bladder wanting to release as the fear was rising within me.

I didn't have my phone on me; it was by the front door. All I could think was that I needed to get to my phone. I saw movement on the couch, and I walked faster. As I walked past the first bedroom, I noticed movement out of the corner of my eye. I felt like I was on a treadmill walking in place at a low speed. I was trying to be as quiet as I possibly could be. The trailer seemed like it was getting darker and darker and the smell of the odor was getting stronger.

"Do you always walk into other people's homes uninvited?" I heard right behind me.

I could feel my legs turning to jelly. My bladder was threatening to release. My heart was racing so fast. I took a deep breath and turned around. Although the hall was dark, I could see before me a male. I know that sounds weird to call him a male and not say man, but it didn't fit to call him a man. He was so tall he seemed to hunker to keep from hitting his head on the ceiling. He was broad, so broad that it elicited a sexual response in me. He was heavily tattooed, and his skin was dark. The smell of body odor was heady upon him. It seemed to consume the air I was breathing. The scent was a turn-on.

"I asked you a question," he commanded in a thick, deep voice, stepping closer to me.

"I rented this place, and I was given the key. I was told that no one was living here, and I would be able to live here until I can find a place of my own," I said with bated breath.

"As you can see, this place is not empty and won't be for some time," he said as I felt someone come up behind me.

"What do we have here, Dhareyin?" I hear behind me.

"Well, Roman, it seems we have an interloper. What do you think we should do with her?"

From what I could tell, Roman was just as daunting and masculine. The pheromones were thick in the air. There was an incredible ache in my body that was deliciously wonderful. I could feel myself trying to slip out of control.

"What is she doing here?" I heard from the first bedroom.

"Well, Seth, she says that this place has been rented to her and that no one was occupying it."

With all three of them around me, I was on the brink of an earth-shattering orgasm. I was having a hard time concentrating and I was doing my best to keep my breathing under control. I was brought back to reality when my nipples stood at attention and were rock hard. I was feeling closed in and it was hard to breathe. It was apparent none of these males knew anything about personal boundaries.

"Does she really?" the one called Roman said.

I cleared my throat. "Can you all take a step back, please? You are invading my personal space."

"So, we have invaded your space. You have some nerve, girly; this is our place and you are the invader," Seth piped in.

"Who are you calling girly? You-you-you Neanderthal."

"Neanderthal, hmm. Well, brethren, I don't think we have ever been called that before. Usually, the female of the species, when they sense our awareness, fall at our feet begging us to take them right then and there, not really knowing what they are asking for. What is your name, so I can address you properly?"

"If you must know, Dhareyin, my name is Dabney."

"Odd name for a female."

"I was named after a family friend who saved my mother's life when she was a young girl. I would say it is a unique female name, thank you very much."

"Girl, you have got some sass to you. I like that. I did not mean to offend. Now back to the living arrangements. As you can see, it is occupied, and you cannot stay here with us."

"Well, where am I supposed to go? I was told this was a safe house."

"What would you need a safe house for, and who told you that, Dabney?"

"None of your fucking business, Dhareyin. Let me pass and I will leave you all be." I was feeling upset and scared. I had nowhere to go but here. I instantly went on the defensive and so did my mouth.

"Now wait a minute; if you are asking for a safe place to crash, we can find a way to accommodate you.

"Move the fuck out of my way."

They all stepped to the side.

"Thank you," I said lightly under my breath.

I walked past them all, grabbed my purse and phone, and went out into the night. Wait, how long had I been inside there?

I unlocked my car and got in. I stared out the windshield into the night. The tears flowed down my face and dripped off my chin. I laid my head on the steering wheel. All the pent-up emotions from the past few months rolled out of me, releasing one sob after another.

I didn't even know who to call. I had the rental papers here in my purse. There were no numbers to reach anyone. I wiped the tears out of my eyes and off my face. I was going back in to show them that I had every right to be there.

Summoning up the courage, I walked to the door and knocked. There was no answer. That was strange. I reached for the door and it was unlocked. I walked in and it was as if I was in a totally different place. The whole area was lit up and clean. The air smelled lemony fresh. Not one single note of heady male pheromones hung in the air.

Knock, knock!

I turned around and the man I saw earlier was knocking on the door.

"Star, I am Robert, but you can call me Bob."

"Hey Bob, what can I do for you?"

"Matilda asked me to come over and make sure you got settled in all right. I have some paperwork for you."

As he handed me the paperwork I asked, "Who is Matilda?"

"She said you might be a little forgetful but to let you know things will start coming back to you soon. If you look at your paperwork, it has all new IDs and passport. This is a safe place. No one asks anyone anything; those are the rules. Here is my business card. It has all the ways that you can reach me if you need to. I will be your contact with Matilda. We all watch out for each other."

"Bob, what about the three males that were here earlier?"

"What males?"

"There were three big men in here earlier. Dhareyin, Roman, and Seth. They said that they were staying here, and I couldn't. I came back in, and they were gone."

"Let me check with my assistant Grace. I was told this place was free for you to use. It is why I gave Matilda the key and rental papers. I will be right back, Star."

"My name is Dabney, not Star."

"Look at your paperwork. You have a new identity. Learn it quickly. Let me go talk to Grace. I will be right back."

"Oh no! I gave them my real name."

I watched as Bob walked out the door, shaking his head. As Bob walked down the steps, I could tell he knew who the three were. I perked up my hearing so I could hear the phone conversation with Grace through the door. Except he didn't call Grace.

"Tilly, it is Bob. What were the three doing here today?"

"How do you know the three were there today, Bob?"

"Your new client Star saw them in the place she is renting."

"That is not possible, Bob. No human can see the three unless the three want to be seen."

"Well, she saw and spoke with them. She forgot and told them her real name."

"We need to take a closer look at our Ms. Star. If she can see and speak with them, then we may have to rethink some things. Keep an eye on her. You know those three have a way of doing things they shouldn't."

"What do I tell her about them, Matilda?"

"Act dumb. Tell her you don't know what she is talking about and that Grace has no one else listed for this place. I would like to say that I could discipline them, but that would not be possible without starting a war."

"Goodbye, Tilly."

Knock, knock!

"Hey, Star. Grace doesn't have anyone listed with this place but you. I am not sure who was here, but please tell me if they show up again. Be careful. Don't speak to anyone else about them, okay?" he said as he handed me more papers. "These are for groceries, prescriptions, and takeout deliveries. Matilda has people everywhere protecting her clients. We suggest doing the deliveries until you get more settled in and feel more secure with your surroundings and identity. It was great meeting you," he said as he walked back out the door.

I shut the door behind him. After hearing his conversation with Tilly, I knew not to trust any of these people too much. Something was not right with this situation. What did it matter now? I had a safe place that put a roof over my head. Speaking of takeout deliveries, I was starving. It had been a long day. Looking through the takeout menus, the ramen soup shop seemed like the best place for tonight. The soup was filling and comforting. Plus, the broth would help me to heal even more.

The next few months seemed to just float on by. It appeared that no one was looking for me. Which meant I was not followed here. My injuries had healed somewhat on the surface, but the mental part was still a problem. The anxiety from PTSD was harder to treat. Matilda was providing a therapist so I could work through the attack and learn how to reclaim my power. There were no signs of the three males. Thank heaven for that. They were a lot to take on.

The daily routine I set for myself was getting more manageable, and it was helping me to regain some control I felt like I had lost. This helped me to feel more at home here. I was moving forward in my life the way I wanted to. Matilda required that all her clients take self-defense classes, fencing, and to learn how to shoot and handle a gun. She felt it was just as important to learn how to disarm an assailant. It was Mathilda's mission to help us to reclaim our power by becoming efficient in self-defense and combat. They were all there for different reasons, and this regimen seemed to work the best. Some came from abusive relationships and they were hiding from their spouses or ex-spouses. Some had witnessed a crime.

Every one of us had to leave loved ones and friends behind. We weren't allowed to keep any of our connections on social media. We were off the grid, so to speak. It could not be avoided. It was simple; those that wanted to find us would love to do that. They wanted to take our voices away. They wanted no witnesses left to their crimes. I honestly thought I would feel more alone. I was enjoying finding my true self and reclaiming my power.

We tend to second-guess our choices. Even though I was conflicted about what had taken place over the last few months, I knew I was where I was supposed to be. My world had been turned upside down. I used to think it began with me figuring out that my company was dumping toxic waste. I'd had plenty of time to think lately, and I knew that wasn't true. My life had been one hiccup after another my entire life. Matilda, whoever she was, had been more family to me than my original family. I knew that her help would not always be around, so learning all this self-defense made me feel better about myself.

They were starting to hint that it was time to revisit the forest. Apparently, the owners of the Heart of the Godz Forest were waiting patiently for me. She said that it was vital for me to understand the ramifications of my company's actions and how important I was in saving the forest and the beings that live there. I didn't know how I was such a big part of this.

Sitting on the front porch with my neighbor Sally felt normal. We weren't allowed to talk about our old lives or why we were there. We enjoyed talking to each other about the present and what we would like to see for the future. When Sally went back to her place, I couldn't help but remember how I was treated at my last job.

I was not sure I would have done anything even after they threatened my job. When they tried to frame me for their shit was when I took action to move away. I had no clue they would send someone like Daegorth to kill me. I could remember the gist of what happened to me but not all of it. I wasn't sure it was safe going back to the forest.

It was time to turn in for the night. I was still afraid to sit outside alone in the dark. I drew myself a bath and threw in some vanilla bath salts. I intended to relax with a glass of wine and a new book I found at the local bookstore. It was a book by one of the indie authors I met on Twitter. Last night I was able to get through the first three chapters. Stepping into the hot bubbly water was so relaxing. My hair was pinned up so it wouldn't get wet. I was able to get through several more chapters. I was out of wine, so it was time to finish up, get out, and put on some of my favorite lotion.

My favorite was cocoa butter vanilla lotion with sparkles. It made me feel sensual all over. I didn't have a man in my life to take this extra measure for. One day last week I realized I did not need a man to be like this. I could be like this for myself. I put on a silky nightgown and grabbed another glass of wine.

I walked from one end of the trailer to the next, making sure everything was locked up tight, which was hard sometimes when it was so hot. I was grateful for my air conditioner. There were two essential things that I always checked on before going to bed: the front doors had to be adequately secured, and my backpack had to be reachable in case I needed to make a mad dash to my car. It was a ritual that helped me to feel safe.

I climbed into my satin sheets and read for a little while longer. I felt my book fall into my lap as I dozed off. I snapped awake. I was not prepared for who was standing next to my bed. I felt my heart instantly start to pound. A big smile came across his face. I could see him a lot clearer this time. What I couldn't get past were the horns on his head. They were naturally a part of him as the hair on his body. His eyes were intensely black but filled with color. His pheromones were starting to consume the room and the air was becoming quite heady. I could feel my entire body responding to him. The lower parts of me were lit up and ready to go.

"How is it you can see me, Dabney?" he asked as he points his finger at me.

"What do you mean, Dhareyin? Are you telling me that others cannot see you?"

"No, they cannot."

"My name isn't Dabney. It is Star."

"No, it is, Dabney, but you are in hiding, so I will call you Star. You really did need a safe house that night, didn't you?"

"How did you know that?"

"I read your mind. One of my many talents. Why aren't you falling at my feet, beautiful one?"

"Why would I fall at your feet?"

"My pheromones have a magickal effect on earthly women even if they cannot see me. You are a strong beautiful goddess. Your energy is mesmerizing and stunning. I would love to taste every inch of you," he said as he slid his finger up my inner thigh.

"You have some nerve, you dirty perve."

"Do you not have desires, woman? I have craved you from the moment I heard you walk into this place. Have you not craved me?"

Never in my life had a man talked to me in such a manner. I felt stunned beyond belief. Here I was in my bed in a silky nightie and this delicious man-beast was sitting on my bed, sliding his finger up my inner thigh. Why wasn't I running?

"Yes, I do have desires, if you must know. Do I crave you? Not in the least. I have not given you a second thought."

He looked at me and laughter began deep in his chest.

"You lie to me, beautiful one. I won't embarrass you by probing your thoughts too much, but you do crave me. I can smell your desire for me. Are you not honest with yourself?" he said as he dropped his pants.

I couldn't help but look downward. The man was supremely built. All of him was mighty. I looked up and caught him watching me.

"Do you desire me, beautiful? Do you want me? Can I pleasure you, my sweet?"

This was all a little too much to take in. After what happened with Daegorth, I was not sure this was even possible. With all the damage that he did to my body having sex might prove more painful than pleasurable. On the other hand, I had this incredibly sexy man-beast who wanted me. I didn't sense anything bad from his energy. Could I even go through with it? Why should Dhareyin pay for what Daegorth inflicted upon me? Good hell; I just mind-fucked myself with all the questions. That was one hell of a workout. Maybe this would begin a deeper healing process. Hell, why not? He was divine and delicious.

"Bob said I am supposed to let him know when you show up again."

"Don't tell Bob a damn thing, you hear?"

"Before you rudely interrupted me, I was going to say that something isn't right with that whole situation. The answer to all your questions, Dhareyin, is a solid yes," I said to him as I threw the covers back and invited him in.

He climbed in with me, touching me and tasting me. Then he stopped.

"What is wrong?"

"Not here, my sweet. I want to take you to a realm where I can show you what desire really means outside all human emotions. I want to taste you in ways you never thought possible," he said as he reached his hand out for me to take.

I hesitated for a moment. What if this was a trick? Why did he crave me?

"Because I do. Are you coming or not?"

Am I safe?

He penetrated my mind with a clarity of not safeness but honor, respect, and trust.

"Trust yourself, Star; it is time! I see you have been hurt and betrayed. For that I am sorry. It is an experience I understand that most if not all humans go through. That does not make your experiences less painful, my lovely, but it makes you forget to trust yourself. When you completely trust yourself, most things easily fall into place. I showed you that trust and I see it touched you."

"Yes, it did. I always want to feel safe. I never realized that completely trusting myself is what safe feels like but freer. I am not relying on anyone to make me feel safe ever again."

"Do you trust yourself with me, Star?"

"Not completely, but I would like to, Dhareyin. One day I will tell you what happened to me, but not today. I know you can read my mind, but I would rather you didn't dive into that part. I am not ready."

"I would never dishonor you by going against your wishes. Take my hand and come with me. Let me show you where I come from."

I took his hand and we traveled to his realm. Some of the surroundings looked familiar. I was so intrigued by the places he took me. We walked through what I would describe as the garden of Eden but more. There were blossoms of all colors but beyond my comprehension. He walked me through what I would call a maze, but he referred to it as a labyrinth. We held hands as we walked through incredible paths of delight. It was then that I realized he was touching all my senses in desirous ways.

The scents in the air created a desire within me. The air upon my skin felt like I was being touched all over. I felt the most delightful touch upon my inner thighs, and yet there was nothing there. As we approached the center of the labyrinth, I found I was filled with the most delicious desire I have not ever experienced before.

At the center of the labyrinth, there was an angel bench. As you sat in it, the angel wings would surround you and bring you comfort. I allowed myself to feel openly. I trusted those feelings completely with no expectations. He sat down and pulled me on his lap. Immediately the center began to move down. I looked at him. He looked back at me in a way that said, *Trust yourself completely.*

I don't know how far we went down, but it seemed to go on forever. The scenery was breathtaking. All I could think about was Eve and the devil.

"Who is this devil you refer to, my sweet? Dhareyin is my name. I am no devil. I may have horns, but that is a part of me like your breasts are a part of you. I am not human, nor do I strive to be. This is not the human realm. You must stop seeing it as such, or you will miss out."

I took in all the sights. If I looked at it from a human standpoint, it was just greenery. When looked at through all my senses, it was so much more. My heart was satiated. If my heart could have an orgasm, that would have been next.

He reached out and plucked a piece of fruit off a tree. The fruit was foreign to me. The texture was akin to a nectarine or apricot. The flavor profile was a mix of apple, pear, and peach, with a hint of caramel flavor.

The air was heavenly. It smelled like the purest form of freshly mowed grass. The scent was absent of gas fumes, weed killer, and fertilizer. It honestly smelled like a fresh, ripe, cracked-open watermelon. The roses were the size of dinner plates and the smell was perfectly unexplainable.

Dhareyin's pheromones were getting stronger. This time, instead of body odor, the pheromones were musky and masculine, feral, and earthy with a hint of sweet pine. Sweat and salty, crisp, and clean. Heady like before but delightfully arousing.

I watched him close his eyes and smell the air a few times. It took me a bit to realize he was sniffing the air for me. My scent was musky and feminine with hints of vanilla, peach, cocoa butter, and cotton candy in its purest form.

The closer we got to whatever realm this was, the more I found myself aroused and wanting. I caught myself smelling the air for him. I wanted to be wrapped up in his arms. My thighs wrapped around his waist, I was being touched and pleasured in ways beyond human awareness or comprehension. I was hot and wet.

We met our destination with eagerness. I stood up and my legs were weak with desire. Dhareyin stood up next to me.

"Come, my sweet."

I followed him, completely trusting myself and my instincts. He wouldn't let me follow behind him; he kept me by his side. As we walked past various beings, they bowed. He must be important for them to bow to him. Should I have bowed to him? Is that what he meant when he asked why I didn't fall at his feet in front of him? I felt myself changing with every step I took. He led me to a chamber. He whispered to the females that were standing by the door.

"Go with them, Star. They will prepare you. I will see you soon," he said as he walked away.

I turned and stared at the women. They were different but gorgeous. They had different types of horns, long hair, voluptuous bodies, big eyes, and long pointed ears that were black on the tips. They were fanned out like big leaves. They had petite noses and full lips. Their cheekbones were high and covered in hot-pink and purple freckles. They had what looked like my hands and feet, but they were slimmer and longer. They had the cutest coiled-up tails on their backsides.

They bowed to me.

"No, you don't have to bow to me."

They waved for me to come forward into the dimly lit room. One was on the right and the other on the left. They each took down the straps of my gown, letting it fall to the floor. The scent in the room was heady and intoxicating. There was a substantial heart-shaped pool filled with multicolored water. I didn't even know how that is possible. Distracted by the pool, I was unaware of the women touching me until one took my nipple in her mouth. I damn near came undone.

Was this why he brought me here? "Trust," I could hear in my mind.

I became aware that the other woman was gone. I was looking around when I felt her move my legs apart. She placed her mouth upon me and did wondrous things with her tongue. She stood up and looked me in the eyes as she licked her lips. She reached forward and placed her lips upon my own. She was kissing me and allowing me to taste my scent upon her lips. I felt like I was being devoured by her desire for me.

The other woman took me by the hand and walked me to the pool. Both women on each side of me walked me in, touching and caressing me as the water sang to me. I felt myself becoming different. I felt impeccable. The things I used to be concerned about as a human did not bother me anymore, it must be this place. I wish I could bottle it and take it home and help people. The women bathed me and at times were intimate with me. I was washed in ways that were unfathomable to my psyche. I felt beautiful, silky, and whole. Suddenly, the women seemed upset and they rushed out of the room.

Dhareyin hurried in, concerned. He took one look at me and seemed to be at a loss for words.

"You have returned," I heard in my mind. "Step out of the water!"

"No, Dhareyin, enough."

"Now, Star!"

I stood up feeling like a goddess. You know when you see a beautiful woman step out of a pool and she is so sexy and confident? That is how I felt. My hair felt longer, and I smelled different. My body moved with a sensual grace. I felt something substantial upon my head. I could see things in a crisp, clear clarity. Dhareyin watched me walk out of the pool. He was instantly erect.

"You have returned. We thought you were lost to us a long time ago. We must prepare."

"What do you mean, Dhareyin?" I said in a husky smoky voice.

"Look in the mirror, Aoroia."

"My name is Dabney; well, I mean, Star. Why did you call me Aoroia?"

"Look in the mirror and see for yourself."

He turned me toward the mirror. What I saw before me shook me to my core. I was tall like Dhareyin. I had beautiful horns and the most incredible hair that was black with purple, neon greens, pinks, and slight yellow highlights. It reminded me of the aurora borealis colors. I had big colorful eyes, full lips, and my ears were small and pointed. I had large breasts and a voluptuous hourglass shape. I was lean and had incredible, sexy, defined muscles. My fingers were long and slender and my nails long and feminine. I was naked. Dhareyin was behind me and I could feel how excited he was for me. I felt every part of my being responding to him.

"Aoroia, I must get you back to the surface. No one can know you have been found. Unfortunately, we have a leak within our tribe, and you are not safe here."

"What about the women who serviced me?"

"Serviced?"

"Let's just say they have tasted me in ways only you have dreamed of."

"Dara and Fera will be punished. Did you enjoy it?"

"What a ludicrous question. Of course, I did; who wouldn't? They are great at what they do. Will they say anything about me?"

"You enjoyed the women so much—does that mean you don't want me anymore, Aoroia?"

I turned around and faced him. I looked him in the eyes, which was a lot easier now. I took his hand and placed it between my thighs.

"You tell me, Dhareyin."

"You are so wet. I want you just like before."

"What are you going to do about it?"

"Come with me."

I followed him to what looked like an oasis with a waterfall. There was a colorful pool below that the waterfall dropped into.

"It is beautiful, Dhareyin."

He took me in his arms. He brought back all the memories of our trip to this place. He picked me up and carried me into the water.

"You are so magnificent, even as a human. We must use protection for it would be wrong for me to get you pregnant."

"I cannot get pregnant—and no, I don't want to talk about it. How am I going to hide up there looking like this? Is there a way to turn back to a human?"

"Is that what you want to do is to turn back to a human? All you have to do is think about it, and you should be able to shape-shift."

"I want to make love to you in human form, Dhareyin." As I said this, I transformed back into human shape.

"What in blue blazes happened to you, Star?"

I looked down and the scars on my chest, abdomen, and back were still there. They were the deepest wounds. Plus, the ones connected to my sex. I looked up and noticed tears running down his face.

"Who did this to you, Star?"

"A little over a month ago I was attacked by a being called Daegorth, flesh-eater from the Heart Tribe. Long story short, my old boss hired him to murder me. He chose to take his time doing it. He flayed and brutalized me. I didn't know that he was doing all of this because he had a numbing agent in his saliva. I was about bled out when they found me. The scars have struggled to heal. They say it is because of the bacteria in his saliva. A week into my healing, I released from all my orifices some weird masses. I was originally a redhead with green eyes, and my skin was pale. As you can see, that has changed. I could feel these changes on a cellular level. All my senses have become enhanced. Before I left there, I heard him say that I was his and that he would be coming for me with no mercy. Wow, my memories are coming back to me more and more. Dhareyin, why would it be wrong for you to get me pregnant?"

"I am not concerned with that anymore. I want to heal these

wounds for you as much as I can. I cannot take away what happened to you, and you would not want that. It has brought forth a strength that will be needed when they know you have been found."

"I had a guardian come to me and a female presence claiming to be my mother. She is the one who told me about him being a flesh-eater. I am not sure who warned me when I was being tortured."

"What warning?"

"The voice told me what to call him to stop him before he implanted inside of me. I am curious—where have you brought me and who am I, really?"

"I have brought you to the center of the Heart of the Godz. In a sense, it is a forest, but it is so much more. We are here on another realm or dimension — a realm within a realm, to be more exact. Have you heard the term the space between space? Not to change the subject, but did he implant inside of you?"

I could see that the idea of this happening was bothering Dhareyin, but why?

"The Heart of the Godz is where my company was or is dumping the toxic waste. I was sent back here to help stop them. I am supposed to meet someone—I think his name is Ramsey. They took my memories, but that name seems to stick out for me. As far as Daegorth goes, I told you I could not get pregnant. It has been that way for quite some time. They say it could have been when I was born or from being assaulted when I was younger. It took me a long time to get used to that, because I would love to have children. There was a mass that came out of my vagina. You mentioned earlier that you wanted to heal me. They said that the one that did this to me is the only one who could heal these wounds."

"I am a healer and shaman of this tribe. We are immortal beings, but to live in this place and time we are blood, flesh, and bone as well. We have had to learn how to heal the flesh. It sounds like he did implant with his saliva, but it did not take. My saliva can heal your wounds as well but not as deeply as he could."

He walked to the edge of the water. He bent over, pulled a root out of the bottom, and crushed it between rocks. He waved me over to the bank.

"Bend over!"

"Excuse me?"

"This is a healing poultice for up inside of you. I need you to bend over so I can insert it into both places."

"Dhareyin?" I said with my cheeks blushing bright red.

"Please, my love, let me do this for you. When he was flaying you alive, he went deep and caused wounds and scar tissue to form up inside of you. I want to help you heal those wounds so you can function fully again."

I bent over and he lovingly inserted the poultice up inside of both places. As he touched my body, I could hear him chanting what sounded like an ancient language. I instantly felt a soothing take place. Before I could get a grip on what he had done, I felt him lick one of the scars on my back. It sent shivers all the way down my legs and calves and all the way up my body. He proceeded to do this with every wound. As he licked them, I could feel the healing taking place on the surface of my skin. Dhareyin took me by the hand and led me to sit on a rock next to the waterfall. I knew that he could not heal me completely, but what was happening would be enough.

"Let us sit here for a while. The waters are quite soothing and healing as well."

"Who am I, Dhareyin?"

"You are Aoroia. That is all I can tell you for now. The more I tell you, the more you return to who you truly are. Once that happens, the tribe will become more aware that something is taking place. It won't take long for them to discover you or figure things out. We have got to keep you as safe as possible. The markings you saw on your body earlier when you became Aoroia—they tell the story of your clan and your family line. As I speak your truth, those lines will fill in and everyone will know who you are. Someone is hell-bent on destroying this forest. We cannot let that happen. I didn't answer your question earlier about why I couldn't get you pregnant. That is something I will have to answer later. Right now, let's get you healed as much as possible before I take you back. You are going to need all your strength to help us."

I sighed heavily as the frustration set in from the lack of answers. I could sense there was so much more he wanted to tell me. As much as I hated to admit it, the time was not right for answers!

6

We never did make love. He took me back to the surface and tucked me into my bed. He kissed me on the forehead, and I was out. I tried not to overthink what happened down there or wherever it was. It finally made sense why I never felt like I fit in or belonged. Even if what he told me was true, I knew I wanted to focus on healing and to finish my training. For the time being, I chose not to say anything to Bob about Dhareyin; after all, what could I really tell him, anyway? There was nothing I could do until I was let in on the secret of who I am.

It was time to start working on a new book. The events unfolding in my life would make a great story. Changing my pen name was easy to do. It was time to head to the store and purchase a new computer and printer. I understand why they had to gut and get rid of my other ones, but it still irritated me.

All I could think about was Daegorth's last message to me. It made me so nervous; I squirmed, and my bladder wanted to kick in. The idea of losing control was not helping my self-confidence. It was time I took control back over my life. My instructor Griff should be able to help me with that. I had learned so much from him, but there was this knowing inside that no matter what I did I could not defeat Daegorth. How the fuck can you train for something like that?

So deep in thought, I didn't hear my disposable phone ringing at first.

"Hello?"

"Star, it is Bob. Have you had any contact with the three men you described to me when you first got here?"

I couldn't help but lie. I did not wholly trust Bob or this Tilly, whoever she was. "No, I haven't. Why do you ask?"

"There is a lot of whispering going on in the Bureau about you making contact again. Tilly asked me to call you and confirm one way or the other."

"I thought the Bureau knew everything about my whereabouts. So why all the questions?"

"Well, as with all agencies or big businesses sometimes the right hand doesn't know what the left hand is doing. She doesn't know what is going on. Therefore, she doesn't like it when she hears news about one of her clients that she is not privy to. What can you tell us, Star?"

"I cannot tell you anything, Bob. If Tilly wants to know what is going on maybe she should go find out what the others know. There is a new story brewing in my mind, and I am in desperate need of a computer and printer. I am headed to the computer store now. If you or Tilly need anything, I am sure you know where I am. If you find out who is spreading rumors about me being in contact with the three, please let me know. Goodbye, BOB!"

I wished I had an old phone so I could slam down the receiver. I felt like sending this one across the room. Don't get me wrong; I appreciate their help, but they were less than forthcoming, and I am sick of it. I would keep my contact with Dhareyin a secret for now. Enough thinking about the Bureau and Daegorth. It was time to start taking my life back, a little bit at a time.

Driving to the computer store, flashes of what Dhareyin showed me were surging powerfully through my mind. I could write it as it happened. As I pulled into the parking lot, a sense of personal power was flowing in me. I was doing something on my own without the Bureau's permission. There was no need for me to hook up to the internet until the book was done.

I didn't have to worry about money. I had plenty from the sale of all my belongings. I could buy whatever type of computer I wanted. I would have to find a way to protect my story. I knew what I wanted to buy. Every single guy hit on me in the store. I got asked out like six times, all by different men and one woman named Kat. I wasn't interested, plain and simple. If Dhareyin had shown up and asked me, that would have been different.

I walked out of the store happy with my purchases. Now I can focus on my training class. It was something I have come to enjoy. It is a definite bonus that I feel more powerful after each session. My body was in the best shape of my life. I felt alive and healthy for the first time in months. I looked back over my life since this all began, and I realized that even though it seemed like I was moving forward, they were tiny baby steps. My divorce hit me the hardest and I did miss Rex so much.

Today was my fencing class. Where would I ever need to use those skills? I might not understand Tilly's idea of training, but it had made my whole body stronger. Plus, my response time has gotten way better.

"Star, can I talk to you a minute?"

"Sure, Griff." Griff was my lead trainer at the Bureau. He seemed serious-minded today. Had Bob been telling him about my possible chats with the three?

"Some of the top people at the Bureau want to add in different types of training for you. We will start those next week."

"What types?"

"You will be learning geology, runes, some witchcraft, herbal medicine, and shamanism. They want you well informed before you meet with Ramsey and his people. There are a lot more things they want to teach you, but I am not allowed to know what those are. Ramsey and his people will be teaching you those things in private. We are not allowed to interfere with your sessions. Your physical training will be concluding over the next two weeks. You are welcome to come here at any time and work out. If you want to spar or fence with someone, just call and let me know. You have amazing skills, Star, and we want to keep them fresh and tight."

"So does Tilly know about this?"

"I don't think so. I work for the Bureau. That means all the top people are my bosses. If they tell me to do something, then I do it. No questions asked. Tilly isn't the main person; there are others. I think she has tricked herself into thinking she is the top dog, but I know for a fact there are others that are far higher than her. She has her place in the organization, but it is nowhere close to the top. She does not know this, though, so that has to be a secret between us Star."

"Griff, I don't know what to say. It all sounds so covert to me. How did I end up in this world? I wanted to talk to you as well. I am struggling with a situational memory and it leaves me feeling vulnerable, helpless and at times out of control. I was hoping you had some advice to give me on the subject."

"What is the situation, and we will go from there."

"You know my history and what happened to me when I almost died. Before I left the Bureau, I was warned by Daegorth that he wouldn't stop looking for me. I don't know how to feel safe. How do I defeat this monster, when he is obviously far more evolved than I am?"

"Star, you must never think of yourself as less, or you give your power away. I did hear what happened, and I can understand how you are feeling. When you try to run from your vulnerabilities, it just makes you more vulnerable. You have got to learn to trust yourself. Trust your strength, your power, your wisdom, and your intuition. Trust that you will know what to do should you reencounter the monster. The biggest monster in this scenario of yours is fear. Fear can eat away at our self-esteem and strength. It can cause us to doubt our skills and it can destroy our trust in ourselves."

"Thank you for reminding me about trusting myself. Someone just recently told me the same thing. Somehow, I forgot it for a moment. I will work on it with every step I take. Thank you again for everything that you have taught me. I hope we can stay in contact."

"Wait right here; I have something for you."

I couldn't help but think about how I would miss him. I knew they would have me so engrossed in my lessons that he would fade into the distance.

"Here—I hope that you have a friend that you could take. It will be a heavily guarded place, so you don't have anything to worry about."

He handed me five pit pass tickets to the Demolition Derby this Saturday at the local fairgrounds. "This looks like a lot of fun. Do you want to go with me?"

"I have my own tickets. My daughter's husband is one of the derby drivers. These are pit passes so you can come visit and check out all the cars. I hope to see you there, Star. It is time you brought some fun back into your life. It is usually pretty hot during the day, so make sure and bring plenty to drink and eat. Bring a jacket, because it can get chilly later in the evening."

"Thank you, Griff. That sounds like fun. I will have to find some people to go with me. See you Saturday."

I walked away, full of energy. Finally, something I could look forward to and I was happy about it. There was that added sense of security, since it would be heavily guarded. I felt like I was skipping back to the car. I knew that my inner child was excited about going. So, the question was--who would I take with me? I would leave that decision for a bit later. In the meantime, I would go to the grocery store for dessert and wine and order take out from my favorite Jalisco restaurant. A giant burrito stuffed full of skirt steak, rice, green bell peppers, and onions sounded delicious.

Walking into the trailer I immediately noticed there was something off about the energy within. I could smell strong body odor, just like the first time I walked in this place. Was it just Dhareyin, or were the other two with him as well? No, this smelled different from last time. It was a more profound, stronger smell.

"Hello? Is someone here?"

I felt an energetic presence swirling around me. It was heavy and black. I felt like I was underwater, trying to breathe. The pressure in my chest and ears was unbearable. Then everything became more transparent. It still sounded like I was underwater, but it felt like I was at the center of a storm. It was all calm. The silence was deafening. I felt like I was on the verge of collapsing. *Trust yourself, embrace the vulnerability. Center yourself and breathe.* I could hear in my mind. How did Dhareyin get into my head?

"We will get to Dhareyin in a moment. Right now, we will discuss what is to come next for you, Star."

"Ramsey, is that you? Why don't you just show yourself?"

"Not Ramsey but Seth. Ramsey is my father. I am here to discuss your training. You are not to go near Dhareyin again—do you hear me, girl?"

"First off, I am not a girl. I am a woman. Don't you ever tell me who I can talk to. I met your father; he was a nice man."

"He is no man. You disrespect him when you refer to him in such ways. Don't refer to him in that manner again."

"How was I supposed to know? He introduced himself and he looked like a man. So, what is he, then?"

"He is the leader of our particular clan within the Heart Tribe. You will take note of that, so you do not offend and lose your head."

"So many rules, and yet no one bothers to inform me of such things. I was not trying to offend. It is obvious that I am not in the loop; nor do I know what is going on here. Why do you want me to stay away from Dhareyin?"

"He seems to have taken a liking to you, and we cannot have that. He is the shaman of our tribe, and he cannot lose his reputation by getting involved with a human."

"You act like being human is a disgusting thing. I find that offensive and rude. I haven't seen Dhareyin since that night we met."

"You lie, Ms. Star. Don't do it again, or I will punish you."

"I am not sure who you think you are. You have no right to punish me. Maybe it would be better to deal with your father. You and

I are not compatible at all. You are a big smelly brute, and I don't like you."

"Well, at least you are honest. I do like your fire and your sass. Starting next week, we will begin your studies. You will be learning from our top scholars. They will come to you. We will give you the meeting place and you will be there. Do not ever be late."

"Why are you all going to so much trouble? Why do I need to learn all of this stuff?"

"Dhareyin recommended it. He felt it would help give you an edge when it comes to helping our tribe."

"Funny thing is, I didn't know I was helping some tribe. I was told I was helping the owners of the forest. All the secrets you keep—it is amazing you get anything done."

"I told you to watch your mouth," he said as he grabbed me by the neck and slammed me up against the wall. "You just don't know who you are talking to, and you will learn some respect. I am next in line to rule our clan. You will think before you speak, or you will get a hard lesson in manners," he said as he sat me down.

"You are no better than Daegorth. You think you are supreme. Really, you are just a big nasty brute who likes picking on women. Why don't you go fuck yourself, Seth?" I knew I had pushed it too far when he turned back into black energy and consumed my body. I felt like there was a battle going on inside of me and that my death would be imminent. No thought could form in my mind. I knew that if I survived this, it would be a miracle. The pressure left, leaving me big-eyed and breathless. I saw stars. I looked up to see Seth planted firmly up against the wall by none other than Dhareyin. He turned and looked at me as I whispered his name.

"You pushed too far this time, Star. You are damn lucky he didn't kill you. What were you thinking?" he asked rhetorically.

"You will take your hands off me, Dhareyin. Know your place."

"I could say the same to you, Seth."

"What does that mean, Dhareyin?"

He let go of Seth and walked to me. "I have to tell him who you are. I have seen your death by his hands. If he killed you, it would mean the end of our magick."

"Can he be trusted?"

"We will find out, won't we? You shouldn't have pushed him, Star."

"Stop telling me this is my fault. He was saying shitty things to me. I was sick of it. He is no better than Daegorth, and I stick to my truth on that." As I finished my sentence, I was consumed again with the dark energy, and this time I knew I was done for.

"No, Seth! You cannot do this."

"You are next, Dhareyin—be prepared."

"She is the only one who can save us. Are you telling me you want to kill our chances of surviving?"

"If you are telling me that some human woman can save us then we might want to rethink your role in our tribe."

"Seth, she is one of us. Show him, Star!"

"I don't want to show this brute who I am. What if he is the bad guy? Then I end before I even know what is happening."

"Do it," Dhareyin commanded me.

I closed my eyes, and I remembered the time down below or wherever it was at. I remembered Dhareyin calling me Aoroia, and I focused on my appearance.

"I don't believe it. How is this possible? You are dead. This is a trick."

I looked down at myself to see if I had transformed or not. Sure enough, I looked like I did that night with Dhareyin.

"What now, Seth?"

"Dhareyin, this is not possible. How long have you known she was alive, and why haven't you told her father?"

"You know we have a mole in our midst. Do you really think it is safe to tell them when she does not fully know who she is? She wouldn't stand a chance against the traitor. She would be dead before she was fully transformed. Is that what you want?"

I was sick of them talking about me as if I wasn't there. "Who is my father, and where is my mother? I want some answers from both of you. This is ridiculous. How can I ever help myself if I am not being told the truth? Who are the liars now?"

"I almost killed you. Do you know what would happen if you were to die?"

I shook my head no.

"When SHE takes her place, if all is not in place then the magickal world will always stay in the dark."

"Who is SHE?"

"We are not allowed to speak about HER for her name is unknown to us at this time. All we can hope is that SHE takes her place, willingly."

"I don't understand what part I play in that."

"We thought that part of the prophecy had died with you. All hope was gone for our magick, and so others were consumed with hatred and have turned against their own tribes."

"I still don't know what that has to do with me."

"How much should we tell her Seth? You know the more she knows, the more her tribal will begin to etch itself darker upon her skin."

"She has to know. You know the spells to keep her safe and protected. Do an invisibility spell, Dhareyin, so she remains unseen."

Something changed within Dhareyin. He became something I cannot describe, other than to say he was far more beautiful than before. He was standing before me in robes heavily etched in symbols I did not understand. He was speaking under his breath words of a language I did not comprehend. I had heard this language at some other place. When Dhareyin finished, I felt more protected than before but pissed off.

"You son of a bitch. You sound just like Daegorth, do you know him personally?" I said to Dhareyin as I slapped him hard across the face. "Don't you even try to justify yourself to me right now. I fucking hate you both. I hate what you are and who you think I am." I stormed off to the back of the trailer. I shrugged off Aoroia.

"I am so sorry that I could not tell you about Daegorth. I hoped that you would give yourself a chance to know me before you knew the whole truth."

I turned and looked at Dhareyin. Shaking my head, I turned and faced the window again. "I am nothing more than a pawn here. I thought I was important to you. For fuck's sake, Dhareyin, I was going to have sex with you. Hell, I was misleading myself. You are the first man that I would allow to touch me since Daegorth damn near murdered me."

"Dhareyin cannot be with you, Aoroia, and he knows that."

"You and your fucking pheromones. Well, that would have been nice to know before I met you. Why is it that he cannot be with me?"

"He knows why and that is all that matters. For already being with you, his punishment will be brutal."

"He hasn't been with me. As soon as he realized who I was, he brought me back here, and I haven't seen him until you tried to kill me."

"Took you where Aoroia? Tell me now?"

"I took her down below. I wanted to show her where we reside. When she entered the bathing pool, she started to transform. I did some healing work on her from her attack. I did not disgrace or disrespect her, Seth. I would not do that. I know how important she is to our people."

"Where is my mother?" I demanded.

"After you died, she asked that her journey here be over. The current flesh-eater consumed her magick, and she was able to go home among the stars. She left her other five children and her husband because she could not live without you."

A sparkly energy filled the room. Seth and Dhareyin seemed oblivious to it. Taking shape in front of me was the one who called herself my mother.

"Oh, my beautiful girl. You must tell them something for me. Tell them that I intentionally left this life so I could be here for you now. I didn't want you to be found, so I gave you away. I wanted you to

have a chance and to give a chance to our people. You must decide if you want to take your place at the head of our tribe. Only then can we move forward."

"What do you mean, the head of our tribe?"

"You are queen to our people."

"How is that possible if I have five other siblings that were born before me?"

"Right now, Ramsey oversees the tribe. In the prophecy, it was written that you would become queen to the Heart Tribe, no matter who was currently on the throne."

"What is going on, Star?"

I proceeded to tell them what my mother had told me.

"How do you know these things?"

"She just told them to me."

"That is not possible. Your mothers' journey ended; she cannot contact anyone on this plane."

"Tell her that. She is standing in front of me." I described her to them. They seemed surprised that I would know that.

As I finished talking, her light became brighter, and she appeared before them. Both bowed to her. I could feel the level of respect they had for her.

As they all got reacquainted, I stepped into the shadows. I watched them, feeling like an outsider. I felt all the pieces coming together and I couldn't stop the transformation. I felt divine and deliciously supreme. Instead of coming out of the shadows, I slipped further in, knowing it was where I belonged and where I thrived. My light was like a beacon within the shadows that surrounded me.

"Where did she go?" I heard my mother ask.

"I don't know; I cannot sense her anymore."

"What do you mean, you cannot sense her anymore? How is that possible, Dhareyin?"

"Seth, I don't know. It is like she is gone. I don't feel her human presence etched on her as a child and I don't feel the Aoroia presence either."

I watched from the Shadows. If only they knew what I was capable of. I was not sent here to save our magick. I was sent here to destroy. What an incredible turn of events. Me, a killer. The idea was ludicrous. I knew about the one they won't speak of, and there was another as well. We all must align because we were all sisters sent here. If you think I just lined everything up impeccably, you would be wrong. In life, there are always twists. Whether my mother knew it or not, her sending me to have my light destroyed was the best thing she could have ever done for me. I could feel the power building inside of me, and I wanted to use it. Somehow, Ramsey knew I was a weapon. I was here to destroy those inflicting harm upon our tribe. The question was, how did Mother escape, and how could I return her to that place?

I stepped out of the shadows, naked and fierce. My horns filled with color, and the tribal upon my skin was forever changed. For it did not match anyone else's. My eyes were black, and they glowed. I walked out and with the power within me, I grabbed Dhareyin and Seth by the throat. I kept my eyes on Mother. The energy I expelled from my being held the two man-beasts in place. There was a look of complete surprise on their faces.

"My daughter, what have you done?"

"It is not what I have done, Mother. It is what you have done. You unleashed the true meaning of the prophecy. I am a destroyer! You made me when you thought you were saving me. Don't you realize there was nothing you could do to stop this? How are you still here? You should have died when the flesh-eater did his ritual."

"He was learning, and he must have done something wrong because I have always been able to watch over you. You are a good girl, Star."

"Don't ever use that name on me again. Before we are through, you will be on bended knee bowing to your queen. Who was this flesh-eater that messed up? He must be destroyed."

"It was Daegorth."

With a flick of my head, I sent her flying across the room. She slumped to the floor. I turned and noticed Dhareyin and Seth staring at me. Neither one of them had pure thoughts running through their minds.

I slowly slid my eyes down their big masculine bodies. I was hungry, and my appetite was ferocious. I looked at Dhareyin with one eyebrow raised. There was a sexy tug to the smile that was lighting up my face. Dhareyin's eyes were not the only things getting larger. Both men possessed massive erections. They seemed uncomfortable.

I had many ideas running through my mind of what I could do with those two. I licked my lips slowly. "No, Star!"

In a voice so loud and forceful, I relayed once again that my name was not Star. It seemed to shake the foundation of the trailer I was standing in. The funny thing was that no one knew what was going on, because of Dhareyin's invisibility spell.

"What would you like me to call you, then?"

"Don't call me at all. I could skin you all alive slowly for what you have done. You will pay greatly for your acts of treason upon me. That monster should have been destroyed when I told you what he did, Dhareyin. Seth, your father Ramsey knew about Daegorth, and yet nothing has been done. When I am done with your tribe, there will be nothing left to save."

I dropped them both to the ground. "Now get out and take that bitch with you," I bellowed at them.

I watched Dhareyin size me up. He grew a mighty set and walked up to me.

"I know I have wronged you. Please do not take it out on our people."

"You don't understand Dhareyin. I am not from all of you. This body may have been born into this tribe, but I am not from your realm. I come from a star system far away from here. Do you honestly think that someone of your tribe could fulfill a prophecy as important as this? If you do, then you are wrong. I am not your kind. I will tell you a secret, Dhareyin," I said to him as I wiggled my index finger to come closer. "Before I am through, I am going to kill each one of you slowly. None of you can stop this. The one who has betrayed you all will die in the most brutal way possible. I will skin Daegorth alive over and over until there is no essence left in him. When I am through, I will take the one who calls herself my mother, and I will rip her fucking head off her shoulders," I whispered to him. "Take them both and get the fuck out of my sight. You will be seeing me soon enough, Dhareyin."

"What do you mean by that?"

"It means you are mine. I will do whatever I want to with you. I happen to want to watch you scream in ecstasy. I see you don't have a problem with that," I say as I point my finger down to his erection.

The look on his face was priceless.

"No, I do not have a problem with that."

I trailed my finger down his chest and reached inside of his pants. I grabbed his erection and pulled. "I am happy you and I are on the same page."

I stroked him repeatedly. I could feel his eruption about to take place, and I squeezed harder.

"When I want you to release, I will tell you." He never took his eyes off mine as I rubbed lightly over his dewy tip. "Touch me, Dhareyin, like you wanted to from the beginning when you thought you were superior to me."

"Not with your mother and Seth watching. I will not do it. Your attempts to control and humiliate me have gone on long enough."

I smiled slowly. I took my hand out of his pants. I left him thick and wanting. I sliced my nail across his chest slowly. The blood oozed out, dripping faster and faster as the cut became deeper. I brought my finger up to my mouth and slowly licked the blood off. Not one time did I take my eyes off him.

"You taste good, Dhareyin. I know you want me. I can smell it on you. You want to taste me, like I have tasted you. You want to touch and lick me like Fera and Dara. I can hear it in your heartbeat. NOW TOUCH ME!"

"NO, I won't do it."

With one big swipe of my hand, I cut a deep trench in his chest from left to right. He looked at me, wounded. His eyes were defiant. I swiped with the other hand and laid his belly wide open. I dropped to my knees and slowly licked him over and over until I was drenched in his blood. His wounds instantly healed.

"Oh, this is going to be fun. Do you think Mother or Seth heals as easily as you do, Dhareyin?"

He looked at them both. They looked at him in shock.

"So, they didn't know you could instantly heal. What does that make you then, Dhareyin? Are you truly one of them or something more?"

I walked over to my Mother and offered her my hand to help her up. She took my hand and she stood. She was too trusting. I would have to teach her a lesson about that later. I took her over by the door and left her there. I waved for Seth to come over to me. He got up reluctantly and walked toward me. "You tried to kill me tonight."

I knew I had to teach Seth a lesson. With my full body, I stepped into his. I wasn't playing around and just using my energy. I was allowing him to feel on a deeper level what he made me experience.

"Aoroia, do not do this. Let him live."

"I am a goddess, Dhareyin. You will do well to remember how to address me," I said as I released the hold I had on Seth. "Get them out of here. Not a word of this to anyone. I have got some work to do."

He took them both out the front door. I headed into the kitchen to grab a glass of wine. As I shed the destroyer, I was intrigued at the brutality I could inflict. I went into my bathroom and stepped into a hot shower — time to get Dhareyin's blood off me.

Was I this cruel goddess? I felt like I went rogue for a bit there. It was good to know what I was capable of. I did not feel bad at all for ripping him to shreds. My power was coming full force. I could shape-shift anytime I wanted to. There was this incredible ambrosia smell to my essence.

"You took a big chance in there, Star," I heard behind me.

I turned, and it was Dhareyin. Did he not learn his lesson the last time? Was he back for more? As soon as she told me some of the story, it all fell into place for me. They needed to know what they were up against. I didn't even show them all my capabilities.

"Do you mind if I join you?"

I waved him into the shower. "Would you mind scratching my back? It itches like no other."

He started to scratch my back, and the more he did, the more it itched. "UMM, Star, your skin is falling off and there is something underneath working its way out."

As he finished, I felt something in my back expand. "Get out, Dhareyin, and give me some room." He got to the bathroom door when I let out a blood-curdling scream. A big set of jet-black wings shot out of my back. There was not enough room in my bathroom to extend them fully. I closed my eyes and thought of being outside in the open. I reached for Dhareyin as I disappeared outside. I wrapped my legs around his waist. I could feel his erection between my thighs. Oh, this was going to get interesting. As I moved my wings up and down, we went higher and higher.

He cupped his hands on the back of my head and brought my lips to his. At first, he went slowly and then intensified when I tried to pull away. He was using his tongue on me and inviting my tongue to do the same. With one hand, he reached between us and started to caress me slowly and deliberately. What I wanted was him inside of me. I wasn't sure I was going to give him that pleasure quite yet.

"Not yet, Dhareyin. I would love to have you pleasure me but let's wait until I figure out what is happening with me."

"I respect your decision. I am not happy that you cannot get out of your human frame of mind for just one moment. Take us back down to the ground."

I took us down to the ground. My wings tucked back up inside of me, and I was back in my etched human form again. This shapeshifting was going to be a huge learning curve.

"We probably shouldn't stand around out here naked. Will you come inside with me so we can talk? I have a question I would like to ask you."

He followed me back into the trailer without saying a word. I could feel his eyes on my backside. We both got dressed in silence.

"Do you drink alcohol, Dhareyin?"

"I have been known to have a whiskey occasionally. That is what happens from hanging around humans. We do have a beverage that is a higher alcohol content that we make ourselves from the fruit trees."

I poured us both a whiskey on the rocks. I was more of a wine drinker, but I did like my occasional whiskey. Rex got me hooked on scotch.

"What do you want to talk about, Star?"

I turned to face him on the couch. He was sexy; that was for sure. His eyes were so captivating. "Now that you know what I am capable of, why are you still here? Do you know that I could kill you at any moment?"

"I am still here because I have a feeling about you. I embrace all of you. I am sure Seth has taken matters to Ramsey, and you will have to deal with him soon. I do not think you know what you are capable of, but I do."

I scrunched my eyes up, looking at him. "I do know what I am capable of, Dhareyin. I could feel it."

"When you decide to destroy another life, even one from your tribe, then you will know what you are capable of doing. What matters is the place you choose to come from when you make that decision. I have always known this was who you are. I understand the prophecy like no other. Even though we are missing a chunk of the prophecy, as a shaman, we know all. We work in all realms. I know who and what you are. It is why I didn't want you to push Seth so much. You were not ready to blossom, nor is the world ready for you to be in it. You are still learning about your power, and you are out of control with it."

I watched him as he spoke to me with determination and kindness. I could see his gentle side coming forth, but there was a strength there you would not want to challenge.

"It is getting late. Are you finished with your whiskey, Dhareyin?"

He handed me his glass and headed for the front door. I came up behind him and tapped him on the shoulder. He turned around slowly.

"Any chance I could get a hug, Dhareyin?"

He took me into his arms, and we seemed to melt into each other. I could hear him breathing into my ear and smelling my hair. I cherished what he was offering me. I could feel something healing deep within me. He took a step back and pushed me away from him.

"Would you like to stay the night? Not for sex but to sleep in the same bed."

He was about to answer when I heard a loud horn. He looked at me in wonder. "I am being summoned by your father."

"I figured as much. I just heard a horn going off."

"You heard the horn? Then you must come as well. Only those summoned can hear the horn. Come on, Star, let's go." He summoned a portal, and he took me through it. We came out in the center of the forest. Was this the Heart of the Godz?

"I am not sure why you were summoned here tonight, Star. I cannot guarantee that I can protect you, so please be careful. Seth and your mother have had time to tell them about you and what you pulled earlier. I will put protection around you, but I cannot guarantee that will work with your father or Ramsey. You should be able to shape-shift. I don't want you going in shape-shifted—do you hear me? He needs to see you as a vulnerable human. You will know when you have to transform."

He had already changed back into his primal self by the time we walked inside. Right inside the cave, several beings were sitting there waiting. I knew Ramsey, Seth, and Roman. My mother's energy was sitting there with five males. Another male was standing at the front, watching me intently. I was nervous; I will not lie. I had to believe in what Dhareyin told me and be vulnerable.

I was doing my level best when the hair on the back of my neck stood on end. Every cell in my body slipped into protective mode. It took everything I had not to shape-shift and rip that fucker's head right off his body. It would be my luck that Daegorth could grow a new one.

I looked up, and Dhareyin was watching me. *"Are you okay?"* I could hear in my mind.

"Yes, but I am about to crack. Did you know Daegorth was going to be here, and can anyone else hear this conversation?"

"No, I didn't know. No one else can hear us; that is the beauty of the protection I placed around you. No one can hear your thoughts. Keep yourself under control."

"Please, everyone, sit down. I want to introduce our special guest we have tonight. Star, will you please stand?"

I could not believe that Ramsey just gave my identity away with Daegorth in the room. What were his motives here? I stood and looked around.

"Star is the one who reported the dumping of toxic waste in our forest. She has agreed to help us find the dumping location so we can stop these illegal actions before the toxic waste reaches the Heart!"

That was strange—did Seth not tell his father who I was? I could tell that Daegorth was keeping who he was at bay. He was having as hard a time as I was.

"We thank you for coming to help us, Star. Is there anything that you would like to say to us?"

I looked at Dhareyin. He nodded his head forward as if to say it was okay to speak.

"I am glad to help in any way that I can. I do know where the dumping was taking place. It has been quite a while since I have been here, so maybe they have stopped."

"Where did you go?" Roman piped in.

"I moved to get away from them, and then they sent a hired killer after me. He almost succeeded, but I am stronger than he knows. I have been taking time to heal my body and mind."

The man who was eyeing me earlier stepped forward.

"I am Raffen, and these are my sons: Duke, Randall, Victor, Albert, and Samson. I use human names because our language is hard to understand. They will be your protectors during your assistance."

"It is so nice to meet all of you. I mean no disrespect, but I already have my team of protectors: Dhareyin, Seth, and Roman."

"That is impossible!"

"Well, those are my terms. If they are not part of my team, I will rescind my offer to help."

I could see by the look on Raffen's face that he was not used to being disobeyed or questioned. It took him a moment before he answered. "I will agree to your terms, Star, but I am going to add one more name to your list. Daegorth will be a part of your team as well."

I looked straight at Ramsey and waited for him to say something. I don't know why I was surprised by his silence. I looked at Dhareyin, in hopes he would say something. These males were going to disappoint me tonight. Then an idea came to me. In my heart, I knew what I was going to do. "That will work just fine, Raffen. When do we get started?"

"We will start tomorrow. Your protectors will meet you at the forest entrance so you can show them the way. Once you have done this, your help will be over."

I nodded my head to him in acknowledgment. I walked out of the cave and stepped into the portal that appeared before me.

"I will be there in a moment," I could hear in my mind.

"Don't bother!"

"Woman, you know I had no choice in there!"

"Do not woman me. You know who I am. I will do what I must do. I cannot guarantee what will come after that. Now leave me alone, Dhareyin."

I walked inside my house, irritated. Heaviness surrounded me.

What was I to do if Daegorth showed up? I was too tired to worry about this shit anymore. If he came after me, then I would do what I could. I had a busy day ahead of me. As my head hit the pillow, I knew that would be it for me tonight.

What I didn't know was that Dhareyin slept outside of my trailer all night long. The next morning, I stepped outside to grab the morning paper. Dhareyin followed me back inside. The silence hung heavy in the air. I took a shower and got dressed while the coffee was percolating. Dhareyin poured us each a cup and set it on the counter.

He walked over and stood in front of me. He brought me into his arms and held me close. "Don't ever shut me out like that again, Star. I won't have it. We are a team, you and I."

"Some team. You let that murdering bastard become part of our team. Neither you nor Ramsey stood up for me. You both know what that monster did. I will help you out today, but it ends there. When it is over, I go my own way, away from all of this."

"I didn't stand up for you because he wouldn't have changed his mind. You challenged him, and he had to have the last word. You fucked yourself, Star. Why couldn't you accept your father's offer of your five brothers for protection? You talk about being done. What about the prophecy and what you are becoming?"

"Why didn't you tell me it was my father? There will come a day that I will have to do something you won't like. I already know this in my heart. Your tribe will die one by one. Is that what you want from me?"

"What are you talking about, Star? Why does anyone have to die?"

"I am the destroyer; what do you think that means? Last night it was revealed to me what would come to pass. It may even come down to killing you. I don't want to do that. That is what will happen if I stay here."

"You cannot run from your fate. It has already begun to play out. There is no stopping it. I want you to stay and to fulfill the prophecy.

It will bring a better world to this planet."

KNOCK, KNOCK!

"Who the hell is that?" I asked Dhareyin.

I opened the door and was not happy about who was standing there. "What can I do for you, Bob?"

"There have been some strange things going on here. Did I see one of the three walk into your home?"

"Yes, you did, Bob," Dhareyin said as he came around the door. "I was sent by Ramsey to pick Star up so she can help us out today. Do you have an issue with that?"

"No, but she was supposed to tell me when she was in contact with you."

"I just showed up this morning to get her. As you can tell, she is not happy to see me this early."

"Where will you be taking her?"

"She is going to show us where they were dumping the toxic waste. After that, she will be off the hook."

"Star, check in with me when you get there. Tilly will want to know."

"I will, Bob. Thanks for stopping by."

I watched him walk out the door. I was happy to be rid of him. Hell, I would like to get rid of them all.

7

The ride over to the forest was a strained one. I could tell that Dhareyin wanted to talk to me, but I wasn't in the mood. I was not looking forward to seeing Daegorth. I desired to kill him. No, I wanted to shred the flesh from every inch of his body. I cannot seem to keep this hatred at bay. No one can know my identity until the time is right. I will enjoy taking care of Daegorth.

Pulling into the Heart of the Godz entrance was bittersweet. So many changes in my life since I lost my job.

"You have been awful quiet, Star. What is going through that beautiful mind of yours?"

"I thought you said you could read my mind?"

"I usually can, but for some reason today, I am not able to reach you. Where do we go from here?"

"Dhareyin, take the next right and follow it back to those trees at the end. You should be able to see where they have been dumping the waste. I am not certain how long they were dumping, so they could have started somewhere else. The day I saw them, they were down there."

Dhareyin drove slowly and we finished our ride in silence. A few vehicles followed behind us. The trees quickly came into sight. There was this weird haze around them. There were places that the trees were growing a mysterious substance on them, and some of them were dead. I got out of the car being careful to keep my distance from the rest.

"*I am going to kill you, bitch—slowly tearing you apart piece by piece. You will beg for mercy, but there will be none for you to have. I am going to flay you wide open, except this time, you will feel every slice. I will enjoy your blood, and you will be awake for all of it.*"

"*Bring it on, motherfucker. Want to do this now?*"

"*You are playing with fire, woman. You have no clue who you are messing with.*"

"*You are the piece of shit who couldn't finish the job, all because I called you by your name, Daegorth.*"

"*Keep talking; you are turning me on. I am fantasizing about what I am going to do to your body.*"

The destroyer who demanded flesh for flesh was rising within me. If I didn't get the destroyer under control, there would be a massacre here today.

"Stay here, Star. We are going to see how much damage there is on this end."

"Don't worry about me. I will stay here and keep a lookout."

They all walked away from me in search of answers I didn't have for them. There was something behind the trees. It was worth checking out. To be safe, I stayed out of the toxic area. The trail took me back behind the trees. I passed a sign that signaled a Heart Pond of some kind. I was curious to see this pond. It would be my first time back here due to restrictions to hikers.

So much of this forest was so magnificent. I was excited to see what beauty would cascade itself out in front of me when I got to the pond. Something was not right. As I came up to a beautiful rock formation in the middle of the trail, I could see that I was in for a surprise. The rock formation looked like crystals and geodes that had been cracked open to show case their beauty. They were all sorts of colors, but instead of being bold and bright, they were all murky. I could feel the energy within them. The toxins depleted the life that sustained them, and they were struggling to stay alive.

The trail split off and went to the right and left. It looked like the trail curved around the rock formation. I suppose the trail ended up at the same place. For some reason, the path to the left was calling to me.

I listened to my intuition and took the trail to the left. The sign ahead directed me to Heart Meadow. How interesting. I walked less than a quarter of a mile when the path opened into a meadow. What I saw next was excruciating. The meadow was not dying, it was dead. I could taste the bile in my mouth as I fell to my knees. It took me a moment before I realized I was sobbing uncontrollably. As my tears hit the ground, I could smell the most disgusting smell imaginable. I could feel the anger boiling up inside of me. I placed both of my hands upon Gaia, and she was screaming in agony. I could hear her cries and her pleas for help. I was so disgusted with the people who did this. I was at a loss about what I could do. *I will be back, Mother. There is something I must check first before I tell the others about this.*

I went back and took the right path this time. I knew it would lead me to the pond. After what I discovered in the meadow, I was not sure what I would find. I came upon a marker telling me about the Heart Pond being three hundred yards ahead. I was apprehensive with each step. What could this mean for the future of the forest, should the pond be lost? I kept stumbling along the path. It seemed something was keeping me away. I finally looked down and noticed all sorts of colorful crystals and stones lying on the ground as if that were their resting place. I was paying such close attention to the path that I didn't notice that I had reached the pond. The smell was so strong it acted like a battering ram, knocking me off my feet. I felt like I was dying inside. I felt so sick about what this meant for the pond, and whatever water source was feeding it.

I was determined not to stop. I got to my feet, and I instantly called in protection from somewhere. I don't even know how I knew how to do this. I rushed forward into the haze. What happened next was surreal. Somehow the pond was protecting itself. It was fascinating to watch. I walked to the edge and peered in. There were geodes of all kinds that made up the walls of the pond. I cannot describe how incredibly beautiful and powerful the pond was. I could see that it was tiring out. Little bits of the toxins were slowly leaking in. The other thing I noticed was that the pond was in the shape of a heart, and so was the meadow. As I looked back over my shoulder, the rock formation was the bottom point of a much larger heart.

I put my hands in the water. I could feel how strong and powerful its life force was. I could feel the energy contained within this water. I had this incredible urge to go swimming inside all those beautiful geodes. Standing up, I stripped out of my clothes. I walked into the water with the power of the goddess within me. The water seemed to carry me and then dropped me. I fell to the bottom of the pond. Somehow, I could breathe under the water. Something was sustaining my breath as I explored around.

It was so amazing; with every twist and turn, a new color or energy was waiting for me to explore. There were caverns upon caverns, and this pond was vaster than I could fathom in my mind. Then I saw what they wanted me to see. One of the caverns was dark and sad. The energy coming from it was heavy and dangerous. It was being kept back for the moment. I could no longer feel the natural energy coming from that cavern. I could feel the destroyer coming to the surface. I swam until I could see a bank covered in what was once grass. I surfaced and walked out of the water. When I looked up, I saw all the black gunk on the cave walls. The waterfall that was once there became the sludge slowly leaking into this water source.

I could feel the anger surfacing. It was much worse than the other night. I was ready to kill whoever did this. I could hear talking. Then, out of the corner of the waterfall, Dhareyin and the rest walked in. I don't know who was more surprised to see whom. Thank heavens, I had on my bra and underwear, and the black sludge that covered me suited me well. The destroyer raged below the surface.

Dhareyin gave me the once-over and rushed over to me. The others were behind him by a couple of minutes. "What are you doing down here, Star?"

I stared him straight in the eyes. "You keep forgetting who I am. I swam here through all this gunk and toxic waste. The pond is protecting itself, and only this cavern is infected. Gaia is tired and needs help."

"You act as if you know what is going on. How do you know all of this?"

"She told me. The thing you should know is the meadow is completely dead. Mother is screaming for help. She does not have much time left."

"The meadow is gone. How is that possible?"

"I asked myself the same thing. I do not know. Right now, we have to figure out how to help the pond."

"You are more mellow today. Have you calmed down since the last time you surfaced?"

"You would not want to be around if I were to catch one of those men dumping here today. I cannot guarantee I would stop with them. The anger building in me is getting hard to control. There is a knowing inside of me getting ready to surface. I believe it is something to help all of this heal. Did you find out what you wanted?"

"It hasn't reached the Heart of the Godz, yet. If they had kept dumping, we wouldn't have been able to save her."

"Well, well, well. What do we have here?" I heard behind me. I was overtaken with brute force, intensity, and focus. I could feel the color of my eyes shift to a metallic black, and I could almost see the flashes of red flicker at the corners. I turned and faced the voice. I shed the black goo, so I was standing in front of him raw and partially naked.

"Star, what happened to your body?" Seth piped in.

It was what I needed to push her down. I knew the day would come when Daegorth and myself would go head to head. I couldn't guarantee I would win, but he would be sorry he met me.

"Ask Dhareyin," I said, diving back into the water and heading back the way I came in.

The more I swam, the more the water cleansed me. The water healed me repeatedly until it tuckered me out. It was a great feeling.

By the time I reached the surface, I knew what to do for the meadow. I walked out of the water, clean and ready to get to work. Slipping my clothes back on over my wet body was proving to be more than I could handle. I left them at the rock formation and headed to the meadow. I reached the meadow in record time.

First, I offered a prayer of love and forgiveness. I knew it was the only place I could begin. For what one cannot and will not offer, another must take his place and do it for him and the well-being of humankind. I gently walked to the center of the meadow, making sure I wasn't hurting Mother. I put myself into a standing position, casting a sacred triple circle of protection, love, forgiveness, and healing in all directions. I was no longer Star. As much as I wanted to fight my existence as Aoroia, I knew I couldn't anymore. Something in the pond took care of that.

Spinning in a circle three times with my hands stretched out, I chanted the words that came so easily to me:

For deep within this heart of mine
I bring forth the fire of destruction and rebirth.
To cleanse and heal what man has inflicted upon Gaia.
I cast this fire in all directions in a starburst pattern,
Reaching within mother and without, without and within,
From the front to the back, top to bottom, and side to side.
I am asking this fire of destruction and rebirth, to cleanse and to heal Gaia now.

When the cleansing and healing have taken place, then I call upon the water gods to drench this meadow in their love and light, casting a downpour to penetrate, cleanse, and heal deeper than my fire, bringing forth rebirth on a higher vibrational level. Cast your waters upon Gaia, impregnating her with your energy and life force of renewal.

I watched the flames come out of my entire being, including my fingers and toes. What I didn't realize when I was spinning was that I rose above the ground. My fire burned everywhere. It burned so hot that it burned the dirt and broke seeds out of their little homes to bring new growth and life to the meadow. I could see the fire going deep below the surface, ebbing its way along the root system of the Heart Meadow. I could hear Mother crying tears of sadness for what was lost. She had tears of joy for what was to come. I was the center of this fireball. I cannot imagine what it must have looked like to Dhareyin when he came in at the tail end of my ritual. The look on his face was priceless. He stared at me in amazement and lust.

The fire destruction was complete when a single raindrop landed on my third eye. I slumped to the ground as the moment consumed the last bit of energy I had to offer. I felt Dhareyin catch me before it was lights out. I am not sure how long I was under before a vision came to me.

I was standing in the middle of the meadow, looking at what I had consumed with fire. I could feel the energy of Gaia coming back alive all around me. I could see her vibrating under the top layer of soil.

"See what you have done with your magick of destruction. To destroy can mean many things, Aoroia."

Then I was transported to the cave where the sludge was entering the pond.

"You know what to do, and you know how to fix this mess."

"Who are you?"

"We are the Council of Magick. We are a collective of beings governing HER return. You know what you must do. I know you hate him, but to save the pond, you will need him. He does not know what he is capable of, but you can show him who he is."

"Do you mean Daegorth? I would sooner slit his throat than show him anything."

"You are letting your pain blind you, Aoroia. There will be time for redemption when SHE returns."

"I will decide about Daegorth in a moment. Who is this 'SHE' you are talking about?"

"That is a question best answered at another time. Other things are needing your attention and focus. You must be careful, Aoroia.

Daegorth is not what is dangerous to you. It is those that have put a hit out on you. They think they know what you are capable of, but they have no idea. They do not know your power."

"My power has scared me. I am afraid when I dip into the shadows."

"Don't be. To fully become yourself, you must embrace all of you. Everything that you have ever experienced in this life so far will help you to make important decisions. There will come a time where you will have to make a dreaded decision. Do not take it lightly. It will call into question all your human beliefs, thoughts, feelings, and emotions. Choose wisely!"

"I am supposed to tell Daegorth... what?"

"You are stubborn, Aoroia. You know what to do. Now wake up and do it before it is too late. There are caverns in that pond that are extremely important to the lifeforms on this planet."

I awoke in Dhareyin's lap. He was stroking my cheek softly. The way he was cradling me was so tender. I could hear him whispering to me. "Thank you, Star, for saving the meadow. Your transformation is going so fast, and I don't know if I can protect you," Dhareyin said with his eyes shut, rocking me back and forth.

"Dhareyin, open your eyes."

I could see tears running down his face and dripping off his chin.

The miracle of what came next was breathtaking. The landscape had changed entirely. In a matter of moments, the whole scene was reborn. You could see new growth everywhere.

"Gaia is starving for water. Where does the water come from to supply this meadow?"

"The cave we were in before you left us. That is why Gaia is dying. Her water supply was so badly tainted. Do you have any ideas on how we can heal the pond, Star?"

"Yes, I do. I am not happy about it. Gather the guys together. Send Daegorth into the cave where I was when you showed up. I will meet you there."

"We will all meet you there."

"No, send in Daegorth alone. We must settle something. You are not to tell him who I am."

I watched him walk away as I admired the new life growing. I could hear Gaia's urgency about needing water. I decided to go for a swim again, and I wanted to surprise Daegorth. He was way too arrogant. I wasn't exactly sure what I was supposed to do with him, but I knew it would come to me. As I reached the surface, I could hear Daegorth ranting and raving at the top of his lungs. He was not happy about being down here alone. I walked out of the water naked. It was best to face him scars and all.

"Thank you for meeting me here, Daegorth." I barely got the words out of my mouth before his hands were around my throat, and he had pinned me against the cave wall.

What came next was without mercy as he ripped and sliced at every inch of my body. He went for my face this time, and I let him brutalize me and I thrived on it. I welcomed it with open arms. I chose to be fully awake this time. The scent of my blood was thick in the air. Who was I becoming that I would enjoy that? I should have bled out by now. I knew the reason I hadn't. My body was replenishing the lost blood faster than he could extract it from my body.

I watched him working on me. One slash at a time. So brutal and unhappy. So ferocious and primal. He was wearing himself out quickly. I could see that someone had turned him against his beautiful true nature. When those beings that wanted to free their essence made that decision, they would go to Daegorth to eat the flesh from their light. It was all tender and loving. That was the reason for the numbing abilities in his saliva.

Someone had turned his true nature into something brutal and ugly. I could see that now. I also knew the other part of who he was, and it ripped my heart out.

When he finished with me, he threw my limp body in the corner. Embracing the irony of the situation, I lay there with tears flowing down my cheeks. My heart filled with sadness as I looked up, and my blood was everywhere.

"Let me in there, Roman," I could hear.

"No, Dhareyin, you don't want to go in there. It is bad, so bad. We should have listened to her."

He must have gotten past Roman because I could hear him getting closer. Who was I kidding? I could smell him getting closer.

"OMG, Daegorth, what have you done?"

I looked up just as Dhareyin fell to his knees. The sound that came next was out of this world. The pain released in his scream caused me more pain than everything Daegorth put me through. It was more than my appearance to him. It was the truth about Daegorth that gutted him the most.

As every cut and slash came back together, I knew I was stronger than before. I could feel the healing taking place at a cellular level. All my parts came back together perfectly aligned. My face was taking a bit longer to heal because Daegorth did the most damage there. I should be feeling pain as this process was taking place. I felt cocooned in my healing juices that soothed and calmed.

I don't know how I saw anything at this point, considering how much of a mess my face was. Then I realized I was using my third eye and higher senses to see. Roman and Seth were huddled around Dhareyin, comforting him. What an odd scene. They all had the look of horror on their faces about what had transpired. I could hear their heartbeats, and I listened to their thoughts. None of them looked in my direction to see what was happening to me. Their grief surprised me. That grief was not for me, which to be honest, was offensive. The anguish was for Daegorth and what he had become. They knew the Heart Tribe would call for his permanent execution to never exist again when they found out what he had done.

"We have to take him to Ramsey. He will know what to do."

"No, Roman, not yet. I must gather my thoughts. We must take care of Star properly. Wait—where did she go?"

I didn't realize that when the cocoon happened, I went invisible.

The blood that covered my entire body hid my new ability from the men.

"We have to get Daegorth out of here. Take him to the surface. I am going to search for Star. She has got to be in so much pain."

Roman and Seth headed to the entranceway of the cave with Daegorth. Dhareyin walked around, trying to find me. I waited for the three at the entrance, healed and invisible. I wasn't angry, although I should have been. I knew I needed to teach Daegorth a lesson. Roman tried to shove him through, but he was met with resistance. With the flick of my hand and wrist, he went flying across the room. Seth knew my capabilities and he stepped out of the way. Daegorth was dumbfounded.

"Star, no!" Dhareyin screamed.

I came into full focus as I stood in front of Daegorth.

"How is this possible? I ripped you apart! You should be dead, you filthy human."

Knowing it would do no good to have a conversation with him, I went to work. I allowed all the anger to surface that I had been feeling since the beginning of time. I unleashed a wrath so brutal that my power began to burst forth, overtaking the essence of who I was and hurling me closer to the one I was to become. I could taste his blood in my mouth, the warmth overwhelming my senses, and I loved it. I slashed, and I ripped with such force that my hand entered and exited through his body. I flung him all over the cave, each strike an echo that reverberated for what seemed like an eternity, mixing his blood with mine, covering me from head to toe. What was born in me next was always meant to come forth. As my teeth sunk into his neck, I could taste the iron and copper in his blood, my body thriving on the taste. I took my eyes off him and stared at Dhareyin, who was in shock. Levitating three feet off the ground and in a quick spin, I scattered all remnants of blood, muscle, and flesh in every direction. I watched Daegorth slowly heal just like I knew he would. My fluids could destroy and heal.

"Are you ready to get to work, Daegorth?"

"Who are you?"

"You will know soon enough. Daegorth it is time you took your place by my side."

"What in the hell are you talking about?"

"Come to me, and I will show you."

He walked to me slowly. We never took our eyes off each other. He stood in front of me, unsure of what was to come next. I placed my hand on the back of his head and on his third eye. I showed him a vision of who he was always meant to be. A flicker of recognition flashed across his eyes.

Daegorth of the Heart Tribe
In this cave
On this night
I call forth
Your true essence
What was
Will no longer be
Shape-shift Into your destiny
With every swipe
Of your claws
And flicker of your tongue
The sludge is reversed
And will feed
Your greatness,
You will not stop
Until you are done
Begin now
Daegorth, my HELLHOUND.

We all watched him transform into a beast three times the size of a grizzly bear with the face of a werewolf. Talons adorned his feet and his claws could disembowel you in a single strike. He had a mouth full of teeth that could cut through steel and an elongated tail covered in spikes. He had a growl that was the mix of a bear and the chuff of a tiger. Daegorth was as dark as night when the sky was without illumination and he shimmered with iridescence, not your typical run-of-the-mill hellhound. I watched him slurp up all the sludge in the cave, like a suckerfish. He proceeded to drink from the pond. All the muck that had leaked into the pond he consumed. As his body separated the sludge from the water, scales appeared to release the water back into the pond. When he was done, he walked over to me and kneeled before me.

I stood before him, looking at his strange beauty. He licked my face. His tongue was velvety soft and warm. He put his paw out in front of me, and I climbed on board. There was a special place for me to sit that was soft and furry. My knees tucked in beautifully at his sides and some of the scales turned outward for my feet to rest upon and keep me safe.

The walls instantly became a thin shell of black onyx, black tourmaline, black obsidian, blood stone and labradorite with flecks of blue turquoise, carnelian, and amethyst. The walls seemed to shimmer with colors from the dark end of the rainbow spectrum. It was a beautiful sight to behold.

"No, Star, you cannot go with him. I don't understand what is happening. You cannot take him away."

"Dhareyin, you will soon learn I can do anything I want to. I will be back one day. You should all be ready for my return."

Daegorth dove into the water with me on his back. We explored all the caverns and learned the secrets of the Heart Pond. At one point, one of the caverns led into a private wilderness lake that was larger than all the caverns put together. You wouldn't know its size, because only a small amount of the surface was visible. The pond went on forever. It seemed like it was linked to many water sources. There was an energy of importance around this cavern and lake. He surfaced where I left my clothes. As he came up out of the water, he vibrated the water off and wings appeared. He took us higher and higher until we were soaring above the clouds. When we were done exploring, he flew over the forest. The pond and the meadow were safe. What I saw next was beyond belief.

My old boss was dumping in another area. This time, it was so much closer to The Heart.

"Fly low, my hellhound, and scare the hell out of them. When you get close enough, consume the toxic waste. Do not swallow it. I have an idea."

He swooped down and scared the men. He gathered up the toxic waste and waited for instruction. I leaned forward and whispered in his ear. He took off in flight and before long we reached our destination.

"Now, Daegorth!"

He spewed every amount of toxic waste and sludge all over my ex-bosses' home, cars, and property. It may seem stupid of me to do this, to dump toxic waste on Gaia, but what you don't know is I asked Daegorth to add protection fluids with the debris so that if it landed on Gaia she would be protected from its destruction. For now, my ex-boss needed to learn his lesson.

"Take me home, Daegorth. I need food and rest."

He took me home. No questions asked, he turned and left. What he and I must discuss could wait until another day. I walked into my home and headed for the shower. I needed my girly soaps and lotions. I wanted to feel normal again. Today was off the charts and no matter what, I could not change what I had become. I felt like a beautiful monster.

As I rubbed the sparkly lotion all over my body, I felt like Star again. Well, I should say, Dabney. Hell, how did I end up with three names? One of these days I would have to choose one and stick with it. I was able to transform back into my human self fully. It was getting more natural to shape-shift. Shapeshifting into Aoroia's body I stayed away from. I was born to the Heart of the Godz Tribe, but I was so much more than that. Right now, not transforming into the body that was like my mother's was the safest for me. After today, I was not sure who knew who I was. Would Gaia and the pond spill what they knew about me? I was curious to know if the Council of Magick was in contact with my tribe.

I needed a glass of wine after the day I have had. Walking to the front of the trailer, I ran the events of the day through my head. There was a part of me that was concerned about what Dhareyin thought of what happened. Another part of me did not give two shits what he thought. The Council of Magick had been silent since the meadow. It was probably for the best. I was not in the greatest of moods.

It was only seven. I could have sworn it was much later than that. I decided to order some Chinese food and pour myself a cold glass of wine. I got the food ordered and stood at the kitchen sink, staring out the window.

"Where have you been, Star? You need to report to the Bureau right away."

I was not surprised by Bob. I knew he was there the whole time. I was not interested in what he had to say or starting up a conversation with him, so I ignored his presence.

"You know where I have been, Bob. I have had a long day. I am going to enjoy this glass of wine, eat my food when it gets here, and read my new book." There was no point in arguing with him about going in. There were only a few who knew who I was. The Bureau did not need to know. "I will go into the local office tomorrow. If you will excuse me, I am going to get comfortable for the night. Next time, wait until I invite you in."

I watched him get up and walked toward the front door. He took a well-secured manila envelope out of his pocket. "This was on your front steps when I got here." He handed it to me and walked out the door.

I opened the envelope cautiously. There were only a few that knew I was living here. Dhareyin would have just shown up. It would not surprise me if he was lurking in the shadows watching over me. There was a letter inside from Matt.

THE FATE OF MAGICK

"Dear Star,

I hope all is well with you in your new place. I am writing to you because I felt like I had to warn you. There is something strange going on here at the Bureau, and you seem to be right in the middle of it. Matilda is not happy with you keeping secrets from her. She has been talking about booting you out of the program. I don't want anything to happen to you, my beautiful Star. I would not want that maniac Daegorth to find you again. I hope no one has intercepted this letter before you read it. Please heed this warning.

Love, Matt

P.S. There is something dark and sinister happening here at the Bureau. Something to do with the higher-ups and Ramsey. WATCH YOUR BACK!"

I took a picture of the letter and envelope with my cell phone. I shredded the actual letter and envelope in case Bob decided to enter my home again without permission. I wish Matt would have given me a way to get a hold of him. It would be nice to talk to him again like we used to on Twitter. My handsome friend who brought me back to life after my divorce from Rex. Nothing went on between us. It was the way he treated me that opened my heart back up. Where the heck is my food? I am starving.

Knock, knock!

There it was. I paid for my food and headed out into my back yard. I wanted to be out in the open and under the stars. When I first got here, I bought myself a cute picnic table and chairs with an umbrella. I headed back in for my wine and book. I grabbed my phone and locked the front door. I don't need any more surprises waiting for me. At some point, I needed to change my locks whether the Bureau liked it or not. I enjoyed my food and my wine. The book I decided to save for later when I was in bed. I didn't want to have my light going. After today I needed to soak in the night, place my bare feet upon Gaia, and gaze at the stars. I could feel something rejuvenating within me. The connection between the earth and the heavens was getting stronger and stronger. I could hear the world calling for HER return. I might not know who SHE is, but I was going to help in any way that I could.

8

After going to bed, I didn't get much sleep. I had one fitful dream after another. I knew where I needed to go today. It was the only way to make the nightmares stop. I had to go back where the Council of Magick reached out to me. Usually I would have a shower and eat breakfast. This morning there was an urgency pushing me to the Heart Meadow. I had a third-eye headache that was excruciating and zapping the energy out of me. I rubbed some citrus essential oils on my third eye and temples and drank a stiff glass of chocolate milk.

The drive there seemed to take longer than usual. I could feel all these emotions rising in me. I couldn't place them; they were becoming too many. Walking the trail to the Heart Meadow was calming in a way that felt like I was in another time and place. As I came into the clearing, I was astonished at how fast things had grown since I was here yesterday. The colors in this meadow were indescribable and out of this world. There were colors there that I have never seen. They looked like they came from the darkest and lightest points of the color spectrum. The colors seemed to vibrate back and forth, mixing several colors together. I was delighted to see and feel that Gaia was happy again. I walked towards the center of the meadow, where I used my magick. Every step I took, I felt more and more despair. When I reached the center, I collapsed to my knees. I knew what I was experiencing was on a human level. Instinctively I knew I had to feel what I was feeling. If I didn't allow this to happen, it would always be a hindrance to my purpose here. It could cause me to react from an overly hurt place. I had come to realize that it didn't matter if I was Aoroia or not; the human experiences would always be with me. Honestly, I didn't want them to go away. Those experiences have made me more diverse than anyone expected.

The tears fell from my eyes and hit the ground softly. With my abilities to hear, it sounded like thunder clapping in the distance. I cried my tears and snuggled the earth. I knew that I needed to feel Gaia on my body. She nurtured me with her heavy blanket of love and awareness. I fell asleep quickly.

"Why are you crying, Aoroia?"

"I am so afraid of who I am becoming. The things that I enjoyed when Daegorth was ripping me apart make me physically sick. To think that I enjoyed tasting his blood in my mouth is beyond what I can handle. Is this who I am meant to be? I feel like a monster. How am I any different from Daegorth? All my human instincts are telling me that there is something wrong with me."

"I understand your concern, dear girl. What you experienced yesterday was on a primal level. You were in control. You could have stopped Daegorth at any moment, but you chose to experience it in full. I know why you did this. The last time it happened, you were in and out of consciousness. You knew that you would heal, and so you allowed him to show his true colors. To begin with, I think you wanted Dhareyin, Roman, and Seth to find you that way so they would punish Daegorth. After a while, you came to realize some things about him, which then allowed you to realize that he had been broken. I believe you meant to have mercy upon him until he insulted you. It was then that you allowed all you had experienced through the entirety of who you be to unleash upon him."

"I feel so angry about this whole situation. I know that it is a human experience, but that is what I have been raised to be. To be taken away from my family and put into a home that was unloving as it possibly could be was unfair. Knowing that the only reason I

am being brought back is because this place is in trouble is offensive as hell. Then my mother, who handed me over to the monsters who were a part of raising me, thinks she did me a favor. What is even harder is taking off on Daegorth's back like we had been friends forever. How fucked up is that?" I said as the tears flowed like a torrential downpour down my face.

"It is not time yet, but you will learn more about your life. All the puzzle pieces must fit together for this transition to be successful. Allow yourself to feel the emotions. If you must do some of your training to work it out, then do so. You might want to ask Dhareyin to help you with that."

"I don't know who I can trust. They all seem to be coming after me or want something from me. How did Daegorth get involved in being hired to kill me? Is there someone from the tribe who is involved in the toxic dumping?"

"Start tuning in to your true essence. Listen to that knowing inside of your being. It will begin to tell you who is trustworthy or not. You must be open to it, Aoroia. Denying who you are is not helping you."

"If I take that name, then everything will start to fall into place, and they will know who I am."

"Then, don't tell anyone. Continue to go by Star but acknowledge to yourself who you are. I know you want to figure yourself out for a while. Ask Dhareyin to do another protective bubble around you so that you can step into your essence fully. Let him help you. You are more powerful than you realize. You don't have to take on your family's look. Look at what you accomplished yesterday without looking like them. You are so much more than their daughter, Aoroia. It is up to you to figure that one out. Find it out soon because we don't have much time before SHE returns."

"I have feelings for Dhareyin, and I don't know what to do about them. It makes it hard to reach out to him when every time I see him, I want to rip his clothes off and consume him. He tells me he is not allowed to be with me. I can see that he wants me as well, but he keeps himself under control. He worries about me getting pregnant and what would happen if my family found out. I feel confused by it all. Thank you for helping me to see that I was strong and powerful without changing into their look."

"Like I said, there are things they do not know. What happens between Dhareyin and yourself is your business. Pay attention to all your senses, Aoroia, including your heart. You are going to find out what Daegorth means to you. You will have a tough decision to make because you haven't been told everything about him. In hellhound form, he can be trusted. Watch out for him when he takes on his other form. There is an influence over him that he doesn't always have control over. We are cloaked from being able to see who exactly has been doing this to him. As far as other things concerning Daegorth, that is someone else's truth to tell. If you ever want to reach out to us, ask for the Council of Magick. I am speaking for the collective consciousness. You need to wake up; Dhareyin is coming this way. Remember we are here to help you and that we love you."

As I came awake on a rush of energy, I could hear Dhareyin headed my direction. I hadn't talked to him since yesterday. I wasn't sure I had the strength to deal with him today. Sitting up was proving to be extremely hard. I couldn't move. Maybe I was in the wrong position for far too long.

"I know you are here, Star. I can hear you breathing. Where are you?"

Why couldn't he see me? "I am right here, Dhareyin. Can you help me? I cannot seem to move?"

"I cannot see you. It looks like Gaia has wrapped you up tightly. Ask her to release you. I don't want to cut away what she has beautifully wrapped you in."

I closed my eyes and focused on my connection with her. *"Gaia, mother of this planet, thank you for nurturing me in my time of need. Please release me from your loving arms so I can get up."*

As I finished the last word, her blanket upon me started to open and release me. What a trip that was. Gaia had been healing me as

I was talking to the council. I sat up, and Dhareyin offered me his hand and helped me to stand. I wanted to see what Gaia had been up to, and I turned around to check it out. It looked like she had woven a blanket of grass and flowers over the top of me. The grass was so green and had a freshly cut watermelon smell to it. The flowers were tall and of all colors. I could hear the grass growing, the bees buzzing in delicious delight of pollinating the flowers, and the flowers welcoming the bees with their petals open. Why did the thought of that make me think of Dhareyin standing next to me?

"We need to talk, Star."

"Not now, Dhareyin. I have places I have to be. Matilda and the Bureau are pissed off at me because they think I am keeping secrets from them. I don't know who I can trust, so I am keeping them out of the loop as much as possible. Someone from my old company hired Daegorth to murder me. They knew what he was capable of. Have you ever wondered if they are connected to the tribe? Think about that and meet me at my place around seven tonight. We will have dinner and talk," I said as I walked past him.

"Come on, Star; you have got to talk to me," I heard as I kept walking away.

I was not going to deal with that big sexy man right now. All I could think about was how delicious it would be to ride that sexy face of his.

I needed to go deal with the Bureau and maybe get in some time with my instructor. I was sure I would have some frustrations I need to unleash.

The drive to the Bureau was intense and hot. I was not panicked as much as unsettled. The air conditioner was on, but I was sweating. I didn't know what to expect when I got there. So, I was going to be okay with the unknown and listen to my intuition. I have been pretty good at hiding what is going on with me so I should have no problem today doing the same thing.

Getting out of the car was harder than I thought it would be. Shutting the door with a slam, I barely missed my hand. Standing up tall, I walked with confidence through the front doors.

"I am here to talk to my field officer, Bob. Will you please tell him Star is here?"

Waiting was excruciating, so I walked around a bit and explored the landscape. They had a beautiful greenhouse made from wrought iron, and it was filled with the most beautiful plants and flowers. The air was robust and an earthy smell with different flowers blooming. The smell was so intoxicating it would take your breath away. There were some flowers growing that looked like they belonged in the Heart meadow. How did they get here? I could feel the hair on the back of my neck standing at attention.

"It is about time you showed up, Star. Why didn't you report in last night?"

"I remember you. You are Matilda. I had a busy day yesterday and needed time to regroup. To be honest, I am sick of people thinking they can tell me what to do and where to go. I know you have helped me out, and I am grateful, but that does not give you any right to control my life. I have nothing to report other than going and pinpointing for them where I saw them dumping the toxic waste. I got home around seven last night. I am sure Bob filled you in on that. By the way, you don't have a right to walk into my place of residence without my consent. It makes the Bureau look creepy and untrustworthy."

"We have been getting some intel that does not match what you are telling us. If you are not going to keep us in the loop, then we will have to end our association with you. The only way we can protect you is if we know what is going on. What we don't understand is how you got mixed up with the three?"

"Who are the three, anyway, Matilda—or should I call you Tilly? They were waiting for me when I got to the destination your people sent me to. The three came and got me to help them find out where the toxic waste is being dumped. Then I hear they are going to take me out of my regular training for something else. Why don't you tell me why Daegorth is connected to the three and was hired by my company to kill me? Something is really off here, Tilly, and I don't like it."

"All we know about the three is they are powerful men. We leave them alone because we have no jurisdiction over them. Only Ramsey has that job. I didn't know Daegorth was a part of Ramsey's people. It does make you wonder what is going on, doesn't it, Star?"

"Yes, it does, Tilly. I hope we get things figured out before I am harmed. I am going to work out with my trainer. I need to get some practice in and let off some steam. Maybe you can dig around and see what you can find. Until then, keep in touch. I want no more visits from Bob being in my home. If it happens again, that is a deal-breaker for me. I will find a way to take care of myself."

"Bob shouldn't have been at your home or even inside of it. I had Matt send you a letter. I have never asked Bob to go in your home uninvited. I will have a talk with him about it later. Go train; you look like you could use a good go-around. I will call your instructor and let him know you will be there in a few minutes. Please don't hesitate to call, Star. Here is my private number should you ever need anything, no matter the time of day. I am glad you remembered me."

I took the business card from her. Her touch was warm and friendly. Walking away from her felt empty like I wanted to talk to her more. What more could I say to her, when I was not entirely sure of what was going on. The drive to the gym was a weary one. I felt like I was trying to grasp what I knew, and it was out of my reach. The new stuff was just as much out of reach. Dinner with Dhareyin could prove exciting tonight.

I was hoping to be greeted by my instructor. Instead, I bumped into the receptionist.

"We are closing up early today, Star. Griff said to have you go back and wait for him. He had to make a phone call and he will be with you shortly. Do you mind if I lock up?"

What was going on? Should I be concerned that Griff wanted me locked inside with him? Tilly did say she was going to call him.

"No, that will be fine. I will go get changed into my workout clothes and warm up. Have a great evening, MoraKat."

She walked away from me. I watched her lock the doors. She had the funniest name I had ever heard. When Griff first told me, I couldn't believe my ears. He introduced her to me as MoraKat Moonpye! She had turned most of the lights off, so getting back to the locker was proving to be a bit difficult.

Once I was all changed, I decided to go out on the mats and stretch. Griff could be quite tough on me, and I wanted to make sure my muscles were stretched and warmed up. I could feel the tears below the surface, but this was no place for those to come out.

Griff was taking a long time. I suppose he could have forgotten I was here and left. This would be a great time to meditate on the last few days. Sitting in a lotus position, I found my center easily. I focused in on everything that had been happening since I came to this town. I was getting goosebumps as if the temperature had dropped twenty degrees. The hair on my neck and arms was standing at attention. This getting in touch was kind of interesting. I never felt anything like this when I learned how to meditate from my dear friend James Lucien. I knew him growing up. He was about fifteen years or so older than me, and we were neighbors until he moved. If not for his friendship and support, I would have turned out a lot worse than I did. I made it a point to get back to Savannah as much as I possibly could.

The last time was right after Rex and I got married. Rex was gone all the time, and I was experiencing anxiety more and more. I called James, and he invited me down to stay for a week. I was excited to go because he married this amazing woman, Layla, and they had a couple of beautiful children plus her grown sons. I had not thought of James this whole time. I wondered if anyone let him know that I was dead. When this was all over, I was ready to go back and spend some time with him and his family. I love being around their incredible energy. I can focus on him this afternoon instead of the drama in my life.

Deep breath in through the nose and blow slowly out the mouth. For the life of me, that was about as far as I got. Unfolding my legs, I lay down on the mat and let my mind wander. I was acutely aware of someone else's energy in the room. I lay perfectly still, not giving away that I knew the person was there. I opened my eyes slowly and detected movement in the corner in the shadows. I was ready for whatever was about to happen. With stealth mode, he landed heavily upon the mats at my feet. I could hear him breathing heavily and powerfully through his mouth. I could feel him stalking all around me. I was waiting for him to pounce. Arching my back and bringing my knees up with my feet on the floor, I was able to flip upright and land on my feet. He came flying at me, and I was able to do a handless flip through the air, landing on my feet and ready to go. I opened my eyes a peep and noticed it was completely dark. How long had I been in here? Where did Griff go? I opened all my other senses. I stood there waiting for him to make his next move.

I could feel him behind me. How did he get there? He was just in front of me! I could feel him in my energy and my space, nudging me from behind to move, rubbing himself all over my legs and my back. Then I felt a lick across my face. His tongue was warm and velvety. Soft and wet. His breath was sweet. He was nudging my hand to rest upon the top of his head. Why wasn't I scared? This was Daegorth we were talking about.

As he knocked me off my feet and straddled me with his body, I felt consumed.

"Mistress play with me. Please dominate me like you did the other day. I am always yours. How can I please you?"

This was an interesting turn of events. There was this part of me that wanted to punish him and torment him. Would it be wrong for me to dominate him? He continued to lie on top of me like a big lap dog. Licking my face and being lovey with me was not how I pictured my relationship with Daegorth being.

"Do you know who we are to each other, Daegorth?"

"No, Mistress. I want you to punish me for hurting you, especially the first time. I was quite brutal with you the last time. I need you to hurt me over and over for an eternity."

As much as the old part of me wanted to oblige him, the new part of me felt conflicted and sad.

"Daegorth, are you turned on by the idea of me punishing you?"

"No, Mistress!"

"Are you lying to me?"

"Yes, Mistress."

"Do you want me to have sex with you?"

There was complete silence in the room. I could feel his attraction to me, but I needed him to admit it.

"Yes, Mistress."

"You know I cannot have sex with a beast. It wouldn't be right. You brutalized me; how do I get over that?"

He was starting to get upset. The growl began low and got louder and louder. "We are not alone, Daegorth," I whispered.

He stayed on my body in protection mode. All the lights in the gym went on. "We will speak again, Mistress," he said as he licked the side of my face, neck, and ear.

"What the fuck is going on here, Star?"

"What do you mean, Dhareyin? I was meditating when Daegorth came in to talk to me."

"Where is he, Star?"

I could feel him. He was still there but had gone invisible. That ability was a good thing to remember. "You better never go invisible on me and come into my home, Daegorth," I whispered under my breath. All I could hear was a light chuff.

"Never mind; he is gone. What are you doing here? I was supposed to be training with Griff, but no one showed up. MoraKat locked me in here and told me to wait for Griff to get off the phone. Why are you in such a huff?"

"It is after midnight. We were supposed to have dinner together, remember?"

"There is no way it is that late. I got here a little after three. It has only been about forty-five minutes. Where is Griff?"

"Somebody tripped the alarm system, and Griff tapped into his cameras and saw you. He called me to ask if I knew why you were at the gym. I told him that I didn't, so I got in touch with the Bureau. I was told that you came here for a training session with Griff. I called Griff back and he knew nothing about it. I came over to see what was going on."

"The receptionist knew I was here. Why would she mislead me? She has nothing to gain from all of this. No harm came to me; what purpose would she have for locking me in here? I am at a loss here, Dhareyin."

"Let's get you home. I have food waiting for us. It is cold, but it will be good. You can ride with me, and we will come get your car in the morning."

"No, I will drive it tonight. There is nothing wrong with me. Why do you keep thinking you can tell me what to do?"

"I was trying to be considerate, Star. Stop biting my fucking head off."

"Be careful, Dhareyin, what you say. I could literally bite your head off. So, back off. I will see you at the trailer."

I got into my car. I was so not in the mood for any of his bullshit tonight. Where did all that time go? Was that Daegorth's doing? I turned up the music and rolled down my windows. It felt so good to have the midnight air blowing through my hair and kissing my skin. I put my forearm and hand out the window. Twisting and turning my hand allowed the breeze to blow lovingly through my fingers. It was renewing my energy. I thought I was in for a fight with Dhareyin. Pulling into my driveway, I was not surprised that Dhareyin beat me there. He was leaning against his souped-up black cherry 1970s Dodge Charger. They looked like they belonged together.

He opened my door, which generally I wouldn't mind, but I wasn't quite ready to get out of my car.

"Do you mind? I was not ready to get out."

"What has got you in such a sour mood tonight, Star? You are the one who invited me over for dinner. Why take it out on me?"

"Fuck you, Dhareyin!"

"I would rather fuck you."

"Excuse me!"

"You heard me," he said as he pulled me out of the car and pushed me up against the back door.

He put his hand around the back of my neck, pulling my mouth to his. He was passionate and in a hurry. We were matching each other tongue for tongue. Kissing me in the crook of my neck, he worked his way inside the front of my yoga pants, kissing me and doing pleasurable things to my body. The night was chilly, and my nipples were at attention. He couldn't see them because it was a pitch-dark night. His kisses were filled with a fever begging to be released. He took my hand and guided it down to his trousers. He wanted me to touch him and to know how turned on he was. I could feel the orgasm building in me.

"I want you, Star. Do you want me? If not, you had better tell me now."

"I want you, Dhareyin, more than I ever knew."

That was all he needed. He lifted me up on the trunk of the car and pulled my yoga pants off. He bent down, kissing, and licking me until I was begging him to be inside of me. He unzipped his pants and slowly withdrew his massive erection. He filled me completely. Slowly sitting up on my elbows, he took my nipple into his mouth. As he grabbed my ass, I instinctively wrapped my legs around his waist as he drove deeper into my hot body. The fever consuming us both was hot and passionate. With one last thrust, he exploded inside of me, causing me to release my engorged tensions, and soaking us both. Dhareyin collapsed on me, and we held each other for a long time, it seemed.

"Do you have the key to your back door, Star?"

"Yes, it is on my key ring—why?"

"I am going to pack you in the way you are. I doubt you want your neighbors to see you in your disheveled state."

"Great idea; why didn't I think of that?" I said as I watched him pull up his pants over his sexy ass and tuck away his enormous shaft.

He grabbed my keys out of the car and packed me to the back door. I opened the door and he set me inside.

"I will be right back. I have got to grab your clothes and the food."

I walked to my bedroom, went to the bathroom, and cleaned up, and put on some clean clothes. I felt giddy inside. I realized I should go unlock the front door so it would be easier on him. As I opened the door, I noticed an envelope taped to the screen door. Who the hell was this one from?

What was taking Dhareyin so long? Walking down the steps of my six-by-nine-foot porch, I felt a strange stirring in the air. Something was off. The energy surrounding me seemed to snap and crackle in various colors. I felt myself slipping into the dark side of my shadow. Opening all my senses, I could not sense Dhareyin anywhere in the vicinity. What I heard next was gut-wrenching. I could hear blood pouring onto the ground and bones breaking. I could smell the copper and iron in the air. The screams were barely audible due to the person slipping into unconsciousness. I walked slowly down the circular drive. Going invisible had become a natural shift in energy for me. I felt myself becoming lighter and lighter, as I could barely keep my feet on the ground. I knew I must hurry. I hoped I was not too late. I knew it was a trap, but I didn't care. I wasn't foolish; I was saving a life.

I knew it was her all along. I don't know who was hurting Sally, but they were going to wish they had stayed home.

"I didn't do anything wrong. I told you everything about her. I informed on her just like you asked me to do," Sally said as she was struck across the face.

"Sally, she denies everything. You have been lying to us. We told you to keep an eye on her and to befriend her. We needed to know where she was going and who she was visiting. You will lose your life due to your lying."

"No, please, don't!"

Not a one of them was any the wiser that I was in the room. I didn't love the fact that Sally had been spying on me. I thought we were becoming good friends. Goes to show how much I know. How did she get caught up in this mess, anyway? I was shocked when I saw who was in the room with Sally. I would deal with them in a moment.

She was bloodied and broken. Open wounds on her face showed knife marks. Her shirt was ripped to tatters in the back like she had been whipped. It looked like they were attempting to pull some of her fingernails off. She had slash marks all over her body, and she smelled like lemon juice. Her right forearm had a bone protruding through the skin. Somehow, they had created a compound fracture. The smell of urine and feces was strong in the air. She endured so much pain; no wonder she was in and out of consciousness. I knew the only one who could help her right now was Gaia. They all had their backs turned, so I walked over to Sally and touched her lightly. My invisibility transferred to her as well. I bent down and picked her up and carried her outside. I laid her upon the ground.

"Gaia, I need you to help my friend. Please protect and heal her." Before I turned around to go back up the stairs, Gaia was already covering Sally in a protective blanket of love. Before long, she would be hidden completely, and that was the way I wanted it to be. There was no point in her seeing what was going to take place.

Walking up the steps slowly, I listened to make sure they were not aware that she was gone. I walked in and took her place and shook my invisibility cloak to the side.

"I understand you motherfuckers are looking for me. I see you get off on hurting women."

"Where the fuck did you come from?"

"Wouldn't you like to know? Now what is all the fuss about?" I could tell that I had taken them by surprise. I knew who a couple of the people were, but there were others I did not know. Griff, Matt, Mark, Bob, and Tilly were there. "I know who you four are, but who would like to introduce me to the other three?"

"It is not necessary for you to know who they are. Where is Sally?"

"Tilly, you will never know where Sally is again. You won't ever hurt her again because of me. You will stop this behavior right now."

"Who do you think you are?"

"I am going to show you who I am. Then you will know not to mess with me again." Turning my head side to side, loosening up the muscles and getting ready for battle felt great. The anger in me was rising higher and higher.

"What is going on in here?" I heard on the front steps.

"This is none of your concern, Dhareyin. We have some business to settle."

"I beg to differ, Tilly. You three had better get out of here before Seth and Roman show up. Tilly, don't ever show your face around here again."

"You cannot tell me what to do. She needs to give us Sally back."

"Star, where is Sally?"

"Sorry; not telling you, Dhareyin."

"You had better start talking before the rest show up."

"Time and time again you underestimate me, Dhareyin. Don't think that because we fucked on the back of my car that you have any right to tell me what to do. When I know Sally is safe, I will let her go, and not a moment sooner."

The look Dhareyin gave me was cool anger. The veins in his temple were threatening to burst he was so angry. I was not afraid of Dhareyin. "You don't know who she is, Star. Give her back, NOW!"

The last thing I did before I went totally invisible was cast an incredible "fuck you" with both of my birdie fingers. I walked right passed him and he couldn't do a damn thing about it. I walked outside and went to where Gaia was protecting Sally.

"I don't care who you are, Sally. If you want to survive the night, you will let Gaia take care of you. I will be back later to check on you."

"I am really sorry, Star. I hope you will let me explain tomorrow."
"All in due time, Sally. Now rest and be safe."

I walked back to my place, grabbed my bag, got in my car, and drove away. I had no idea where I was going, but it didn't matter for tonight. I felt so empowered and full of strength and determination. I didn't know who Sally was or why she was spying on me. At this point, I do not care. Could that change when she explained herself? I honestly did not know.

9

I didn't know where I belonged anymore. I thought once I figured out these powers and who I was that it would change how I felt. I was finding out that it didn't matter, because I still felt like an outcast. I wanted to get as far away from this place as I possibly could. Hopefully, there was a fast food place open, or a grocery store, because I was starving. Hell, I could use a stiff drink. A couple of glasses of scotch sounded pretty good.

There was a twenty-four-hour convenience store and liquor store open. It was right next to a place that rented little cabins in the woods. I found some excellent food to eat, and instead of the scotch, I bought some peaches and cream MD 20/20. I checked into a little two-bedroom two-bathroom cabin that was tucked away in the forest. It was called the Enchantress! I checked in under Dabney Vaughn and I paid cash. They hesitated at first until I explained that I was running away from an abusive husband. I got settled in and hid my car in the little garage behind the cabin.

I sat and ate the deli sandwich, chips, and fruit pie I bought. I poured myself a drink and sat on the bed waiting for sleep to take me. I enjoyed thinking about my sexual experience with Dhareyin. I had hoped for another round, but I was not sure if that was even possible now. I would check on Sally tomorrow. I went to sleep with a lot of heavy subjects on my mind. I would make a list when I woke up.

"Aoroia, you have to give Star back. You don't know who she is. If you are not careful, you will start a war amongst the humans

and the tribe. It is morning; you have to go back and free Sally from Gaia."

I had a fitful night, and the message I received did not help my mood any. I was on my time schedule and no one else's. They could wait. If they were so bloody hopped up on starting wars amongst themselves, then let them do it. The damage that had been done to her body and mind needed time to heal. I took a shower and had a cup of coffee. I decided I would keep this place and never stay at the trailer again. I would gather my things discreetly and move here. The owners offered me a great price, and it wasn't like I didn't have plenty of money floating around from my other life.

I didn't want anyone tracking me, so I turned off my phone. My car wasn't new enough to have Lo Jack. I finished my coffee and turned my phone on. Not only were my text messages full, but my voice mails were as well. It looked like fifty people had tried to call. I wasn't returning any of them. I headed back to Sally. It was early enough; hopefully, no one was there.

I was mistaken. As I pulled up, my car was surrounded by a mob of angry people I didn't even know. I wasn't afraid, and that surprised me. I got out of my car and was met by Dhareyin.

"Where have you been all night, Star?"

I shoved by him without even one word. I was on a mission. When I got to Sally's trailer, Ramsey was there in a frantic state.

"What have you done with Sally, you evil girl?"

I ignored him as well. That did not go over well at all. I was almost on top of where I laid Sally down when I noticed movement out of the corner of my left eye. I made no sudden movements, but I did turn slowly to face my attacker. Seth was coming from the left and Roman from the right. Both were in attack mode and neither looked like they had any mercy to show me.

"Stop where you are, or I will show you what I am truly made of."

They both stopped, looked at each other, and pounced on me like a jaguar would his prey. I was able to move into and tumble around where Sally was hidden.

"Gaia, it is time to release my friend. Thank you for all you have done," I said in a whisper.

I was distracted long enough for Seth and Roman to advance on me. They both grabbed me and were quite rough on me.

"Leave her alone," I heard at my feet.

"This is a miracle. Where did you come from, Sally?"

"Star saved my life after they tried to murder me last night. She asked Gaia to protect and heal me. I have been wrapped in Gaia's blanket all night. I am perfectly healed this morning."

I looked at her and was sick to my stomach. Her face was struggling to heal. We would have to do something about that. Before I could suggest anything, I was let go and they took Sally away. Maybe one day she would be able to explain to me what this was all about. I could see that this wasn't exactly over. Ramsey, Dhareyin, Seth, and Roman were in a private chat. They kept looking in my direction, and I knew something was up. I started walking toward my trailer. I wanted to pack up my stuff so I could leave. I didn't make it past all the men as they stepped in front of my path back home. I tried to walk around them, but they wouldn't let me.

"Look, fellas, Sally is doing a lot better and she needs some help healing the rest of her face. I can recommend some things if you don't have a clue. Why don't you ask your brilliant shaman here what to do?" I said as I pointed to Dhareyin.

I was in a feisty mood, and I was not backing down.

"Let me by, you bunch of bullies."

Not one of them would budge. What did they want, and why weren't they speaking? Dhareyin reached for me and I dodged his hand.

"Don't touch me. Don't ever touch me again, Dhareyin. So, help me God, I will rip you into pieces."

He took a step back, clenching his jaw. I knew I had hurt him, but I would not tolerate being treated the way he was treating me.

"We wanted to thank you for helping Sally. That was all we

came to say. You can go now."

"Thanks, Roman!" I said as I walked away from them all. At this moment, I didn't care if I ever saw Dhareyin or anyone from this tribe again. I know I was being a shit and reacting instead of responding, but I didn't care. I was tired and pissed off. Once again, I was being kept in the dark about everything. Walking into the trailer, I was shocked to see the state of my home. It had been ripped apart and savagely mauled by persons unknown. I could feel the rage building in me. I headed to my bedroom, where most of my stuff was. I was not prepared for the carnage that awaited me. My bed, bedding, pillows, and clothing had been ripped into shreds. My makeup, lotions, soaps, and other toiletries were thrown and busted, sitting in the corner. My laptop and printer were broken into pieces. My bottles of perfume were shattered in the sink. You could see the remnants of glass and perfume running down the drain. Thank heavens most of my stuff ended up in storage. I reached into my secret hiding space and grabbed my mini external hard drive and walked away from it all.

I walked down the stairs and headed to my car. Dhareyin was waiting for me.

"I am sorry about your place and things, Star. I told you to give her back. These are the consequences for not listening."

I could feel the rage, anger, and venom surging in my veins. His words did nothing but stoke the fire that was already raging inside of me. "I am going to kill you all. When I am done, there will be nothing left of this town or your tribe. If you would like me to demonstrate, I can start right here?" I said to Dhareyin in an enraged whisper. "You have all fucked with the wrong woman, and you know it. Yet you do nothing to change how you treat me. I am still a human to you all. Don't let that fool you."

"I know I shouldn't say this, but I am actually terrified of you right now. I know your heart, Star, and you couldn't kill all of these innocent people."

I started laughing hard. It felt good to release it. "You know nothing about me, and I prefer it that way."

I could taste the bile in my mouth. I didn't like how I was feeling or talking. I was allowing my hurt to fuel me, and I had to figure out how to shut it down before I unleashed my shadow on all these people. It didn't help that I was confused about my feelings for Dhareyin.

"Don't do this, Star. What about the prophecy? What about your mother and the role you will play here?"

"I am moving away, Dhareyin. I have no answers for your questions."

As the words flowed out of me like water shooting down a rain gutter after a significant rain, I felt sadness in my heart. "Who is to say there is even a prophecy? No one has shown me one so why should I believe what you say. As far as my mother—well, there are feelings about her that I am having a hard time coming to terms with. None of it makes sense, and there is something more going on here than anyone is letting on."

"What about us, Star? I cannot believe you blurted out to everyone what we did on the back of your car. There will be consequences for what we did last night. I am sorry I put you in that position."

"You know what I know, Dhareyin? I know that I am a grown woman, and I don't need anyone dictating who I can and cannot sleep with. If you were so concerned about it, then why did you have sex with me? Do you regret your time with me last night?"

"No, I don't regret it. Why did you have to go help her? Her of all people. All you had to do was stay at your place--but no, you had to interfere. You showed them that we are even closer than we have been telling people. There is no getting out of it. I will have to face this alone, because no one knows who you are."

I could feel my blood boiling. More secrets and no willingness to divulge. I could feel the anger rising in me. This time around, it felt different, and I couldn't control it. I could feel the pain in the palm of my hands from clenching my fists together. They were starting to feel damp. It was getting warm and sticky. I could hear the wetness hitting the ground drop after drop. It sounded like a leaky faucet. I could smell the blood leaking out of my palms.

"Star, what have you done to yourself?"

"I need to see James. I don't know when I will be back," I said to him as I opened a portal that led to James.

"Wait for me," I heard as Dhareyin grabbed my hand and stepped into the portal with me.

Going through the portals was not always an easy thing to do. A portal was an opening of a space between space. It was like these intense blue colors spiraling and working together. The energy inside was sparkly and friendly. The temperature never seemed to change inside. It was always a cool seventy-five degrees Fahrenheit. The smell inside was neutral. The disorientation could be quite mind-numbing. I was feeling nauseous and dizzy. Whether I told him or not, I was grateful Dhareyin was with me. I needed to talk to James and see if he could help me get the anger under control. I was always surprised at how precise these portals were. We landed outside James's home.

"How long have you been pulling portals?"

"I have played with them a little bit. I didn't figure it was anyone's business, so I never told anyone. I knew there would come a day when I would have to face Daegorth again and I wanted a way out. I am sure it will come in handy in other places as well. James is a dear friend of mine and I ask that you surround his home and family with protection to keep them safe. PLEASE!"

"Anything for you, Star!"

I wondered if he really meant that. I would text James and see if he was home. If not, we would have to go to his studio, which was not too far away.

"James, I am standing in your front yard. Are you home? It is Dabney!"

It seemed like forever before he answered.

"Wait, you are here? This is a joke! YOU ARE DEAD."

I sent him a photo of me standing outside of his house.

"I am just getting done with a reiki session. Give me about fifteen minutes and I will be there."

"Actually, could we meet you at your studio?"

"We? Is something wrong, Dabs?"

"Yes, I am in trouble and I need you, James. I don't want to involve Layla and the kids."

"I will see you in fifteen minutes."

It didn't look like Layla was home, so we snuck into the trees so we could pull another portal. It would take us a lot longer than fifteen minutes to get to James on foot. Being back here brought back so many good memories. I knew that James would understand, but how would I explain everything to him?

"Don't worry, Star. Everything will be all right. I am not sure why we are here or why you need this James, but I have got your back."

I looked at him as he softly put his hand on my shoulder, showing me a sign of comfort.

I knew there was a small grove of trees outside of James's office. I opened it up and we went for a light-speed ride. I didn't really know how I was feeling with all these emotions crashing around inside of me. I felt sick over how I had talked to Dhareyin. He could have divulged my secret when he found out, but he was keeping it to himself. It was shitty of me to lash out at him last night and tell everyone we had sex. There were other things rolling around inside of me that I couldn't put my finger on. I felt like a sad love CD was playing over and over in my mind. If I stayed mad at him, would that keep me from letting my feelings for him grow? So many questions and not enough answers.

We came out in the clearing, like I thought we would. What I didn't expect was for James to be standing outside. He saw us walk out of the trees. His eyes were big and bright. He shook his head as I walked toward him. I couldn't tell if he was happy to see me or not. I was beginning to question whether this was the right move.

I stood in front of him, wondering what would come next. He

looked at me and then over my shoulder at Dhareyin. He pulled me into his arms and held me for the longest time.

"I was so devastated when I heard about your death. Rex called me and let me know. I am so happy to have you standing here in my arms, Dabs," he whispered softly in my ear. James released me and put his hand out to Dhareyin. He took it reluctantly.

"James, this is my friend Dhareyin."

Dhareyin gave me a look of surprise. He decided to use this time to speak to me telepathically. "You know I am more than that. Stop denying it."

"It is nice to meet you, Dhareyin. Why don't we all go inside where it is cooler. Dabs, you can tell me what has been going on with you."

We went inside. The air conditioning was a blessing, considering that Savannah this time of year was hot and humid. I explained everything that had been going on with me. I could see he was a bit skeptical, but he kept listening. I simply forgot Dhareyin was in the room. It was like that with James. It was as if he created this space that was between you and him. He was powerful and had a magick of his own. Dhareyin never said a word. I think he wanted to hear what I had to say as well.

"What you have told me is unbelievable, and had you come to me a few years ago, I am not sure I would have believed you. I feel like there is something you are not telling me. Without that information, I cannot help you as much as I would like to."

I had left out the parts about Daegorth and me. I wasn't sure if I should tell him about the Council of Magick. There were things that Dhareyin did not know and I wasn't sure I wanted him to. I wasn't entirely sure he could be trusted. All this was playing out in my head. I could feel myself in deep thought. *"Tell him everything, Aoroia. He can be trusted. He knows more than you realize. It is why you had an urgency to get to him today."* Damned Council of Magick slipped in whenever they wanted to.

"Dabs?" James was saying as he was clicking his fingers, trying to snap me back to the present.

I looked up at him. I was seeing him differently. He had this sparkly aura, and there was light around him that I was not privy to before. His light was pulsating and alive. The love that was emanating from him was all-consuming.

"I am here, James. I need your help. There are some things that have happened that I haven't told Dhareyin about yet. I am not ready to do that currently. What I came here for was for you to help me, like you always have. I am scared and I feel alone. I have so much going on inside of me; I don't know what to do with it."

"I need to see what you can do. I am looking at your energy, and it is spectacular. I do not see anything off in your energy field."

I looked back and forth at them both. I looked up and around to see if I had enough room to do what I knew I could do. I was going to do damage. I wondered how he felt about that.

"Stand back, both of you. Dhareyin, protect him. Put him in a bubble and protect yourselves. Don't hate me for what I am about to do. It will be all right. Have faith in me, and trust that I know what I am doing. I have cast a circle of protection around the property so nothing and no one will be hurt. Only the three of us know what is going on. Are you both ready?"

I closed my eyes and set the perimeter. I opened my eyes, and I could feel the destroyer step forward. I heard James gasp. My skin took on a blue-black sparkle, and everywhere there was a scar, it took on a blue-black rainbow color. I could feel those invisible scars on my face shine brightly. My eyes were like the dark cosmos. They were dark, liquid pools of endless night. My body was beautiful, and I felt fluid. I arched my back, rotating my arms and placing my palms upright. Raising my arms up brought my body with it. I was levitating off the floor. The energy I was creating gave my hair and clothes the appearance of a fan blowing on them. It was time to introduce myself to James and Dhareyin. I looked at them both.

"I am Aoroia the Destroyer. Are you ready?"

They both nodded their heads yes. I looked at them and made

sure they were safe. I rechecked my perimeter and all was safe. I could feel the energy building in me.

I started off slowly by throwing things around the room—casting them about, breaking them. I could see that James was in shock. Was I going too far? I had not even begun. I lifted them both up and spun them around, playing with them. I set them back down in a better place.

I started to spin, and with my spinning, all the objects I had busted into pieces. I took a deep breath in imploding his building and released my breath and exploded James's office out into a million pieces. I kept it all contained in the destruction field, spinning around and around. Why could I smell the faint smell of blood in the air? I looked at Dhareyin and James to see if it was them. I spun around and there she was. Layla was lying on the ground impaled by some of the debris. She was bleeding out quickly. I looked back at James. He looked at me and knew something was wrong. He peeked around me and fell to his knees.

"Dhareyin, let me out of this bubble—I need to get to her."

"NO! Don't do it, Dhareyin. James, stay put. Have faith in me, my dear friend."

He nodded his head in acknowledgment. There were tears running down his face, and I could feel his pain and helplessness. While the destruction remained in the air, floating around and around, I slowly brought my feet back to the ground. I sat down on the ground facing Layla, taking the lotus position. I placed both hands on the floor.

"Gaia open up your body for my dear friend Layla. Bring her to me slowly." Once she was in front of me, I placed my hands strategically on her body to start the healing fluids flowing. "Place your blanket of protection above what impales her. I must put back what I have destroyed," I said to her in a chant.

I went to work putting James's building back the way I found it. Piece by piece, it was coming back together and taking shape quickly. With all things, it takes a bit of time to put everything back together; that includes all the tiny fragments that were created. I was keeping an eye on James and Layla. When the building was completely back together, I had one more thing I needed to do. Knowing this and what I could do helped me to realize that I no longer needed to be afraid of what I was capable of.

"Gaia, remove your protection so I can help my friend."

The blanket Gaia placed upon Layla slowly lifted off her. What I saw next was shocking. Lying next to her was her spirit family Aeryana and Wolf. They were holding her suspended in a peaceful sleep. They looked at me with tears in their eyes. Was she dead? Had I killed my friend? The tears erupted out of my eyes with such force that everything I had been feeling was laid out on the floor before me. This was my fear that I would destroy what I loved. How could I become that being? I fell to my knees, sobbing at the truth before me. My tears fell, turning into a pool of water and filling the grave that held Layla.

"All is not lost, Aoroia. What has happened here today not only opened your next level of gifts, but Layla has been reborn into who she was always meant to be. That is why Wolf and Aeryana are here with her. They knew back when they came into her life that this would be where she was meant to go in her life's journey. You know what to do. You just needed the fear to be released from you. Now embrace your destiny and help her out."

I stepped into the pool with her. Everything about me changed. I had become a translucent color, shining all colors of the rainbow. My eyes turned into the color of the Milky Way. My tears were still falling from me into the pool. I could feel the love in the water. I went to work pulling out all the debris. I could see her entire body as if I was an X-ray machine. I could see clear to a cellular level. I knew what had to be healed. I could see her healing things on her level as well.

"Layla, rise and take your place amongst the magickal beings of your tribe."

As she became fully vertical, I could see the changes taking place within her and on the outside. Everything was changing for her as she accepted her position amongst magick. I let her continue to shift and change. I needed to see how James and Dhareyin were doing.

I turned to face James. I didn't know what to expect, but I knew I had to take responsibility for what happened, even if it was meant to be.

"Dhareyin, let him out."

James tried rushing toward her when he was stopped by Aeryana and Wolf. "No, James, not yet. She needs time to heal and transform."

He turned to me and took me in. He walked closer to me. I stood my ground and was ready to take whatever he dealt out.

"I am speechless. I want you to know I don't blame you. You did everything you could to protect this environment so you could show me what you have become. I am not sure I can help you, Dabs. What is happening with Layla? I don't understand; she is changing before me. Is this why you came here?"

"I don't need you to help me anymore. Give her a few moments and we will talk. Let's give her some space while she transforms. I am so sorry, James. I did not know she was here, or I would have brought her in here with us."

I could see a transformation taking place within him. I did not expect this at all.

"I always knew there was something about you, Dabs. I know that what you carry in you can be scary and powerful. Don't hate it. The more you hate it, the more you will fight it. There are so many things that come back to life after destruction. Take a forest fire and how it burns away the old to pop open the seeds so new trees can come alive. I never thought one of those things would be my love."

"When I saw what I had done to Layla, my beautiful friend, something broke free from within me. I knew I was afraid of what I was becoming for this very reason. What if I became so hard and cold that I just killed people? That is what they were trying to explain to me is that there is a balance here and I had to find it. I can still be the destroyer and find compassion and empathy. It is a delicate balance and what happened here today destroyed the fear I have carried my whole life."

"James, what happened?"

He got up and went to Layla. He hugged her tightly for a long time. "I thought I lost you."

"That would have never happened. I was in good hands."

"What were you doing here, Layla?"

"You weren't answering my phone calls, James. I wanted to let you know I saw Dabs out on our front lawn. I was taken by surprise because we thought she was dead. I wanted to come tell you she was alive. I walked in the front door when I noticed a strange energy go up around the office. Before I could say anything, things were already underway. I had no time to take cover before the debris started flying around the room. How is it you are alive, Dabs? What are you?"

"I will let James tell you. I am so happy you are all right. I am so sorry I didn't see you in the line of fire. I have some things I need to tell you and show you. Do you mind if we go back to your place?"

"I don't know if that is a good idea or not. I wouldn't want anything to happen to the kids."

"I can understand that. Your home and children have already been placed under protection. If you would feel better having your dad take them, then we can wait until you clear them out. It is important we go to your house. Could you have Zane, Zay, Alex, and Heather come over as well?"

"I suppose we could do that. Why don't we have a big BBQ? We haven't been properly introduced. I am Layla," she said as she looked straight at Dhareyin.

"It is nice to meet you, Layla. I am Star's friend Dhareyin. Could we catch a ride with you back to your place? We don't have a vehicle."

"What do you mean, you don't have a vehicle? How did you get here?"

"Through an energy portal."

"I will go call everyone to meet us at our house. James, will you come with me and make some of the calls? Give us a few moments, will you, Dabs?"

She didn't wait for an answer as she grabbed James's hand and walked into the office.

"What is going on here, Star?"

"I only want to explain this once, so can you wait to hear it when I fill them in?'

"I can do that. How long have you known you could do all that stuff?"

"Longer than I want to admit, Dhareyin."

I wasn't sure what was going on in the office, but I was getting nervous. What if they didn't want to have anything to do with me?

"Are you two ready? We have to stop at the store and pick up a couple of things while Layla gets everything set up."

I let Dhareyin sit in the front with James. I needed time to think. I knew that I would have to show them instead of just tell them what they were all a part of. What if they didn't want it? I remembered how I felt when this was all dropped into my lap.

The drive seemed to take forever. I shouldn't have shown James who I was, but I felt like it was the only way I could help him to see. I knew things were meant to be, but that didn't mean that I wasn't upset about it. I was grateful for the release, but what did it all mean?

The grocery shopping went quickly. I noticed that James threw in some of my favorite foods and even the wine I like. Maybe they weren't upset with me after all. I felt at home with them. It was why I made many visits back here. Sometimes I wished I had never moved away, but I also knew that this life would have found me, anyway.

James's yard was full of vehicles. I knew it was to begin. Should I do it before the meal or wait until after? It would have to be after, because there were going to be so many questions that I would have to answer. Everyone gave me their hugs. I had been missed, and that fulfilled me. I loved them all so much. Would that change? We took our time getting caught up and I explained everything that had been going on. Even though they seemed skeptical, I would not be showing them the same demonstration as I had to James.

Eating with people I deemed family felt so good. It lifted my spirits, and I knew it would. They were my true family and I would protect them at any cost even if it cost me my life!

We all sat on the patio sharing stories and living it up. I knew the time had come when the sunset and the dark of the night was starting to set in. I had a demonstration for them that I thought they would enjoy!

"I wanted you all here tonight because I have something to say and to show you. If you can bear with me while I get through this, and then you can ask questions."

"You have the floor, Dabs. Feel free to discuss anything with us."

"Thank you, James. I learned something today and it involves Layla and James and all of you. Not long ago, you were all a part of something not only sad and destructive, but it also created incredible new beginnings for all of you. I want to show you something. Could you turn the patio lights off, Zane?"

I stood in front of them all. I opened my hands and blew breath forward as my hands and arms opened fully. What appeared was luminescent magickal beings. There were Unicorns, dragons, Pegasus, griffins, centaurs, sphinx, and so many more showing their beauty to my friends. There was a phoenix flying in the night sky.

"Thank you, my dear friends, for showing us your true essence this evening," I said to them as I released my hold on them.

I was so excited about what I saw that it took me a few moments before I turned to see what everyone else was feeling.

"Dabs, we don't understand. All those creatures are mythical fairy tales we tell our children about. How is it we just saw all of them?"

"James, that was not all of them. There are so many more all over the world. This magick is global and it is time you knew why I wanted to come here tonight. Follow me, please."

I walked silently down the path, illuminating my way with lightning bugs. This path kindly led us to the pond. What lay beneath knew I was coming. I could feel them calling out to me. I stepped to the edge of the pond and I dove in. Swimming deeper and deeper, I was searching for the hippocampus, a beautiful sea horse. I didn't have to go far; she was waiting for me. She came up to me and nuzzled up against me. I was able to climb aboard her, and she took me deeper and deeper. Through telepathy, I was able to call them all forth and tell them to follow me. They knew what was happening and that it was time to show themselves. She took me to the surface, bobbing and weaving on the way up.

We surfaced first. Then one by one, they all surfaced. They allowed their illumination to shine brightly. The emotion that was coming from my friends was incredible. A few of them were sobbing, with smiles on their faces. I could see all their childhood dreams coming true. On land and water, the magickal beings gathered around and celebrated life with us.

"You shouldn't be showing these humans this, Star. You don't have the right to do this. I don't know how I will ever forgive you. I cannot help you now because you have broken a sacred vow of secrecy. HER wrath will be upon you and humankind when she returns," I could hear Dhareyin saying in my mind.

Such nonsense. He still underestimated me at every turn. I knew what I had to do. I thought of Dhareyin and snapped my fingers. He was on the back of the sea horse before I could comprehend what I was able to do.

I leaned forward and whispered in her ear, "Dive!"

He grabbed me around the waist and held on. She took us to deeper depths than I imagined were in this pond. Of course, James and Layla didn't know it was this deep. There was the bottom, which only the magickal creatures could access further. She took us to a cave where he and I could talk — such an intelligent being.

We both climbed off and she swam away. I wasn't worried,

because I knew how to pull a portal.

"I know you are mad at me right now, and I can even understand your feeling that way. Much like you, I have been keeping secrets. At every turn, you prove that you don't trust me or have faith in me. Do you honestly think, Dhareyin, that I would jeopardize the magickal world?"

"I don't know what to say to you right now, Star. What you are becoming is so different from what our tribe has seen in the prophecy. I feel like I must tell them what is going on. You are dangerous to all of us. I should have listened when you threatened this morning about killing all of us. I had all these feelings for you, and I let it blind me to the truth of who you were becoming. Heart of the Godz Tribe will never accept who you are. Your mother was right in getting rid of you."

I knew in my heart that what he was saying he said from his mind and the old ways. My heart was aching for the man-beast I first met in the trailer. There was fear and doubt in his heart, and that made me sad. I knew that fear well. What would it take for him to release his? I opened a portal that led back to the Heart of the Godz Forest.

"I am sorry you feel that way about me. I can honestly say your attitude doesn't really take me by surprise. Go home, Dhareyin. You do what you must do. There is nothing more to be said here."

No goodbyes passed between us. I watched him walk into the portal and out of my life for now. I opened a portal at the edge of the pond. I was distraught and heartbroken. I was hoping he would change his mind. What would happen when they found out what Daegorth had done and now meant to me in my mission? I walked out before all my friends.

"None of us know what to say, Dabs. You have truly opened our eyes to what is out there. What does this all mean?"

"Let's go back inside and talk. I have some things to say."

The walk back was empty without him. I knew that at some point I had fallen for him, whether it would work or not. I could not focus on that right now. I had plenty of time to grieve what could have been. I watched them all file into the house waiting to hear what I had to say. Each of their energy fields were alive with excitement.

"There is no point in me talking to you about this before I ask if you are up to the challenge. Layla, you were reborn today and chose to come back to be with James. I want to know if you and James would be willing to be the guardians of the magickal creatures on this land? Before you answer, let me finish. The rest of you, I wonder if you would be willing to be caretakers of this land and the magickal beings here? Your task would include keeping magick safe, making people aware of the magick within themselves, and helping James and Layla."

"Are you serious, Dabs? Is that what all of this is about? Is that why you came here today?"

"I came here to have you help me deal with who I am becoming. I had no idea that it was not the only reason I was coming here. I am serious. While the healing process was taking place, I was told what was to happen if you would accept the guardianship. If not, then someone else would have to be brought in. For now, you cannot tell anyone about these creatures. It would not be safe for them, and they are not allowed to be seen. You must promise never to sell this land and to hand it down to your children and so forth. I am not sure when SHE will return, but we must have guardians in place before she shows up. What do you say?"

They all looked at each other. They all chimed in at once: "I am in!"

"I must go, and I don't know when I will be back. You will be called upon when SHE returns, so be ready. I love you guys so much. Be careful! Just so you know, I have increased the protection around your property, home, and each of you. Remember to keep this to yourself."

"What about you, Dabs? Are you going to be okay?"

"I don't know, James. I may be walking into a trap that will lead to my death. Just know that I have lived because of what you taught me. You have all shown me such love, and I cannot ever repay that. I learned a lot from you today, Layla. What comes next for me will be a decision that I am not sure I am ready for. Don't worry about me. You are a beautiful tribe of people: guard and protect it forever."

I blew them all kisses as I hopped back through a portal I set for my car. I thought about just going to the cabin, but I needed my stuff out of my car. As I exited the portal, I knew I was in trouble. I was surrounded by Roman, Seth, Ramsey, Dhareyin, Daegorth, and many others I didn't know. For tonight I was to become their prisoner, and so it began.

10

When they grabbed me, they shot a weird vapor into my face that was fruity-smelling, and I lost consciousness. I don't know how long I was under, but I awoke with a killer migraine. I was in the bedroom that Dhareyin put me in when I visited this place with him the first time. I wasn't shackled or tied down, but I would soon find out that the door was heavily bolted.

It could have been worse. They could have killed me and dumped my body somewhere. Could they kill me? There was an eerie energy in the room. Was someone protecting me from something, or were they protecting themselves from me? All I could do is wait for them to make a move. Until then I would enjoy this incredible morning and the gigantic tub waiting for me.

Hmmm, could I pull a portal in here and get out? I gave it a whirl. Sure enough, one appeared. I stepped in, and where it took me next was not the destination I had picked. It brought me straight into Dhareyin's quarters. He seemed to be waiting for me. The scene was well laid out. He was in bed, bare-chested, sheets up to his waist. He had a smug look on his face, as if he could control me.

"This is not where I opened a portal to. How did I end up here?"

"I linked all portals pulled by you to my quarters. I knew you would try to escape, and I could not have that happen."

"You don't have a right to keep me here, Dhareyin. This is kidnapping. How dare you!"

"It was the only way I could keep you from fucking with magick."

"You should have hung around because you would have found out why I did what I did with James and Layla. Would you like to know, or are you going to continue to be a stubborn asshat?"

"Asshat? You have been calling me some interesting names since we met. What a saucy little mouth you have, Dabney Vaughn!"

"How do you know my full name?"

"I know a lot of things about you. Why don't you come join me and we can finish what we started the night before last?"

"Fuck you, Dhareyin," I said as I pulled another portal.

"Wait—I want to hear what happened last night before you came back."

"You mean before you were an asshole? What happened has nothing to do with you. A new tribe was created to take care of the magickal beings in that area. They all accepted the job. Had you stayed; you would have seen how privileged they were to accept it. Who is Sally?"

"Her name isn't Sally. Her name is Luna, and she was named after the full moon she was born under."

"More to the point—who is she to you, Dhareyin?"

I didn't know what the big secret was, but I could tell he was choosing his words wisely. He sat up in bed and folded his hands behind his neck. "She is my daughter."

I could hardly believe my ears. Was he married? Better yet, why was he screwing around with me? I really didn't know what to do with the information he laid at my feet. I was genuinely speechless.

"I can see you have nothing to say. So, let me explain. She is not my biological daughter. She is my niece. Both her parents were murdered the night she was born. We were lucky that she had given birth and hid Luna in the tall grass. We never knew who murdered them, as we have many magickal beings coming and going through the portals. She is about to marry Seth; that was why they were all on edge the other night."

"Why would Sally—I mean Luna—be watching me for the Bureau?"

"What are you talking about?"

"When I got there, they were beating the crap out of her because of me. She was almost dead. Why do you think I jumped in to help her? She would have died had I not shown up, and they would have let her die."

"I will have to talk to her and find out what is going on. How do you even know her?"

"Sally and I became friends after I moved to the trailer park. Bob introduced us, and we weren't allowed to talk about our lives or the past. I am sick of all the lies. I wish Daegorth would have succeeded the night he tried to murder me. I wish I had never met any of you."

"You don't mean any of those things you are saying, Star."

"You don't know me well enough to know what I mean or feel. Let me go home. I don't want to be here anymore. None of you want me here. Let me go back to my car, and I will be out of your lives for good. I can go back to my life that I was living before all this shit went down. I don't need the Bureau anymore. I have made peace with Daegorth, and should he come after me again with the intent to kill me, one of two things will happen. Let me go, Dhareyin."

"What about your family?"

"I don't have any family here. The only family I have is James and Layla."

"If you feel that strongly about it, then I release you from the binds I placed upon you. Are you sure you don't want to say goodbye to your mother?"

"I would just kill her. Keep her away from me," I said as I opened a portal and came out near my car. I got in and drove away. The tears kept coming as the frustration bubbled up and out of me. I was back to square one with nowhere to go. My condo had been sold, with all my belongings. For today, I would go back to the cabin and rest my soul. Driving back there proved strenuous. The further I got away from the forest, the more clarity I had. I knew what I had to do, but it would be in my own time. I needed to talk to the people who owned the cabin I was renting.

"Is there any property that comes with that cabin I am renting, Meg?"

"That particular cabin is not part of the rest of the cabins. It sits on twenty acres. We use it when our clients need privacy, or we have no vacancies. It was my husband's family's old homestead. That cabin was where his grandmother lived. Why do you ask?"

"I was wondering if you would be willing to sell it to me?"

"Jason and I were discussing that this morning. It hardly gets used, and it is quite large for us to take care of. The pond needs lots of attention, and we just do not have the time anymore. I suppose you would want to keep this hush-hush?"

"Why don't we do this between us? Would that be all right? That way, you can keep more of the money. Talk to Jason and let me know. I should be in all day."

I drove away feeling inspired. The cabin was perfect for me. What were the odds that it had its own pond? I bet it is attached to the Heart Pond. I would have to check the place out tonight under dark skies. When everything got settled, I would send for my stuff in storage. Hopefully, I could hire someone to bring it out to me.

I really felt like I needed to connect with Gaia. The best place for that was between some trees in the front yard. They created enough coverage to give me privacy, but I could see and hear if someone was coming to the house. I slipped into my wild leopard-print yoga pants and a loose black tank top. Sitting on top of the blanket felt like I was preparing for a picnic. I would have to do that sometime. I had no set intentions with this meditation. I just wanted to be one with Gaia and renew my energy. I couldn't help but ask that everything would go smoothly with the cabin.

The sale of the cabin went through effortlessly. It took about two weeks to make sure everything was finalized, but the time was worth it. It was done among the three of us. It was officially mine under the name Starlene Jasper. It was the only name I had identification for. I was told by the title company that I could change the name later.

They allowed me to stay there while they cleaned out their family heirlooms. I was happy to be making this my own. No one knew where I was, and I liked it that way. The title company said that it would be classed as a private sale, so my name wouldn't alert anyone.

There was an awareness growing in my energy field tonight. Images of Dhareyin and Daegorth kept popping into my third eye. I was having a hard time making them out, due to their faces being so distorted. I sat with the feeling for a while. I was hoping I could discover where the despair was coming from, but I was partially blocked. The depth of hopelessness I felt was so heart wrenching I wanted to vomit. Was I really picking up on them or was it someone else? I would know soon enough, and I would have some of the answers I had been seeking for a while. There was no point in trying to figure this out.

It was time to make plans for a little field trip to my pond. I was curious to see what would be waiting for me. With all my heart I desired for my pond to connect to the Heart pond. Can you imagine the novel I could get out of this whole experience? Until I could get down to the pond, I knew I had to go buy some supplies so I could write.

I would have to go buy a new laptop in the morning, and then I could get started. There was a town in the opposite direction about ten miles. They should have an electronics store. I could stock up on some food as well. I was not able to take much with me, considering they destroyed everything. I enjoyed eating out, but it was nice to have some stuff on hand. I liked to snack when I was writing, from chips of any kind to marshmallows and chocolate. I should pick up a few bottles of wine as well.

My eating habits were changing. I got particularly hungry after the destroyer would surface. Until my body could get used to the changes, I would keep jerky on hand to keep my blood sugar balanced.

My day started out uneventful as I enjoyed my trip to town. It was smaller than I expected. There were mountains on all three sides going into it. It almost looked like a dead-end highway. The pine trees were magnificent and majestic. They had those cool family stores operating on both sides of Main street. I decided to try their little diner. I knew I couldn't go wrong with this place when I walked in. The incredible smells of burgers and fries gifted their delicious scent into my olfactory glands. My taste buds instantly started watering. The service was excellent, and Cherrie, the owner, pointed me in the direction of where I could buy a laptop. She insisted I take a piece of chocolate cream pie home with me, on the house. I did not tell her, but that is my favorite. She also told me where I could buy some new clothes.

With all my physical activity lately, I had gained more sleek muscle than before. They destroyed all my clothes, so I needed to replace some essentials — time for some new bubble bath and light scented lotions. I needed to get my routine back in order. It did not seem like Griff could be trusted, so I would have to train on my own. No point in me going to the Derby either. So much for his invitation.

I found a laptop, some sexy underwear, and my delicious lotions. This one store had some vintage clothes, and I had a blast in there. The owner was a hoot. She found a bunch of cute things for me to wear. I was not sure why I bought them. It wasn't like I was going to go out anywhere, but I did have to wear clothes. I think it made me feel slightly normal. The next store had more practical clothes for me, like jeans, t-shirts, yoga pants, and tank tops. I found a perfect pair of workout shoes, flip flops, and some cute heels to go with these beautiful black velvety corduroy pants and a black and hot-pink dress shirt. It was time to head back to the diner and grab my pie. I decided to order another delicious cheeseburger and fries to take home. I was ravenous after all the shops I visited today.

The drive home was peaceful. The sun was setting, and it was gorgeous. I had to pull over and take some pictures of the red, orange, pink, and yellow hues cascading across the sky. In some areas, the orange was so red you could swear a new color had been born. I missed taking pictures. One of my hobbies that brought me such peace was taking pictures of just about everything. There was so much of my life that was changing; I couldn't help but feel a deep sorrow inside my being. Would I have to give all of that up? Could the old and new merge and be one with me?

I was so excited to put all my purchases away when I got home. I found Sally—or I should say, Luna—sitting on my front lawn when I pulled in. How in the sweet hell did she find me? I got out of the car cautiously, not sure what I would come up against.

"You don't have to be worried about me, Star."

"Why are you here, and how did you find me?"

"We need to talk. I have my ways, and you should know they always know where you are."

"I don't see that we have anything to talk about. Who knows?"

"How did you know my name?"

"Your father told me. Now answer my question."

"The tribe and the Bureau always know where you are. You have a tracking chip inside of you. They put it in there when you were attacked before and they had to put you back together."

"Where is the tracking chip?"

"It is on the roof of your mouth."

"Well, that would explain the funny taste and feeling in my mouth. Do you know how I can get it removed?"

"They have a device they use. Dr. Roxanne is the only one who can remove it. She wasn't happy with Matilda when they asked her to put it on you without you knowing. She said it went against everything she believes in. They talked her into it under the guise of it being for your own safety."

"Why were you watching me? I thought we were friends and I cherished that relationship."

"Ramsey made me do it. He didn't like the fact that you could go through portals and sense him when he was cloaked. He wanted you watched because he wasn't quite sure who you were. Matilda tried to control things creating bigger problems for us. I was always meant to answer to Ramsey, my future father-in-law, but he handed that duty over to Matilda. She has become power-hungry. I always knew she would be capable of what they did to me that night. Matilda can be a cruel cat. I truly have enjoyed our friendship, and I am sorry for the betrayal."

"I understand the curiosity about me. I do not understand the brutality that was inflicted upon you because of me. It makes me sick, but not as much as your betrayal. I haven't even had time to process the pain in my heart. Did your father send you here?"

"He told me to stay away from you because it was not safe for me to be around you. I disagreed and came anyway. Why does he feel that way about you, Star?"

"Dhareyin is probably right about it not being safe to be around me. I am glad you came to see me. You have completely healed from your injuries. Are you feeling all right?"

"I see I am not going to get a straight answer out of you, either. I do feel good. Thank you for knowing what to do and for protecting me even from my father. So, the other reason I came to see you is that I am getting married tomorrow evening. I was hoping, as my friend, you would come to the ceremony?"

"What did Seth or Dhareyin say about it? I don't want to cause any problems."

"It is my wedding, and I will invite whoever I want to. You did such a wonderful job letting them know where the toxins were. They should be happy to have you come and celebrate with us."

"I wouldn't even know what to wear, Luna. Check with them first before we decide. Go home and find out."

I watched her open a portal, and away she went. That is interesting. How come Ramsey cannot pull or go through a portal but Daegorth and Luna can? I will have to ask her when she comes back.

I unpacked my purchases from the store. I put my pie in the fridge to eat later after I explored. It was a lovely evening to picnic with a glass of wine. I would have to go to the Diner more often. The food tasted great cold!

I didn't know where my mind took me, but I was lost to this time and place. I was not sure how long I was gone, but when I snapped back, Dhareyin was kneeling before me. It took me a moment for my eyes to come back into full focus. I don't know how, but I must have known he was there, because I was not surprised by his presence.

"I see you found me. What can I do for you?"

"You can tell me why you are trying to influence my daughter."

"Not sure what you are talking about, Dhareyin."

"She wants you to come to the ceremony tomorrow. Are you telling me you had nothing to do with that?"

"When I got home earlier Luna was waiting for me. She stopped by to explain everything to me and she invited me to the ceremony. I told Luna to ask you and Seth first. She told me you didn't want her around me, and I agreed with you. I have no intention of hurting Luna. I wouldn't have helped her the other night if that were my intention. Can we get past how you feel about me, or is this our relationship as we move forward?"

"Your power terrifies me. I don't know what you have in store for our people. If I must protect them from you then I will, whatever the cost to your life. I have always told you there can be nothing between us. I crossed the line the other night. I cannot take it back, but I can make sure it never happens again. I am not saying there isn't an attraction between us, but I do not see the point in being with someone I cannot be with."

"If you don't want me to come to the ceremony, I won't. Honestly, I wouldn't even know what to wear. What is going on between you and Daegorth?"

"How do you know there is anything going on?"

"Last night I could feel you both. What is happening?"

"The tribe wants to end Daegorth because of what he did to you. I have kept the leaders at bay for now, but I am not sure for how much longer. They want to end him so he will never exist again, and it is ripping my heart out," he said as he sat down next to me.

The silence was unbearable, but I didn't know what to say. I could feel the emotions wanting to pour out of him, but he was holding them back. I could sense that he thought that would make him too vulnerable in my presence and he was afraid to do that. I placed my hand lightly on his shoulder to show him he was safe. He looked at my hand and then at me. The stare was deep and intense. He turned away from me. How do I change this thing between us?

I kneeled before him and placed my hands on his chest and pushed him back. There was resistance, but not as much as I thought there would be.

"Take this moment and lie here upon Gaia with me, Dhareyin. Let us both take in the night and the stars above. Let it renew our strength and energies."

Staring up at the night sky on our backs, we were able to take in the spectacular view of all the stars. Occasionally a shooting star would streak across the eternal blackness of the night. He had his hands clasped behind his neck. I rolled over and laid my head on his chest. He wrapped his left arm around me, holding me tightly against him. No matter what came tomorrow, this moment with him was perfect in all ways. His smell was intoxicating and was making me dizzy. It was alluring and seductive. I snuggled in closer to his side. It wasn't long before I was asleep.

"You did well with James and Layla. You have set things in motion in their part of the country. They will do well in their guardianship. I am sorry we could not tell you what was going to happen. You would not have gone. We have visited and explained to them that what happened was meant to be. They do not blame you. They feel blessed that they know you. Aoroia when are you going to take the lead over your people and this tribe? You don't have much time before your next mission is in place. There will be things that happen next that make no sense to your mind, which was influenced by your human upbringing. The one that you want, the one lying next to you, is afraid of you. He is terrified that you are here to destroy everything he holds dear. You have one chance to change that. The time will come sooner than you think. Your people need a leader, and you must accept your place. If you don't, it will end in chaos

and disorder. All pieces must fall together like a puzzle. SHE is coming, and what you decide to do here will impact HER decisions on a deeper level."

"I don't know what to do. I feel like no matter what I choose he will never be able to trust me. I don't know how to fix this."

"There is only one way. You will know when that time comes. Make a balanced decision from both aspects of who you are. Daegorth will come to you. You are attracted to him, and you don't think you should be. Let him in and figure things out. I know that you don't want to because of what happened. This must happen for a decision later. He wants you to punish him because he knows that what he did to you was not his nature. He allowed his hurt to make him a target for hate. It changed who he was. What he was choosing had to be changed, and he doesn't understand that. You must be willing to truly see him and take that chance to understand what was always meant to be. You have until the wedding tomorrow night to decide what you will do. The only questions are what will that mean for you, this planet, James and Layla, magick and your tribe?"

"You don't lay it on lightly, do you? How do I contact Daegorth?"

"He is waiting for you. Just open to him and invite him in. I know that sounds scary, but it is the only way. He doesn't necessarily understand the changes that are taking place within him, either. You need each other to understand that. Wake up, Aoroia!"

I could feel someone shaking my shoulder as I came awake. I looked up and watched as Dhareyin loomed over me.

"You fell asleep, Star. You were mumbling in your sleep and fidgeting. Is everything okay?"

"I was dreaming. Thank you for waking me up. I am sorry, Dhareyin, that we have ended up in this place of fear and distrust. I don't know if this will ever change. I want you to know that I am so grateful I met you. There has not been a moment when you have not been on my mind."

"I want you to come to the wedding tomorrow night. I will have Dara and Fera bring you clothing and get you ready. It is important to my daughter that you are there. I will deal with Ramsey and Seth. There will come a time soon that you must accept who you were always meant to be. I know we haven't figured out who the mole is, but something must be done before everything is lost. It is time for me to take my leave. I will see you tomorrow evening."

I sat up on my elbows and watched him walk into the woods. A bright blue light flashed in the distance and I knew he had pulled a portal open. It was late enough that I wanted to go explore the pond. I headed down the dirt trail knowing the path would be illuminated for me. When I walked up to its edge, its surface looked like a mirror, it was so deep and dark. I sat down and closed my eyes. I opened myself to the energies of the night. I heard a sound in the distance that sounded like a beast. I kept my eyes closed and allowed it to come to me.

The beast sat next to me and I felt him shift into a manly form. I knew I could not show my fear, or he would run with it. I could hear a growl deep in his chest.

"Mistress, why have you been ignoring me?"

I took a deep breath. I knew I had to be careful how I handled this.

"I think we both needed some time to think over the changes that are occurring in both of us. I have yet to figure out what it is you are meant to be for me. I was hoping you had some answers for me, Daegorth."

"This tribe and what they believe in is outdated. I knew this the day you were sent away. What happened to you made me angry inside. I was angry with your mother for giving her baby away to such horrible people. She sent me out to find the most horrible people I could find. She made me believe that it would be best for you. I wanted you to be safe and protected. I couldn't see how these horrible people could provide you with that. I was distraught when she simply gave you away. Your mother knew that one day you were meant to be something special to this tribe. Her fear blinded her to your power. She was so concerned that they would figure out who you were meant to be and kill you."

The more he conveyed what had occurred, the emotions and feelings from a little girl's lifetime welled up and burst forth easily, flowing down my face and into my hands that lay linked in my lap. I had no words, so I listened.

"You were my little girl and I watched over you, even though I was just a little boy. When she took you away from me, something broke inside of me. I lost my link with you because she blocked me. Somehow when you were about seventeen years old you must have opened to your gifts or something, because I was able to track you. The signal was strong enough until I could get to you. I watched you for a long time and was disgusted by how your parents treated you. One night after you had a big fight and you took off; I made my plans. I snuck in through the back door and ripped out their throats while they watched television. I do not regret that decision one moment of my life. I do think that decision put me on a path that led me to hurt you. After that night, I lost you again. Your mother regretted her decision after she gave you away and decided she wanted to leave for good. I was so angry with her; I made her pay. I left enough of her flesh attached to her that she didn't go the way she was meant to. She stayed in a stasis of limbo. I knew what the prophecy was. I wanted her to see how you were going to change everything and that she didn't get to be a part of that. Unfortunately, the despair I felt from the beginning left me open to control by someone unknown. I let that anger and hate consume me, and before I knew it, I was being turned against you and the tribe. Someone has control over me, but I have no clue who it is."

I could hear the sorrow in his voice. I could tell that what he was saying was the truth. He was punishing himself more than I ever could. It was hard to get the cringe out of my mind about what he did to me. It wasn't that I forgot what he was capable of, but I was beginning to understand what happened. I don't know if that made a difference or not. I also knew I was capable of the same brutality because I inflicted it upon him, and I enjoyed it.

"I was quite powerful when I was a little boy. I don't know if I am your familiar or what I am. I know I missed you and I wanted you back every day. I am sick inside with what I have become. Please punish me for what I have done to you and others."

"How many have there been, Daegorth?"

"You and another woman. The one author that sent you the book. I didn't get to her before she sent it to you. That is why I had to show up that night. I killed her and I cannot take it back. I wish I could because it makes me sick inside to think what I have done. She was trying to help you, and I was angry about that. Matilda doesn't have control over her people like she thinks she does. Ginger was never supposed to be what she was for you. Liz stepped over the line. They were next in line. Someone was turning me into a killer, and I LET them. I let that anger blind me to the truth of what they were doing and who I was becoming. I am not making excuses but helping us both to understand what happened."

It was like I was being ripped apart again emotionally. My heart hurt. I felt an attraction for Daegorth I did not understand. I figured there must be something wrong with me.

"Please punish me, Mistress. Take an eternity ripping me apart over and over. Take your vengeance out on me."

"I cannot do that. I don't know what to do. I am confused."

"Please, Mistress, kill me before they do. I would rather die by your hands than theirs."

"Why do you think they are going to kill you?"

"Dhareyin told me that they came to him and were discussing what to do with me. They mentioned ending me, so I would never exist again. I will pay for what I have done, but please be merciful and let it be by your hands. I know I don't have a right to ask for mercy, but please."

"Can't Dhareyin stop this?"

"He is trying to, but he also doesn't want to turn you away by saving me."

"I have nothing to do with this decision."

"You do if you take your rightful place."

Everything that the council was telling me tonight was making sense.

"I need to get a hold of the prophecy. Do you know how to get it for me?"

"I used to have it. Only Dhareyin knows about the prophecy and where it is. I have told no one else."

"How is that possible?"

"The shaman of the tribe foretells these things. Dhareyin has been shaman for a long time. He is what you would class an ancient. Your mother kept you away from him so he couldn't see the signs of who you were."

"He knows who I am. I transformed in front of him one night. He told me to keep it a secret. He has mentioned the prophecy to me. The rest of you have only seen bits and pieces of the destroyer come out. Is that part of the prophecy?"

"No, and we need to keep that hush-hush until Dhareyin can perform the ritual."

"Well, he keeps talking about destroying me because he is afraid of what I will do to the tribe. Why did you ask me for sex the other day, Daegorth?"

"I am attracted to you. When I hurt you, something broke in me. I wanted you to torture me so I knew I could never have you. What you transformed me into that day in the cave I never knew was possible. Had I not become this monster; I do not think I could have truly become what you were bringing forth. We are connected in many ways, and I want you more than life itself. I know I will never have you because you were destined for another."

What do I do with these feelings I am having? I am attracted to him, yet how could I be, considering what he did to me? The monster in me was drawn to the beast in him. I knew even if we did have sex that we would never be together. I wanted someone to balance out my monster, not live my life that way.

When I met Dhareyin the first time, I knew there was something there. I had such strong, deep feelings for him. After the destroyer came out, those feelings went limp. When I ripped Daegorth apart, something came alive in me, and only Daegorth seemed to understand that savagery. The look on Dhareyin's face when he saw what I could do was one of fear and judgment. How could I be with someone who couldn't understand what I was capable of? Was that what he was fighting with? He didn't find me attractive anymore.

I could not deny these strong feelings in me for Daegorth. They were built from fear, hate, anger, resentment, and vengeance. I knew I could handle him, but was it worth it?

"Why don't you smell sterile, right now?"

"That part of me only shows up when I am in transitioner mode. What do I smell like to you, Mistress?"

"You smell spicy, musky, and earthy. You remind me of an aftershave my adopted father used to use called *Old Spice.*"

I knew what I wanted to do. I sniffed the air for him, and I let his scent fill my senses. I stood up and offered my hand to Daegorth. "Do you know where this pond goes? Is there a cave like the one at the Heart Pond?"

"There are many caves built into the ponds. They were meant to be used for sanctuary for us should we have to flee this realm. I am not sure what is contained within this pond," he said as he transformed into my hellhound. "Come, my mistress; let's explore."

I climbed onto his back, and we dove deeper and deeper. We explored cave after cave. Breathing underwater came easy to both of us. I lay upon his back, feeling him between my thighs. I could feel myself becoming aroused as the destroyer came forth. As my body moved upon his, he rolled and turned and showed me what he was capable of. I wrapped my arms around his neck and held on. I felt a love for him that only the destroyer understood, but I knew that by the end of it, I would know it as well.

He found a cave filled with precious jewels and stones. The variety of crystalline structures was breathtaking. He walked out of the water onto land and helped me down. I walked over to the amethyst structure and rubbed my hands and body all over it. I could feel its power radiating through me. I felt wild and free. I wanted to be with him. I watched him swagger toward me as a beast. There was a hunger within him to devour me in the most pleasurable way possible. He was sniffing my body slowly, which made me want him more. As he got to my abdomen, he gradually transformed back into a man-beast. He was kneeling at my feet and had his hands on my waist. He slowly undressed me.

I already knew what he was packing and was not surprised at his erection. He turned me around and started trailing kisses up my inner thighs and all the way up my back. He wrapped his arms around me as he kissed my neck. I could feel his mighty shaft pressing against my sweet spot. He pinned both of my outstretched arms up against the amethyst and kissed me all over my body. He slowly bit my cheeks with slow kisses. He turned me around and finished his job at the junction between my thighs. His tongue was long, warm, and just the right amount of roughness. Daegorth was doing incredible things to my body, and I couldn't help but rock against his face. I had my fingers in his hair, holding on to him as he pleasured me. He trailed his tongue up my abdomen and the sides of my breast. He took my nipple into his mouth and had me arching against him in no time.

He looked at me for the longest time. It was like he was talking to a deeper part of me, telling me goodbye. Daegorth picked me up and wrapped my legs around his waist. He teased me with the head of his shaft before he slowly penetrated the hot, wet, heat at my core. I wrapped my arms around his neck, and he plunged deeper into me. I wanted to taste this man. I sat back and took his face in my hands and brought his mouth to mine. Our tongues worked at each other, creating one thrill after another. The growl in his chest was enough to push me over the edge, and I orgasmed powerfully, rocking me to my core. With one last powerful thrust, he let his release ripple through him, and we came undone together.

We held on to each other for the longest time. I could feel something wet upon my chest, and I raised his face with my hand. The tears were a torrential downpour and all I could do was hold him. It was as if our hearts were breaking and healing at the same time. I knew what he was telling me, but I wasn't ready to let him go. I didn't just love him; I was in love with him. Two monsters in love with each other, and both knew their time was short.

"Daegorth, let us fly out of here. Take me to the stars and make love to me amongst the galaxies."

He transformed and helped me up on his back. We came out of the water and flew high in the sky. We flew out of the atmosphere, using portal after portal, and headed for the Milky Way, determined to have one last time together. We came to rest upon the center of the galaxy, and Daegorth made love to me one last time. We sat and talked with our hearts, making plans for the day when we would be together again the way we were meant to be. We had secrets that only we knew, and we cherished them. He knew he would fly to our home in the cosmos. Should I ever need him, I only had to call, but for now he was going home, and he was free.

"Aoroia, my love, I am giving you an image to give to Dhareyin. You will know when to give it to him. If you ever need me, just call out for me. I love you, and I always have. I have opened a portal that is a straight shot back to your cabin using wormholes. My dear, you are more powerful than even you know. Embrace your power, my sweet Aoroia."

He flew off, happier than I had ever known him to be. It was time for me to go home. I was ready for some sleep. I had a wedding to go to tonight. I would mourn Daegorth for everything he was and wasn't in my life. At some point I would have to tell Dhareyin where Daegorth was. One day soon I would call him back. If he wanted to, he could transform back to his man-beast, but he sought comfort in becoming the hellhound. He embraced his monster and his heart. To set him free was breathtaking. Now it was my turn to set myself free.

I wasn't sure how I was going to deal with Dhareyin, but I wasn't worried about that tonight. I needed some sleep, and I had some decisions that needed to be made before the wedding. For now, I wanted to check the situation out. I might not have to do anything at the wedding but just be there for Luna. I could feel something was off, but I couldn't intuit that knowing. Dara and Fera would be showing up to help me get ready. I was excited to see what they would bring for me to wear. Now that everything was calm in my mind, I could crash for a while before the girls arrived. Dozing off was instantaneous as my head hit the pillow.

I dreamed of far-away places and the place where we come from. Something was going to have to change and I wasn't sure if the tribe was ready for those changes. They were living the old ways and they didn't work anymore. For things to be prepared for HER when she returns, I would have to help them destroy some of those beliefs and rituals. That didn't mean the old traditions weren't important; they just need an upgrade and some updates. I imagined SHE would be providing some crucial downloads to us all.

11

I slept well and had time to myself before they showed up to dress me. I had already taken a bath, but they wanted to bathe me again with their ancient soaps and lotions. The outfit was outrageous and gorgeous, and the shoes were to die for. I imagine Luna's dress will be stunning and I cannot wait to see it.

Once they got me dressed, they excused themselves. I must have given them a strange look because they told me Dhareyin would be there to pick me up an hour before the ceremony. What was I supposed to do in this outfit until he got here? Great time for some selfies. I could send the pictures to James and Layla. As I took each photo, I could see myself slowly transforming in each one. After all the trauma that I had been through the last several months, I wasn't in the mood to look in the mirror. I had no need to take pictures. Somehow my face had become more distinguished and wiser, defined, and elegant with a touch of fierceness. I wasn't just slimmer; I was toned and fit. The hourglass shape I have always had was sexy and taut.

The outfit was glorious on my body. It was cut almost to my belly button and hung down in a swoop at my backside. Somehow it was made to hold my breasts in place. It was tied around my neck and flowed all the way down my body in light layers. It seemed to change colors depending on how the light caught it. One moment it was a light pink shifting into a hot pink. It seemed to take on all the color spectrums of pink. Thank heavens for the layers, or this dress would be sheer. It flowed to my feet effortlessly. The undergarments were just as sexy, with a strapless bustier and short slip. The shoes were glittery and wrapped around my ankle like you would ballet shoes, and the heel looked like tree limbs intricately designed. I smelled like an ambrosia salad with a hint of musk. They put my hair entirely up and back, in a bun that sat high on the back of my head.

"I knew you would look stunning in that outfit."

I about jumped out of my skin and came unglued.

"WTF, Dhareyin! You could warn a girl before you sneak up on her." I could feel my heart pounding in my chest, and I could feel the destroyer wanting to step forward. *Shit, fuck, damn—how do I get her to calm down?* "Dhareyin, help me," I could hear myself saying as she was sliding into place.

"How do I help you, Star?"

"I don't know, but if you don't, she is coming out to play."

He did the most incredible thing and wrapped me in his arms. "I am so sorry I scared you, Star," he whispered in my ear.

His voice in my ear tingled all the way down my body and settled between my thighs. I could feel myself calming down. Was it safe for me to go to this wedding? What if something triggered the destroyer to step forward? He held me for the longest time, and I could feel the love he carried for me. I knew then that was the difference between him and Daegorth. Dhareyin brought out the healer, whereas Daegorth brought out my destroyer. I didn't know if there was any chance to save what we might have had, but I would do my best to change it.

"How are you doing, Star?"

"I feel a lot better now, thank you," I said, looking up into his big, beautiful dark eyes—the eyes that carried so many secrets and mysteries. I reached up and lightly touched his cheek with my hand. He placed his hand on mine and held it there for a moment.

"Why can I smell Daegorth on you?"

Daegorth knew this time would come, and that was why he sent me with the message. I repeated that message in Dhareyin's ear.

"How dare you do this to my brother? You have left our tribe without a transitioner. What have you done, Star?"

"I did what he asked me to do. You know by his message that all you need to do is ask for him and he will respond. Please remember he won't be the same anymore. He is my hellhound and can transform back to man-beast form. He belongs to me now, Dhareyin, and you have to respect that."

He just stood there shaking his head. "What about the one who will take his place?"

"I will take care of that today, hopefully."

"What do you mean you will take care of it today? Who are you to be throwing orders around for this tribe? You won't even accept who you are, and you have no plans to tell anyone who you are."

"Whether you want me at the wedding tonight or not, I will choose the next in line. Why didn't you tell me he was your brother?"

"I didn't think it was your business."

"So many secrets you keep bottled up inside. You might want to think about letting some of them go. What you think of me is not the point. Had you kept me in the loop, things might have gone differently. You asked why I smelled of Daegorth. We flew to the Milky Way and I rode upon his back—and anything other than that is not your business."

I could see that it was bothering him not knowing. I wasn't going to hurt him like that or piss him off. That is all I need to do before the wedding tonight.

"Don't you think we should get going to the wedding?"

"I am not sure I want to take you. What if the destroyer comes out again?"

"Whatever is going to happen will happen. It is time to let life flow again. Let's go, Dhareyin; I don't want to be late for my friend's wedding."

He opened a portal, and off we went. He held my hand. His feelings for me were more profound than he was letting on, but that was a dilemma for another day. We arrived in Dhareyin's quarters.

"I want to go check on Luna. Would you like to come with me?"

"I was hoping you would ask, Dhareyin."

We walked hand in hand to Luna's preparation room. He knocked on the door and we were let in by women who looked a lot like Dara and Fera. They gave Dhareyin a smile but gave me a dirty look.

"Don't mind them, Star; they are just protective, and they do not know you. I am so glad Father has brought you here. You look stunning," Luna said as she walked toward Dhareyin.

Dhareyin and Luna hugged each other and took time to themselves. I was in awe of the bond that existed between them. I was still surprised that she was his daughter, whether biological or not. I could have been so much better off with a loving father like him. Hell, Dhareyin was close to my age. I wonder if he wants any children. If he does, then we won't have a future together. Having the destroyer inside of me could be why I cannot have children.

"Star snap out of it. Are you okay?"

"Sorry; I was deep in thought. I was enjoying watching you and your father spend time together. What you have is beautiful, Luna!"

"It is time for me to get my dress on. Father has you sitting with him if you want to go find your place."

"I cannot wait to see what you look like, my dear friend. I need to talk to you a bit later after the ceremony. Where did Dhareyin go?"

"He is waiting for you outside. He said he wanted to give us some privacy."

We hugged and kissed each other like close friends should. I walked out of there feeling alive and wanted. Dhareyin took my hand once again. I liked it, but it felt possessive. What was he up to?

"I am not up to anything. Most will not understand why you are here tonight. No humans can attend our ceremonies."

"I am not human, am I, Dhareyin?"

"No, you are not! I am not sure what you are. I want to protect my people, and until I figure out your agenda, I am keeping you close by my side, even if that means you share my bed tonight."

"You sure are taking liberties with yourself. I may not be human, but I do know I have rights. I may not have them in your eyes, but I have more rights than you will ever know. Just when I think we are making progress; you turn back into a possessive asshat!"

He looked at me with his lip cocked up and smiling. "I remember the last time you called me that. I should have made you mine then, but I knew I had to take my time with you. I knew you were special the moment you walked into that trailer house. I could smell you and feel your intentions. You are a lot stronger now, and I must watch you. Your powers are so strong, and you are not in full control of them. I would hate to have you get angry and unleash on all of us."

"You are right; I am just learning. This is all new to me, and had I not been given away all those years ago I might have been better trained than I am now. I have no intention of hurting the people of your tribe, as you keep stating it. I am here today for Luna and nothing else. Why won't you let me enjoy this? Why can't you accept me for who I am? I do deserve it—you know?"

He just stared at me for a moment. He showed me the way forward and guided me with his hand on my lower back until we came to our seats. The people of the tribe were starting to file in, and they were staring at me.

"What is she doing here? You know no human can come to these ceremonies."

"Ramsey, when you decided to use my daughter, you opened this door yourself. Those two became good friends. Accept it; I have!"

He walked away mumbling under his breath. I could tell Seth wasn't happy to see me there either. I wonder why he hadn't told his father what he witnessed at the trailer?

"Because as much as he loves his father, he doesn't like how friendly he has gotten with the Bureau. He is quite upset with him about Luna as well."

"Would you stop reading my mind? Good hell, can't a woman have her own thoughts?"

He chuckled out loud. I think it caught him off guard because he was looking around to see if anyone had noticed. It was great to hear him laugh. It was an incredible sound. I looked at him, and he looked at me. I looked deep in his eyes and I knew then that whether we were together or not, our worlds would always collide. I was so angry at him when none of it was his fault. He was an easy target to take things out on.

The ceremony began like most weddings, with one exception. Instead of the fathers walking the bride down the aisle, it was the women in the family. I felt so much pride in my heart at the overall female empowerment being played out as they walked down the aisle together. I watched as tears rolled down Dhareyin's face. We were still holding hands, and I squeezed his lightly in reassurance. He squeezed mine back gently.

Luna was beautiful. She wore a flowing white dress that brushed light kisses across the floor as she walked down the aisle. She was in full tribe mode; in fact, they all were. It was hard for me because I could feel my body wanting to change. I was surprised that they were showing that side of themselves to me. She wore her hair up, and as the ceremony was ending, Seth placed the crown of his family's crest upon her head. It was all so beautiful and reminded me of my wedding. I have been so busy lately; it just dawned on me that I was not sure if I will ever get married again. He would have to be unique.

I am not sure if that person exists or not. Who wants to be with a woman who cannot have children? It saddened me every time I thought about that piece of news the doctor gave me. I really don't believe that it sank in. Lately more and more it had been on my mind.

The ceremony was over, and now it was time to partake in the reception. I was stunned when Luna came up and asked me to meet her in her quarters in ten minutes and gave me instructions on how to get there. I was not sure what she wanted, but it seemed urgent.

"What did she want from you, Star?"

"I am supposed to meet her in her room in ten minutes. I am not sure what she wanted, Dhareyin, but it seemed like an urgent matter."

"If you aren't back in fifteen minutes, I will come looking for you. Something seems off about all of this."

I nodded okay to him as I walked to Luna's quarters. I knocked on the door several times, but no answer. I tried the door, and it was unlocked. I knocked as I called out her name. The only thing I could do was walk in. Maybe she was in the restroom and didn't hear me. Her wedding gown was on the floor, and her room looked torn apart. I felt panicked and I was doing everything possible to keep the destroyer from surfacing.

"She is in here," I could hear Luna saying behind me.

I wondered who she was speaking to. I turned and was surprised to see her dressed in her regular clothes.

"Did you really think I would let a human get away with coming to my wedding? I don't know what you think is between my father and yourself, but it ends here tonight."

I was shocked at how she was speaking to me. She was the one who invited me. I saw movement behind her back. I peered over her shoulder and Matilda, Ramsey, and Dr. Roxanne were standing there.

"What is going on, Luna? You asked me here and to your wedding. There is nothing going on with your father, and if there were, that would be between him and me."

"He is promised to another." As the words came out of her mouth, my heart fell.

"I did not know that. He has never said anything about another."

"Why would he tell you such things? You are only a human!"

"What are they doing here?"

"They are here to take you away for good. We don't want your kind here." She turned and looked at Matilda and Dr. Roxanne. "Get her away from here. I don't want to see her around this town ever again. If I do, your heads will be on the chopping block."

"Somebody is riding high on some power. You probably should talk to Seth before you start pulling power moves like this."

"I don't need him to tell me what I can and cannot do. Take her away."

Dr. Roxanne walked over and gave me a shot in the arm. I felt myself slip to the floor. I had no idea what they planned, and I hoped Dhareyin cared enough to come looking for me. They didn't get too far with me when I heard Dhareyin put up a ruckus.

"What do you think you are doing with her, Matilda?"

"They are taking her away, Father. We do not need her here anymore. She has done what she said she would do—and why hasn't Daegorth shown up for my wedding?"

"Daegorth had a mission he had to go on. She does belong here, Luna. I love her."

"No, Father, you are promised to another. How could you love a human? I am so disgusted by you."

"Was she not your friend who you invited to your wedding? What has changed that?"

"She was never my friend. I was using her to get what the Bureau wanted. I brought her here today so they could take her away."

The beating of everyone's hearts was all I could hear. What would happen next? I was surprised to hear Dhareyin admit that he loved me. I could feel the destroyer begging me to let her come out and play. I was tempted to unleash her. Dhareyin would never forgive me if something happened to Luna.

"Let them take me, Dhareyin. I told you I don't belong here. You are all better off without me here." I could feel the anger welling up in him wanting to tell me to shut up. I knew he was coming from a place that was hurt. Until I was ready to reveal who I was, there would be no future between us. "Go be with the one you are promised to. You will be so much happier with her."

"You don't understand, Star."

"No matter what I do or don't understand is not the question here this evening. What matters is that I don't fit in here with any of you. Us being together could never work, despite what you think you know."

He looked at the ground and shook his head. I could tell he was resigned to letting me go—for the moment, that is.

"Whether you wanted me here or not, Luna, I am grateful for what I thought was a friendship. You have taught me things I thought I had already learned. Dhareyin, go enjoy the rest of your daughter's wedding."

I surprised them all by standing up and walking away. I walked until I was alone and then I cast a portal and was back to my home. I made sure when I got there that any entrance coming into my property was protected and safeguarded against any who would try to hurt me. I knew Dhareyin would come to me later that night. It was inevitable. I was not looking forward to it. He might think that I gave up, but that was not the case.

It felt good to get out of these clothes—such a blinding reminder of what took place. How did I not see how much she despised me because she thought I was a human? To hear how Dhareyin felt about me was thrilling. I was disheartened that he was already promised to someone else. Maybe it was time for me to move forward with my life and let Dhareyin move on with his.

I could feel my water tributary calling to me. It was a great night to take a swim with magick. The path was well illuminated and waiting for me. I got to the edge of the water and decided to go skinny dipping. It would feel refreshing and freeing to have the water lap softly across my skin. The water carried and coaxed me deeper and deeper. Breathing underwater was a liberating feeling. I was along for the ride and was inspired by what I saw. Right in front of me was a water dragon. There was something oddly familiar about him, but I couldn't wrap my mind around what it was. He took on all the colors of the sea. He was the normal size of a dragon, but his tail seemed to stretch out. He looked bejeweled and radiant. He shimmered as the water rippled from our movement. I was not afraid of him, whoever he was. He held out his hand for me to take. Dhareyin was already spoken for, so why not?

He took me to a cave—thankfully not the one I went to with

Daegorth. He brought me to the water's edge and helped me out. I had forgotten I was buck naked until then. So much for being modest. I was so busy thinking about what to do in my state of undress that I did not see him walk out of the water. He walked up behind me and wrapped his arms around my waist.

"I meant it when I said I loved you. There is no one for me but you. You showed me today that you could be trusted, and it makes my heart soar. I want to be with you always my beautiful Star."

"Dhareyin?" I asked in disbelief.

"Yes, my love!"

I turned around to face him. He was a spectacular sight--so tall and handsome. Not pretty-boy handsome but rugged and chiseled. Even though we had sex that one time, I never got a good look at him. This man was packing, and just staring at his erection caused an ache in my belly and other places. I looked back up at him with a crooked smile. I wanted him inside of me again.

"Your wish is my command," he said to me as he picked me up and my legs naturally wrapped around his sexy body. "I want to take my time with you. We haven't been able to do that, and it is something I want to experience."

I could feel his erection pushing up against my thigh, probing to go higher. My heat was waiting for him, throbbing for his arrival. I felt an urgency building inside of me.

"Slow down, Star. What is the hurry? We have all night; let's enjoy ourselves."

"We may have all night, but I want you so bad I can hardly breathe. Stop torturing me, dammit," I said with a heated giggle.

I could tell my urgency was not affecting his decision to go slow. I just shook my head and let him continue.

"Follow me!"

"Where are we going?"

"Trust me. I want to show you something."

"Everything I want to see is on your body, what more could you have to show me?"

It started out as a slow laugh and then turned into a hearty one. His laughter was contagious, and I loved to hear it bellow from its depths. It brought to the surface a side of him I had only witnessed a few times. I could always see the potential for it beneath the surface, but I was not Intune enough to bring it out regularly.

"You will love this as well."

He took me farther into the cave. I was impressed because the doorway he took me through was hidden and only a weirdly shaped key could open it. It was dark inside. I couldn't fathom how we were going to see until I heard him tapping on what sounded like glass. As he tapped the room started to light up. I could see a huge aquarium full of sea creatures that glowed in the dark. It wasn't that the aquarium caged them in, it was like they came to see him when he would knock lightly on the glass. I could feel the love between all of them and the love he had for them. As the room lit up it was exposing all that was hidden in the dark.

It was exquisite. Glass walls showcased creatures from the deep, swimming around. It was strange because it wasn't standard glass but clear quartz crystal. It was not manufactured but made by the actions of water against the crystal. There were all these free-standing crystals and cracked-open geodes. It was breathtaking and I could feel them reaching out and resonating with me. What came next was unbelievable. There was a clamshell the size of a California king bed, and it had a mattress. The pillows were all shapes and sizes. The electric-blue bedding was soft and velvety.

"I don't understand. Dhareyin, what is this place? How did you know it was here?"

"I found this place many years ago. I usually use a portal to get to it, but I wanted to take a different route tonight with you. I have wanted to bring you here since I met you. Even though I had plans for us the night you turned into Aoroia, it was not the right time. I want to apologize for the incident on the car. I am not disappointed or ashamed about what we did; only that I did not have more control over myself. Hell, I am sorry for everything that has happened so far. I am so embarrassed by my daughter this evening. I do not know what came over her, but something has changed in her."

"Don't be too hard on her. She has been under the influence of Ramsey and Matilda, and she just gained some new power being crowned. As far as the other stuff, it just seems like we are always out of sync with each other. That night we were both pissed off, and we turned it into sexual energy. I don't regret one moment of it. All the fights we have had simply at this moment do not mean anything. Dhareyin, you are promised to another woman. Yet you are here with me. That is not only off-putting but a turn-off."

I could tell that he was thinking about what he would say next. He stood in front of the aquarium for the longest time. I decided to get on the bed and get under the covers, considering I was in the buff.

He placed his palms on the quartz and put his head on the surface. He had a delicious derriere and I could take a massive bite out of it right now, but I needed some answers. I could tell he was keeping a secret or not wanting to tell me something. Maybe he was just gauging how much to divulge to me. For the longest time it seemed that we would be steeped in silence. It felt so natural to be in his bed that soon I drifted peacefully off to sleep.

"*Aoroia, my dear, what are you doing?*"

"*What do you mean? I am following my heart, and it seems to drift in Dhareyin's direction.*"

"*If that is true, why are you always questioning his feelings for you?*"

"*I don't want to be with someone who is already promised to another.*"

"*Maybe you are afraid to open up to him in a way that comes from faith. Has he ever hurt you?*"

"*I feel like he has hurt me, but I am not sure if it is intentional or if he is doing it to protect me. I want him to see my strength and trust it.*"

"*Why would he, when you don't see your own strength, nor do you trust yourself, and you treat him like he is less than you?*"

"Is he not?"

"No one is less than anyone, Aoroia. We all have our purposes and missions in our existences. Some carry more power than others but that does not make them better. How can you say you are more than him, when you do not accept who you are?"

"Why is it so important to you that I embrace who I really am?"

"I told you, SHE is coming, and there are things that will set magick free when certain beings take their leadership roles on this planet. You are one of those leaders. Why are you so afraid to embrace all of you?"

"I keep waiting for the perfect time. I don't know if that will ever show up or not. These beings are a bit selfish and have horrible ideas about humans. I don't know if I want to rule people who feel this way about them. I may not exactly be human, but I was raised by humans and I thought I was one for all these years. I love them and I don't want them to be less than. I am afraid I will not be accepted by the tribe you say I will lead."

"Only you can change this, Aoroia. That is why you were chosen and why you have come back at this time. Look what you survived and how powerful you are in this human body. All these beings you talk about don't use their power when they take on the look of humans. You can accomplish what they cannot, because of all you have been through in the human world. They do not even understand a quarter of what you have experienced and learned."

"I never saw it that way before."

"Look at the man lying next to you. What more do you need to know? Look at how you are all wrapped up in his arms and how protective he is of you. He is lying there watching you sleep, and it is a beautiful sight. Look how well you fit with each other."

I came awake confused at first. Dhareyin had loosened his grip on me when I started thrashing around. He didn't move or say anything; he just lay there and watched me. I lay back down on his chest and draped my leg over his. I moved in and got close and snuggled with him. His pheromones were overpowering my doubtful mind.

"I want to talk about this later. Do you mind if we just lie here in silence? It is so mesmerizing and peaceful. I am enjoying spending time with you."

He gave no answer other than pulling me in closer. I lay there and watched all the sea creatures swimming back and forth, all lit up. I was lost in thought when I noticed the seahorse I had ridden at James's place coming in fast.

I sat up quickly, jarring Dhareyin awake.

"What is going on, Star?"

"LOOK!"

We both watched as she crashed into the quartz. She seemed like she was hurt before she hit the glass wall. I walked over to the wall and put my hands and forehead on the glass, and she put her head up against mine! Somehow, we were merging, and the glass was giving away to an enclosed tunnel so I could connect with her.

I wrapped my arms around her neck, and she leaned into me. I softly ran my hand down her neck and shoulder.

I whispered to her softly, "What is wrong, my girl? What has happened to you, and why did you come here? Did you come for me?"

As she spoke, I could hear and understand everything she was saying. It sounded like we were underwater, talking. "Someone came to hurt us. Your friends tried to stop them and got hurt. You must come with me to help them. It is your time to shine, beautiful one. It is you we have been waiting for. You must bring the shaman and the water dragon along. You will need his help, as others like him are in an uproar and ready to unleash on the human world."

"Do you know who started this and who hurt you? Are my friends hurt bad?"

"We don't have time to talk; we must go. I can make the trip back, but I do not know if I will survive beyond the trip."

I looked at Dhareyin, who was getting ready to pull a portal. I could see it in his intentions.

"Bring her out here, Star. We will take her through the portal. She will be fine if you are on her back. You might want to consider healing her as we go through."

This time around, we stepped through the glass effortlessly. I climbed on her back as Dhareyin opened the portal. I laid my full body on her as she walked forward. I could feel her pain and hurt. I could see that the wounds were more than physical. She was emotionally grieving for what was about to take place. I consumed it all and I could feel her will for life coming back to her.

"Dhareyin, where is the exit point of this portal?"

"We are coming out to the cave that you and I talked in. Why?"

"We need to strategize before we walk into whatever this is. I need to know how James and his family are doing?"

"I will open up a portal that is destined to a safe protected place within their home. I will scan for life forms before we go see them. We are coming to the end of this one, is she healed?"

"How are you doing, my love?"

"I am well, thank you. We need to talk, you and I alone, before you take off from me."

"As soon as we get through the other side, we can have our conversation. That will give Dhareyin time to do what he needs to do."

We were cautious as we walked out of the portal. It took a couple of moments to collect our wits. There did not seem to be any damage to this cave.

"I will leave you two to talk, and I will go do my thing. Don't take too long. Right now, we have the element of surprise."

My beautiful, brave seahorse took me away from Dhareyin. She seemed to not want him anywhere near us.

"Are you ready to take your place among us?"

"I don't see why that has to be decided tonight. Is there something you are not telling me?"

"It is your time to take your place. There can be no other time than tonight. The Council of Magick sent me to you tonight because you are the only one who can stop what is about to happen. Your power is balanced within you, and we had to make sure that would happen before we pushed you to take your place. There is a choice you will have to make that may destroy what you and Dhareyin are building. Are you ready to make that choice?"

"I don't understand any of this. What could put a wedge between us?"

"Did you see how free Daegorth was when he accepted his beast?"

"How do you know about Daegorth? How many know?"

"Don't be embarrassed, child. What took place between you two was always meant to be. He does not comprehend that he was always meant to turn. I have been in contact with him, because we are friends. He used to come check on us when he had time. No one knew what he possessed inside. He is not the same anymore. What I sense in him is a deep peace with who he has become. He will be there when you need him to be. Something will happen soon that will shake your world, and you will call upon him. For tonight the battle that lies ahead will be between you and the water dragon. Go to him—he is ready but be prepared."

I walked to Dhareyin with apprehension in every step. What could happen that would cause us to battle?

"Let's go, Star. Your friends are holed up in a small cottage not too far from the pond. Some are hurt, but the wounds will heal. Did you not teach them how to use their new powers? I would have thought that even you would have put up protection around this place?"

I could feel the look that was on my face. It was one of disbelief and irritation.

"Fuck off, Dhareyin. I did put protection around this place. At the time, their powers were not ready to come through. Why are you blaming me for this? I had nothing to do with it."

"You have everything to do with it because you chose to involve humans in protecting this place. You refuse to embrace your powers, and you are leaving us vulnerable to attack."

"I had nothing to do with the decision concerning James and Layla. I was just the messenger. Say humans like that one more time, and I will take that smirk off your face. You don't know what you are asking of me. When I take on these powers—there is no going back. I will no longer be Star and I won't be from the tribe like you think."

"What do you mean? You are part of this tribe, and you are who the prophecy talks about."

"There is a part that you do not know, and I cannot share that with you. If I bring her out and fully embrace her, it will be more far-reaching than you could imagine, which means that our tribe and humans are not safe from my wrath. She does not know good or bad, but what is and what must happen. There is no emotional connection within her when it comes to this. If you get in her way and she sees that as a threat to the greater good, she will destroy what is in front of her without a second thought. Are you sure you want to unleash her?"

"I do not believe what you say, Star. You are just afraid of accepting who you are. You don't want to let go of that human side of yourself."

"I figured out why I dread getting close to you. You don't listen, and you have no intention of hearing me. You see things one way and I another. There seems to be a wall between us, and it is not budging. Maybe it would be better if I went to James and his family myself. Open the portal; I am going through."

He said nothing further. He opened the portal and waved me through. I could tell that he was thinking about what I had just told him. I doubt it would make any difference. I knew that things were going to become quite complicated before the night was over.

I was vigilant in making sure that my friends were safe. I was on high alert as I stepped out by the back door of the cottage. I pressed my back up against the cottage's exterior wall. I was grateful that Dhareyin had something I could put on before we left his cave. I wanted to take everything in before I stepped inside. It was quite strange; if I had not been here before, I would not have seen this cottage. It was protected by a strange energy. I couldn't make out much with it being so dark. I lightly knocked on the back door. I was surprised to see all my extended family sitting in this little cottage. I stepped in and checked them all out. All the children carried an angelic glow about them that was serving as a protective shield. I could feel the tears warm against my skin. I could smell blood thick and heavy in the air. The pain and agony were screaming at me. Someone had inflicted a magickal curse upon the wounds. I could feel the anger rising in me. I walked around the corner and found James bleeding out. Zay was sitting next to him and holding a compress on his wounds, trying to slow the bleeding. He had a tourniquet on one leg, and gauze and bandages wrapped sixty percent of his body. Layla looked up at me. So much sorrow and sadness filled her eyes and energy. Her soul begged me to help him. I knew what she was asking me, and for him, I would transform.

"Please, Dabs, can't you help him like you did me and place him in Gaia?"

"Not this time, Layla. Gaia was helping me to make up my mind about something. If I ever need her help, she will be there, but this time it is something I must do. I will transform for him, because I have loved him like a brother, and I cherish his life."

"What do you mean, Dabs?"

"No time for questions. Please, everyone, back up and step away."

I felt the Destroyer and Healer step forward simultaneously.

"Which will you choose, Aoroia?"

"I choose you both. For in choosing you both I have found the balance and harmony in all forms."

I walked over to James and sat next to him. I rolled my hands over as a blue flame-filled my palms. I could hear gasps behind me. I placed my hands upon James. I could feel the healing energies and fluids in his body. My healing flames spoke to what was hurt inside him. I must allow his anger to come forward and survive the healing. The time was coming for a battle to transpire and I needed his unique talents. Those special talents would be born in anger and they would survive in love—the love that he carried for his family and friends. He would come to know the balance and harmony that anger, and love sought in each of us.

"Is anyone else hurt?"

"I am hurt, Dabs. I don't know what happened, but when I was tending James, something attached itself to me. Can you help me?"

Zay and Zane were both special to me. They were Layla's twin sons that she had with her first husband Derek. We had been friends for a long time.

I walked to Zay and scanned his body and energy.

"How long have you been able to feel what others feel? To be able to take the pain away from them. You do know you saved James's life tonight?"

"I didn't know that I could do any of those things. There was this voice inside of me that told me what to do. I have never heard it before. Will I die, Dabs?"

"We will have to teach you how to hone your empathic gifts. No, you won't die. Do you want what you took from him, or are you ready to release it?"

"I want to release it, as long as it doesn't go back to James."

I closed my eyes and asked Gaia to receive from Zay what was not his to carry and to always be an open portal for him to release these energies. I heard him slump to the floor. I could not go to him right now. I was receiving a vision. I felt my eyes turn into orbs of reflection, and my third eye opened more than ever. I could see who started this mess, and I was angry. I knew I could turn this anger into something beneficial. I was not sure Dhareyin was going to see it that way. Right now, I needed to make sure my family was safe. How was I going to do that?

"Layla, how did you guys know to come here to this cottage and that you would be safe?"

"When the shit hit the fan earlier and James was hurt, a being came to us and brought us to this cottage. He said that it would be safe for us and no one would find us but you. The being told us he was your hellhound, whatever that means. He said when you came you could help us, but not to leave until the battle was over. You are to call for him should you need him. He said not to be afraid of you when you transformed and that it would be a beautiful sight."

Daegorth continued to surprise me again and again. Now that I knew they would be safe; I could get back to Dhareyin and let him know what I know.

"What happened here tonight, Layla?"

"Some men and women showed up here tonight and demanded that we give them the magickal creatures we were protecting. If we did this, they would not hurt us. James stood up to them and they pulled out these weird-looking weapons. We ran toward the water in hopes of receiving some help. We were hoping that by leading them away from the house, they would not go after the children. I knew that James was hurt and was scared. Everyone was over here for a BBQ and they stayed inside with the kids. We made a pact with you, Dabs, that we would protect these creatures. We were not trained to do that. Next thing I know, we are being pulled through some sort of vortex and we are in the cottage. The kids and our company were all waiting there for us. He wrapped the children in protective light. We don't know what happened to the people, because he started throwing up protection all around us."

"Are you saying these were humans that you saw?"

"As far as I could see, yes. Although the weapons were weird."

"I have to get back to Dhareyin. You listen to Daegorth and stay here, no matter what you hear. I have called in Aeryana and Wolf to watch over you all."

As I stepped out of the back door, I watched the spirits merge in to be with my family. I accessed the portal once again, and it took me straight to Dhareyin. How was I going to tell him what I saw, and would he believe me?

"Aoroia, be careful. Trust no one, not even Dhareyin. There has been a leak within the collective. We do not know who it is yet, but we have been betrayed. I repeat, Magick has been betrayed. You are not safe. RETREAT!"

As the words ended, I could see a being fading out. What the hell now? I would just tell Dhareyin what I saw but nothing about Daegorth. I won't tell him I have fully embraced myself — no need to give him information that could be leaked. I stepped out onto the sandy cave floor. I looked around, and Dhareyin was nowhere to be found.

With my back against the cave wall, I sat down in the lotus position. It was time to do some meditation. I surrounded myself in protective light and proceeded to go deep within. The past, present, and future were all lined up in front of me. I did not like what I was seeing. I knew tough love at some point would come into the picture. There would be a choice I would have to make, and it could destroy everything I knew. I kept trying to see who I had become as harsh and mean, but she was not. I must believe that there is a reason that I have become her, considering the life I have had among humans. There must be some point in this.

"Star wake up. How can you be sleeping at a time like this? We have wounded creatures everywhere. They were attacked on the surface by humans tonight. We should find those humans and take them out. I told you that you were putting magick at risk by involving your human family."

"First of all, I wasn't sleeping. I was meditating. I hate to tell you this, Dhareyin, but it was not humans that did this."

"Who was it, then?"

"It was your daughter and some other female and male beings."

"My daughter would not do this, Star. I cannot believe you are so bitter that you would throw this at her feet. I don't even know you."

I let him finish and then I placed my fingers on his third eye and gave him the vision that was revealed to me.

"I don't understand why she would do this?"

"Dhareyin, I could feel the power coursing through her veins. She is on a major power trip, and we must figure out how she was coerced into this. How many creatures are we talking about?"

"More than I can count. They have been wounded with weapons.

Where would Luna get weapons?"

"Layla said the weapons were weird-looking. You don't think they are something that was developed at the Bureau, do you? After all, Luna has been friendly with Ramsey. Honestly, Dhareyin, you all have. We have a problem if they are going to try and blame this on humans."

"What are we going to do about the creatures? I am concerned; why aren't you?"

"They are already healed. Turn around and look."

All the creatures were lined up on the cave floor, healed and ready to do battle if necessary. They were looking for insight and instructions.

"Aoroia, they want you to tell them what to do?"

"Why me?"

"You healed them. They have been waiting for you. Don't you get how special you are? Don't you understand that for HER to return completely, you must accept who you are?"

"My beautiful seahorse, I don't know what you know about me, but I would love to know it. I see your faith and trust in me, and it moves my heart to open wider. I will do what I can."

I looked at Dhareyin, shook my head, and let out a slow breath.

"I know you have been led to believe that humans have attacked you here tonight. I have intel that says otherwise. We have some traitors in the magickal world. We do not know their agenda as of this moment, but we are headed back to find out what is going on. I know you have no reason to believe me, but we are doing what we can."

They all bowed before me. A beautiful mermaid stepped out of the water with two legs. "We will await your instructions. While we wait, how do we protect ourselves?"

In a whisper under my breath, I asked, "Daegorth, have you secured the property so no one can hurt them again?" I felt a cold, calming energy slide up behind me. I could tell he was invisible.

"Yes, Mistress. I have taken care of everything. Luna and the others will not be able to penetrate this area again from any direction."

I could feel him slide his arms around my waist. He leaned in and breathed in my scent. "I have made sure your special family is safe. The Council of Magick will be sending the teachers necessary to help them open their gifts so something like this doesn't happen again. Dhareyin doesn't trust you, and you should be careful around him. He seems to be confused about what to do."

"How do you know that?"

"Stay away from Luna. He will choose her every time. You have work to do. Go embrace who you really are. It is so freeing. I will come to you later and show you how freeing it really is."

"Everything is secure. They will not be able to enter here again. Watch over the humans who have been placed into guardianship over you. They will be taught better ways to take care of this place. Until then, they need your help and guidance. They are my family; please protect them when I cannot."

In unison, they all agreed.

"You can reach me anytime. Do not hesitate to call out. If I do not answer, then you will know something has happened."

"Let's go figure out what Luna is up to," I said in a whisper to Dhareyin.

"This is not for you to take care of, Star. I will drop you off at your home. I have to deal with this on my own."

"I have every right to be a part of this. You cannot keep me out. They tried to kill my family tonight. Did you think I was going to let that happen?"

"That is precisely why you are not coming with me tonight."

"How are you going to approach this? My beauty did not come to you; she came to me to inform me of what was taking place. How are you going to explain to them how you even know about James and Layla? That will set them up as an even bigger target—or are you the one that told them about this place?"

"You don't trust me, do you? Well, that makes two of us. I don't trust you, either."

There was nothing more to be said. Without my knowing, he

created two portals—one for the tribe and one for the pond by my house. I was blind to see how I could change any of this. I was so in my head about everything that I didn't notice right away that the path was not illuminated like before. I stopped dead in my tracks and slowed my breathing so I could hear on a deeper level.

It was too late to become aware of my surroundings. I was hit in the head from behind and I blacked out. I could feel myself being dragged by my feet. Even though I was unconscious at one point I was aware of my head hitting several sharp stones along the way. I knew I could call on someone, but that name was not registering for me. I slipped under again and somehow knew I was safe.

12

I do not know how long I was unconscious but when I awoke, I was moaning and groaning. I felt terribly sick to my stomach. The nausea was coming in waves. I was stretched out on a stone bench. I was chilled to the bone, and I would soon realize I was totally without clothing. I tried opening my eyes, but it made my head spin even more. The bench was hard, and my head felt squishy and wet. I tried to bring up my right arm, but a sharp pain shot through my shoulder. It caused me to jump and made me realize there were more things battered than I had noticed. Why was I naked? I could hear someone coming, so I went perfectly still like I was out. I could hear them unlock a metal gate. It registered that I was in a dungeon or a cell of some kind.

"We do not know why she has not regained consciousness, Luna."

"I guess you had better get it figured out, Dr. Roxanne before we decide that you are more on her side than ours. This is your last warning. I don't care if you have to torture her again and wake her up, but I want it done now."

"Does your father know that she is down here?"

"No, he doesn't, and we are going to keep it that way. He is not a part of this, and we are not going to involve him now."

"I will see what I can do. I will have the staff keep you informed should anything change."

"I don't know why he is interested in this puny human anyway.

I fucking hate them all."

"I don't know either, Luna. Go let Ramsey and Matilda know what is going on. I will keep an eye on her."

I heard one of them leave. I stayed perfectly still. Truth be told, I could hardly move anyway.

"I know you are awake, Star. You are safe for the moment. I don't know how much longer I can keep you that way."

"Why are you doing this to me? I hurt so bad; I don't understand. I have done everything they have asked, and I stayed away. Why did they come after me tonight?"

"Oh, my darling Star. You have been in a coma for a month. You are dwindling down to nothing. I am afraid for your life. The Council says you are the only one who can change this."

"Who is the Council?"

"I work for the Council of Magick. They said you would know what I was talking about. Do you not remember?"

"Why do you keep calling me Star? My name is Dabney, or my friends call me Dabs."

"This must be some damage from the beating you took."

"I was beaten?"

"When they brought you here a month ago, Luna had them beat you unconscious again. You have been in a coma ever since. You have so many broken bones, and they won't let me repair them. I am afraid for your life."

"Who is this father you speak of?"

"Luna's father has a soft spot for you. His name is Dhareyin."

"Maybe you can go tell him or get a message to him. Ask the Council of Magick to inform him. I am tired, Dr. Roxanne. I am going to rest."

I could hear her thoughts, which was an exciting turn of events. I knew she had decided to tell this Dhareyin what was happening.

I awoke later to commotion outside in the hall. I could hear a man not necessarily yelling, but his voice was loud and profound.

"Where is she, Luna? I want to see her."

"This has nothing to do with you, Father. You must leave now. How did you find out she was down here?"

"You might wear the crown of Seth's family's clan, but you do not tell me what to do, Luna. Where is she? Take me to her now."

I could hear them walking toward my cell. The sound of the key in the lock was hard on my ears.

"OMG, what have you done to her?"

I felt a presence sit down next to me, not because the stone moved, but because the temperature of the surrounding air changed. I wanted to sink into him, whoever he was, and be lost forever to his warmth.

With soft hands and light fingers, he slowly picked me up and cradled me in his arms. I could feel something wet on my face. Was I leaking? I opened my eyes slightly, and only slightly, because the light hurt my eyes. The wetness was coming from him. He was crying heavily. I felt strange in my body.

"I love you, Aoroia." Something was changing inside of me as he called me Aoroia. "Don't change, my love. Not yet." As the words left his mouth, I felt myself leaving my body.

"Dr. Roxanne, she isn't responding to me. She isn't breathing anymore. You have to help her."

As I watched from above my body, I could see the love this man carried for me. He was mine and always would be, whether it worked for us or not.

The one they called Luna stepped forward and looked disappointed that I was gone. Not necessarily because she cared about me, but she was almost insane in her being. "Throw her body to the dogs. She won't be of service to us anymore."

"Like hell you will. I will take her to the surface and bury her properly. You and I have a lot to talk about, Daughter. Leave us. I don't want to be in the same room with you. If you know what is good for you, this will be the last time you talk about humans in such a way."

I could see her stomp out. She threw Dr. Roxanne up against the wall. "You will have to be punished for your betrayal here today. At midday tomorrow, you will die by the crushing wall."

"I do not regret the actions that I took today. What you were doing with her was wrong in so many ways. I am not afraid to die for Starlene Jasper. She has more heart than all of you put together."

"You will die a slow agonizing death. I look forward to watching your body being crushed slowly. Your eternal soul will scream for its release. Take her away and lock her in the cell next to this bitch."

I watched Dr. Roxanne pull her shoulders back and walk with pride to her cell. The last thing they did was whack her in the back of the head, and she fell to the stone floor. Blood was seeping into the cracks and crevices and puddling around her head. I could feel her heartbeat, and it was strong. I watched the one they called Dhareyin hold me with protection. I could see his lips moving, but I could not hear what he was saying. I decided to get closer so I could hear.

"Daegorth, where are you? She said you would always be available if I needed you. Brother, where are you? I need you more now than I ever have. Please, Daegorth. If you hear me, meet me at Star's cabin. Come on, Star; let's go before she decides she can do something about you." I drifted back into my body slowly. Somehow, he faked my death so he could rescue me. Why did the name Daegorth sound familiar?

He opened a weird light in the wall, and he took me into it. He held me close. He stepped out of the light and we began walking. The path came alive and illuminated our way. He walked slowly but with determination. I could feel him walking up steps.

"Don't be afraid. I will be right back. I am going to cast a protective circle. I should have done it before, but I didn't want to infringe on your place."

He laid me on something soft and covered me with a blanket. The scent was familiar to me. I snuggled in the best I could. I lay there listening for any sign that he was coming back. I did not see him so much as feel him.

"Mistress, where have you been? Why do you look so funny?"

I felt the blanket being removed. I was exposed once again, but I knew that I was safe. What took shape before me was terrifying and beautiful in the same image forming in my mind. What I heard chilled me to the bone.

His scream and harsh response to what he could see was more than my ears could handle. The sound came from somewhere deep. It was primal and angry.

"Take it easy, Daegorth."

"He took the form of a man. Why did you call me here, Dhareyin?"

"I need you to take Star away for good. She is not safe here, and I can see that now. I was so blind to what was happening, and I must take care of this. I have to find a way to help Dr. Roxanne."

"Where would you like me to take her? I cannot heal these wounds."

"She knows what to do. Take her away to the Milky Way, like before. Let her know that I love her and wish that I could have protected her better. I need to get to her friends and protect them. I am afraid my daughter has declared war on the humans, and she isn't working alone."

"Her family is safe, Dhareyin. You do not have to do anything. They were safe before you and Star showed up that night. I have watched over them closely since the attack."

"You were there? Of course—that is how she knew they would all be safe. So, you know who she is, then?"

"What I know is that she is special. She is more special than anyone knows."

"We need her to transform."

"No, Dhareyin, you need her to transform to justify falling in love with a human. She is perfect the way she is. She needed to know that you would accept her as she is, not something she could become. You have been so blinded to the love that was right in front of you. You kept pushing her to become what she never asked for. Star knows she will accept it, but she wanted your love despite what she will become. How would you feel if you were thrown away like trash? To be given to monsters because you fulfill a prophecy. To then be expected to change everything that you have become because it is time for a prophecy to come to fruition and you are expected to save the people who didn't want you? Instead of showing her love, Dhareyin, you showed her your fear. You had no faith in who Star was becoming. She was in balance more than you could know."

"This coming from the monster who brutalized her for enjoyment and because you were hired to kill her. I don't think you have any room to talk, Daegorth."

"I cannot take back what I did to her. I will punish myself for the rest of my existence but somehow, she has forgiven me for it. It is that human heart you keep trying to get rid of. She is complete the way she is. I must show her how freeing that is. I will do what you ask, for her. Why didn't you protect her from this? Why is your daughter still alive?"

"I am in the dark about what is happening here. How do I kill my daughter to where she will never exist again? She will never be able to have children."

"Those are your battles and demons. You have made your choice. Had you taken Star with you like she asked, she would not be in this state."

I was watching and listening to them fight over me as if I were not there. I did have my own words; I just chose not to use them.

"Daegorth?"

"Yes, Mistress!"

"Take me away from here. It is time."

"I am so sorry, Star. I hope one day you can forgive me."

"It is not for me to forgive, Dhareyin. You must forgive yourself. I have a warning for you."

"What is that?"

"You take care of Luna and those involved who hurt my family. If you don't, I will come back and delete you all."

"How am I not supposed to be afraid of you when you talk like that? How dare you threaten my tribe?"

"That is where our issue lies. As much as you want me to fulfill the prophecy, you still only ever see me as human. It isn't your tribe, Dhareyin. It is our tribe. It is not something we own. It is something we are a part of. It resides in our essence, and there are those who are trying to destroy that, including your daughter. I told you once who the destroyer is, and the day will come when you will wish you had not met me. As much as I love you, Dhareyin, at this point it is not enough."

Daegorth opened a portal and took me where I needed to go. He took me straight to James and his family. He walked out of the portal and knocked on the back door. James opened the door and gasped when he saw my condition.

"What happened to you, Dabs? Lay her down here, Daegorth. Can you explain what happened?"

"I have no idea. Star will have to tell you."

I could see their tears and I felt them in my heart. I must have looked a mess.

"Let me take a look, Dabs?"

He went to pull the blanket off me, and I stopped him. "I am not clothed under here, James. Does Layla have something I can put on?"

"Why are you naked?"

"Clothes, and then I will answer your questions."

James carried me into the room where he and Layla were sleeping for the time being. He laid me gently on the bed. Layla followed to help me put some clothes on.

"Do you feel like a bath, Dabs?"

"I would love one, Layla. I am so hungry and cold. My body hurts all over; maybe the hot bath will help that. Do you by any chance have some bone broth?"

Layla ran a bath for me. She immediately stepped into nurturer mode and helped me into the tub. "Just relax until I get back with your soup. James has a nutritional drink around here I will make up for you. Oh, Dabs, I just want to cry. My beautiful girl, what did they do to you?"

I stared at her with tears running down my face. I knew what she asked was rhetorical for now. I lay back and allowed the hot water to wash over my skin. The bubbles were scented with my favorite bubble bath. I did not smell good. Good lord, a month without a bath. The water was starting to sting and burn me, but I knew I needed to wash. I could feel my hair matted against the back of my head. My head was still sore and squishy. I dunked my head under the water, which instantly turned red. I could feel that some of the broken bones had started to heal when Dhareyin called me Aoroia. The blood was coming from my head. It burned and stung and felt oddly enjoyable. The heat on my skin, even though it hurt, was soothing to my battered muscles and bones.

"Let me help you wash your hair. I imagine it is hard work for you right now. Where is all this blood coming from?"

"The back of my head feels all squishy. Can we just wash it for now and check later? I am so tired. I have things to do and not a lot of time to do them."

"I brought you some of that lotion you like. I fell in love with it when you gifted me some a couple of Christmases ago. I also brought you some water and electrolytes mixed up. It is James's personal mix that he created about a year ago. Slowly drink it; we don't want you throwing it back up. You soak for a bit longer, and then we will get you out of there."

I knew what I had to do to heal myself. I just was not sure I wanted to. I was heartbroken over Dhareyin. I yearned for the beast that I first met, the one who wanted me just the way I was. I ached for the monster who took me down below and showed me a different way of seeing pleasure. Why did it change once he found out I was part of the tribe? Was there a chance that he really did want to be with a human? I need to get a hold of that prophecy. As I made this realization the following words poured out of me:

I am Aoroia from the Heart of the Godz Tribe and beyond
I am destroyer
I am healer
I am shadow
I am light
   But one
Aligned together
Perfectly balanced
Harmonious, bright, and true
Not just a woman, nor a queen
   But goddess of the in-between
I am whole and complete
I am Aoroia!

I embrace the destroyer and the healer as I open to the entirety of who I be. I release the Goddess of destruction and renewal within me.

As I spoke each word with intent, every cell in my body was transforming and healing. I choose to live as a goddess within this body on this planet, ready to act and do my part to save magick! I could feel my bones, skin, muscles, and the back of my head healing. Everything about me was changing simultaneously, and ancient writing was appearing upon my body. It looked like the prophecy was unfolding on my skin but was borne deep within me. I did not have to read it to know what it said. It was a piece of the prophecy. Dhareyin must have the other part. I was whole again and glowing. I slipped below the surface of the water completely emerged. I felt myself go invisible soaking in everything I was meant to be.

"Dabs, where did you go?" I heard a moment later.

I came back to the surface and reappeared.

"Well, how did you do that?"

"Could I get a towel, Layla?"

"Sure thing, love. I will leave it on the edge of the tub. Do you need any help getting out?"

"No, I think I have got this. Give me a moment, will you?" I stepped out of the tub brand new—newer than I had ever been. I was entirely transformed. I knew there would be one more transformation, but that would come later.

I dried off and put on the lovely lotion she left for me. I drank down the broth because I was starving. What I needed was meat, preferably rare. I looked at the clothing Layla left for me, and I wanted something different. I could see in my mind's eye what I wanted to wear, and it appeared on my body. My hair was incredibly beautiful. My eyes were big and bright and electric blue! When I went to take a step, I didn't touch the floor. I was gliding.

I opened the door and glided out. I stood there watching all my family. I noticed that Daegorth was still here. It was a lovely sight to behold. My presence quickly became known when Daegorth dropped to his knee and bowed before me. "Goddess, you have arrived!"

I peered deeply into his eyes and I knew I was right in setting him free. I could see all the stars in our solar system dancing in his dark, beautiful eyes. I looked up to see everyone watching me in amazement.

"We don't understand, Dabs. How is this possible?"

"James, my dear friend, I am Goddess Aoroia, but you can continue to call me Dabs. This is who I was always meant to be. It took me a bit of time to embrace the two parts of myself that I always kept separate. It was time, after everything we have all been through, for me to step up. I love you all, and it is time you start your training. Soon SHE will come, and we must be ready for her. I have a question."

"What is that, Goddess Aoroia?"

"You can call me Dabs, James. I am starving and I need meat. Are steaks by any chance on the menu tonight?"

"We were just talking about having a BBQ. We didn't think you would be ready to eat heavy like that, but it seems you have completely healed. Would you tell us what happened while we cook dinner? Daegorth, are you staying?"

Daegorth looked at me for permission to speak. "Would you like to stay and eat with us?"

"Yes, Goddess. It would be my honor to eat with your family."

We all went outside to eat dinner. Daegorth had secured the perimeter so no one could see us.

"After I left here that night, Dhareyin sent me back to my place. I had told him that his daughter was the one that attacked, with several others. I wanted to go with him, but he wouldn't let me. He opened a portal that dropped me off by the water. I was walking back to the house when I noticed that the path wasn't illuminated like normal. I went silent, but it was too late. I was whacked on the back of the head and I was dragged somewhere. I could feel the back of my head being smashed on rocks as they dragged me by my feet."

"Where did they take you?"

"Layla, from what I could tell I was being held in a dungeon in a locked cell. When I woke up, my body hurt so bad, and it hurt to open my eyes because the light was so bright. I could feel a cold rock bench beneath my body. I was naked, broken, and without blankets. I was freezing cold. I guess I never noticed, because of all the pain I was in. I made sure they didn't know that I was awake. Somehow, Dr. Roxanne knew, and she decided to tell Dhareyin what was going on before his daughter tortured me to death. When Dhareyin came to see me, he must have planned something with the doc, because they faked my death. Luna was going to have me thrown to the dogs, but Dhareyin wouldn't let her. I could hear him calling for you, Daegorth."

"Yes, it went on for quite some time. He wasn't allowing me to speak back so I could let him know I had heard him. He didn't tell me what was going on—only that he needed me."

"Thank you for listening, Daegorth. Anyway, I found out his daughter hates humans, and they are going to execute Dr. Roxanne for betraying them tomorrow, midday, using a crushing wall."

"Then her death will be quick."

"No, Daegorth, Luna said she was going to make it as slow as she could go so Dr. Roxanne would suffer. Do you know where this crushing wall is that Luna is speaking about?"

"I do, but you won't be allowed access to it even as a goddess. It is hallowed ground and is protected to only allow those from the tribe in."

"I want you to show me tomorrow where it is. Whether I can get in or not, I will have to try. Will you do that for me, my hellhound?"

"Yes, Goddess. I could go in and save her if you want?"

"This is something I have to do. I am hoping that Dhareyin finds a way to help her out."

"If he tries to help her out, he could wind up joining her. They are very strict on this ritual."

"So, do they use this to punish the people from the tribe?"

"Not so much. Mostly humans."

"You are telling me that the tribe kills humans?"

"Only those who have trespassed into our territory and found out our secrets. It is a barbaric tradition, but no one will stop it. I will take you tomorrow, but for tonight you need your rest. I will leave you to your family."

"No, Daegorth, I want you to stay with me. Is it okay that I ask that of you?"

"Your wish is my command. I will be right back."

I watched him walk into the cottage. I don't know what he had planned, but he was determined. I turned back to my family and tried to hear what they were thinking.

"This is all so new, Dabs. We do not know what to think."

"Are you sorry you accepted the role as guardians of these magickal creatures?"

"Not at all. We just want to be better equipped to protect them. You said that our training would begin—do you know when? Do you know when we can move back to our house?"

"The Council of Magick will be sending those to train you soon. I don't know when you can move back into your place, but we can ask Dae when he gets back."

"We want to talk to you about so much, but we do not know where to begin. It is also getting late, and we have had a pretty long day. What do you say we all head in and go to bed? We could take the kids out of their bedroom so you can have some privacy."

"That won't be necessary, James. I can sleep on the couch."

The size of the cottage from the outside was about five hundred square feet but when you stepped inside those numbers changed. It became a three thousand square foot cottage with a basement that tunneled somewhere. I should talk to Daegorth about tunneling that to their home, so they always had that safe place to go if needed. We walked in single file until we were all inside.

"I will get you some blankets for the couch."

"Thank you, Layla."

"You don't have to worry about that I created a new room for the Goddess. Come this way, Mistress."

I said goodnight and followed him to the bedroom he made for me. When I walked through the door, the room opened into a magnificent sight. There was an enormous bed with curtains around it, covered in pillows and soft blankets. The lighting was perfect. It felt like he was romancing me or trying to seduce me. The air smelled like home, and it warmed my heart that he went to this much trouble. It had its own bathroom with a garden tub filled with warm milky water and gardenias, coconut oil and vanilla.

"I thought you might like to relax in the healing elixirs of our tribe."

"I would love to. Where are you going to sleep?"

"I will sleep here on the floor next to the door."

"There is plenty of room on the bed for both of us. Would you like to take a bath as well?"

"Are you asking me to take a bath with you, Mistress?"

"Yes, my hellhound, come share a healing bath with me. We will both heal our wounds tonight, and you can show me how freeing it is to embrace our wholeness. Come on," I said to him as I offered him my hand.

There were candles lit all around the tub. So relaxing and romantic. I dropped my clothes and he did the same. We walked into the water together. I was at one end and he was at the other. He was right; as soon as my body was fully submerged, I could feel a healing sensation taking place. It was almost as if it were rejuvenating my soul. I felt energetic and happy.

"I hurt you, my goddess. Do you think things will ever be okay between us?"

"There is a stain there. I don't know if that stain ever has a right to be removed. In our human world, I would never go near you again except to see you put in prison for the rest of your life—or better yet, kill you. My eyes have been opened to many things, and while I agree with some of the human ways, I also know that I took my turn ripping you apart with a vengeance. I regained my power when I unleashed on you. I say we start fresh today."

With that, he stood up and walked to me. He was enormous and beautiful. Sexy didn't even come close to what he was.

"I want to heal you. I know that as a goddess, you have healed but there is one thing only I can heal—the wounds I inflicted upon you. I tried to implant in you. How did you get rid of it?"

"It flushed itself out. I cannot get pregnant, Dae."

"I wasn't trying to impregnate you. The implants are what I use to consume the body from the inside out so the spirit can release and go home. The implants are a flesh-eating bacteria but in a good way. From what we know about you now your body must have been healing itself on a mass scale rejecting the implants. Will you stand up for me and turn around?"

I was shocked by what he said. It made more sense than him trying to impregnate me. I felt a calm slide over me, and I did as he asked. I felt like we were on a whole other level of understanding.

"Thank you. Don't be shocked, but I have to lick you, as my healing powers are in my saliva."

He licked me all over my face and then my body, including the hot melting pot between my thighs. He even ran his tongue up the crack of my rear. I could feel the burning sensation in the invisible scars. He then turned me around and licked every inch of my skin. I could not help but shudder at the warmth and softness of his tongue. I could feel a storm brewing at my core. It was hard to concentrate or focus. He slowly took care of each scar, and everywhere he was brutal. I thought maybe he would help my mind and emotions with it, but he didn't.

"I don't want you to forget what I have done to you. Don't ever trust me, Aoroia. I don't know if they are able to have control over me still. I want you to be safe, and the only way that is possible is to listen to your intuition. Your wounds have healed nicely without my help."

"Dhareyin put some mashed-up roots on them. We sat in a healing pool at an oasis."

"I am so glad he was able to do that for you. I am sorry he had to."

"Remember, we are starting fresh. No more apologizing for what happened in our yesterdays. I want to say thank you for all you have done for me today!"

We talked and talked. He washed my back and I washed his. He put conditioner in my hair and ran his fingers through it, playing with it. We laughed and we even cried. He made me promise that if he should be turned again, that I would delete him. When I hesitated and balked at his request, he explained that he would not want to be used as a weapon against me ever again. He would rather die before letting that happen.

"What could I call you that would snap you out of your trance, should they get hold of you again?"

"Call me your hellhound and release your pheromones."

Nothing happened in the tub, for which I was grateful. We both got into bed naked and fresh. We slowed time down so we could fully rest in the way we needed to. It allowed James and his family to get a great night's rest.

I rolled onto my side and stared out the glass doors that reminded me of a looking glass. It allowed me to see all the magickal creatures that had come out to play. I sat up in bed and walked to the doors. I slid them open and walked outside. There was a full moon out tonight, and I wanted to join them. I got to ride on a unicorn named Bleu, and Pegasus flew me to the moon. I could see that my seahorse was waiting for me on the shores of the pond. I needed to find out her name.

I came to find out her name was Nell, and she was the most beautiful seahorse I had ever seen. We dove deeper and deeper, finally reaching the cave where we could talk. It was interesting because she had legs and arms; they were just tucked into her sides when she swam. It allowed her to access land just like the mermaids. She carried me up onto the shore. I got down and we lay side by side. We rolled and rubbed all over each other, frolicking and playing as if we had been friends for ages.

"We have been waiting for you to remember who you are, Goddess. We have all been together for ages. I am so happy you have decided to take your place amongst us. Why didn't you tell me you were carrying life?"

"What do you mean?"

She looked down at my belly. "You know what I meant Goddess."

I looked down at my belly and sure enough, I had a little tiny bump. "The last time I had sex was over a month ago. I should not be showing this quickly, especially for my first."

"Things can sometimes take a quick route in the magickal world. This child will be quite extraordinary. He will have traits of both parents. I know you are confused because you don't know if it is Daegorth's or Dhareyin's. Don't worry about it. In the long run, it doesn't matter who has fathered your child. It is time for you to go back to the surface. You need your rest before tomorrow."

She took me back to the edge of the water, where I found Daegorth waiting for me. He was lounging naked on the grass. He carried a crooked smile of seduction on his lips and eyes. I stepped out of the water and went to him. I lay down next to him in the grass and stared at the moon and stars for the longest time. He stood up, took my hand, and helped me up. We walked back to our room in silence.

He quickly pulled me close. "Shh!" He pointed to the lights we could see bouncing up and down. It looked like someone was looking for something, but they couldn't find it. He wrapped his arms around me and held me tight. "They are wondering what happened to the property they were on the other night. I have made this a secret hiding place, and no one can enter but those of us who are here now. That is why I haven't let your family go back to their home. That protection takes a little bit of time to conjure up. No worries they cannot hear us."

We walked back and climbed into bed. I laid on my back and he was on his side facing me. He placed his hand on my lower belly and held it there for the longest time.

"Don't worry—it isn't mine, Aoroia."

"How do you know?"

"I can sense the DNA, and even though the child is related to me, he is not mine. Why didn't you tell me you were with child?"

"I didn't know until my lovely seahorse Nell informed me. Do you mind kissing me?"

"I don't mind at all. Are you sure?"

I reached my hand up and touched his face. He brought his lips closer to mine. Slowly they met with a fevered touch. He took my bottom lip into his mouth as my upper lip devoured his. As each moment passed, the passion became stronger and more intense. Before long, our tongues were playing exquisite games with each other. He reached his hand down between my thighs, slowly bringing me to a climax. I wrapped my arms around his neck as he pulled me closer. He stopped kissing me and pushed himself away from me just a little bit.

"I know you are in love with Dhareyin. You say that love is not enough. I wonder if you pushed him away because on some level you knew you carried his child. You want him to want you for you, not because of a baby. Which you love, by the way, and you will be a fantastic mother to my nephew. You have been in a broken place for too long, Aoroia. My nephew deserves to have his father in his life, and so do you. I want to make love to you so bad, but you belong in Dhareyin's bed, not mine."

"He doesn't want me in his bed, Daegorth. The pushing away isn't just from my end. Dhareyin will get close and then pull away and say he is afraid of me. I cannot be with someone who is afraid of me. Are you?"

"No, I am not, but I know your truth. There are many unknowns with Dhareyin, and you feel them. He feels the same way. He doesn't know the true you. You want to be accepted for your shadow as much as for your light. When he talks about being afraid of you, your walls immediately go up, and so do his. Love isn't always cut and dried, Aoroia; sometimes it is necessary to work at it. It isn't about who is right or wrong. It is about whether you are listening to each other and communicating."

"I feel like he always wants to shut me down. Like what I want doesn't matter."

"You have to keep trying. I can feel how your heart beats for him and aches for him. Dhareyin is cool-headed and precise. His logic will always come first because emotions can skew the situation. Do you not remember what it was like when you met him that first night?"

"I do remember. How did you know about that?"

"When he came back to the forest, he told me all about it. I could tell that he fell in love with you at that moment. So sassy and full of fire. He said you had a mouth on you and loved it."

"Luna said that he is promised to someone else. Is that true?"

"Yes, it is true. One day she will show up, but until then, why not enjoy yourself?"

"You are not going to tell me who she is?"

"It is not for me to tell you."

"He says he loves me, but he won't tell me about her either. Where is the prophecy? I would like to look at it."

"I used to have it before your mother took it from me. Dhareyin has it hidden. Your mother entrusted him with it. She wanted to keep you safe—and before you say she didn't, that is for another discussion you need to have with her."

"Why hasn't she told everyone who I am?"

"They cannot see her. Only you, I, and the three can see her when she chooses to show herself to us. She does not exist anymore, and her time here is short-lived. You really should go have a conversation with her before it is too late."

"What if I don't want to? I don't have anything useful I want to say other than how much I hate her."

"Even when we don't think we should say something, it is often not true. I feel like it would help you to embrace your part in this tribe. I could set the meeting up, if you would like?"

"I want to take care of saving Dr. Roxanne first; then we will see. Can you talk to Dhareyin about letting me see the prophecy?"

"I will see what I can do. Now let me hold you. It is time we get some rest. We have a busy day ahead of us. I am not sure how the tribe is going to respond to you if you make it through to the execution. Have you planned any of it out?"

"I will play it by ear. I know sooner than later I am going to butt heads with Luna. I cannot guarantee she will come out of it alive. I will lose Dhareyin if she dies, but I don't know how to save her if she won't stop what she is doing. Do you have any advice or insight?"

"Whatever is meant to happen with her will happen. The difference is why it happens. Would you be killing her to prove a point or because it is the only way to keep her from hurting others? You must find that balance and weigh it cautiously. That is all you can do in any given moment and always know the choice is yours."

I laid my head on his chest and fell asleep quickly. It felt good to slip into slumber. My sleep was tattered with remnants of chaos that had been happening since I saw them dumping the toxic waste. I rolled onto my side, and Daegorth spooned me. He held me all night long with gentleness, tenderness, and a bit of possessiveness. I didn't mind; it felt great to be wanted and protected. So how come Dhareyins possessiveness bothered me so bad?

I dreamed of Dhareyin trying to save Dr. Roxanne, and in the process, he was killed. It was so brutal that it slammed me awake.

"What is wrong, Aoroia?"

"Today when I help Dr. Roxanne, you need to watch out for Dhareyin; he is going to try to help her. In the process, he gets crushed and dies. When everything is said and done, please take her to the Council of Magick. She works for them, and they can protect her. We cannot hide everyone out on the Milky Way."

"Is there any way to save him?"

"Knowledge is power, and I have been forewarned about what will happen. I wonder—is there a way you can create a diversion when I need one?"

"I will follow your lead, Mistress. Now let's get some sleep. We have to be up in a few hours."

"I want you inside of me. Is that too much to ask?"

"You are killing me here. I am doing my best to stay strong."

"When I smell you, my loins ache for you. It is a hunger that is hard to quench. I will behave, and maybe it is for the better."

He scooped me into his side. I could tell from his erection that he really did want me. I snuggled my rear in a little just to tease him and make it that much harder for him. Yes, I was a bit of a flirt and a tease. He pushed back slowly, and I returned the favor and before long we were full-on dry humping each other. I could feel myself arching up against his chest, and he took my nipples in his fingers and created a delicious pressure in them. Before long I was releasing that pressure up against him. I could hear my breathing getting deeper and he was following suit. "Aoroia," he whispered in my ear. My whole body shivered as an exquisite jolt rippled through me.

I lifted my top leg up over his, allowing him access to enter me from behind. I didn't have to ask twice as he thrust inside of me with such intensity that I came undone instantly. As our bodies ebbed and flowed with each other, he skillfully played with my nipples. What I was experiencing was scrumptious. He trailed kisses up and down my neck, and sometimes he would nibble at just the right moment and send shockwaves of delight through my whole body. I leaned my head back, and he took my mouth and made love to it with his. The passion and pleasure we experienced, kiss after kiss, was intense and explosive.

He rolled me onto my stomach and started kissing me from my feet upwards. He trailed kisses up my inner thighs slowly. Just as I was about to climax, he would stop and then start again. He grabbed my backside, paying great attention to each cheek. He was biting me seductively until he received the response he was going for. The growls and groans coming from inside of him made me want more of him. He slid his delicious tongue up and down, pleasuring me until I was spent. One release after another left his face covered in my essence.

He flipped me over and went to work from the front. He took my nub in his mouth and played with it until I was arching against his face over and over. He trailed kisses slowly up the rest of my body until he was nestled right between my thighs. I brought my legs up and wrapped them around his waist. I wanted him as close as I could get him. He thrust slowly into my slippery heat, riding me until we climaxed together. He lay on his back and pulled me with him. I was straddling him, and our heavenly bodies were hot, sticky, and wet. The smell of our time together was intoxicating. I kissed his chest and laid my head down and listened to his heart.

"Aoroia, that was incredible. I am sorry I didn't have better control."

I sat up and I could see him clearly as the full moon was shining through the sliding glass doors. I placed my forefinger on his lips and mouthed for him to shh. "I knew what I was doing. I am a grown woman, and I wanted you. You told me to enjoy myself, so that is what I did here with you tonight. I don't regret it, Daegorth, do you?"

"No, I don't regret it. You were delicious, and I cannot seem to get enough of you. Are you ready to go to sleep?"

"Do you mind if I lie on your chest a little longer?"

"I would be honored."

I lay there and thought of what was to come at the execution. For some reason, I was not worried at all. I suppose that was because I had finally embraced my true self. I knew when the time was right, all would be well. I finally have some confidence in myself. It does help that I am able to go invisible.

I slid off Daegorth sometime in the night and dreamed of the Milky Way. I could still get excited and wet remembering my time there with him. I felt like my dreams were all over the place.

"Aoroia, we are so proud of you. The Council has been waiting for this day for a long time. We celebrate and cherish you always. Hail Goddess Aoroia," I could hear from the collective. *"You still have one transformation to make, and it will be the hardest for you. You still struggle because you think your mother betrayed you. The only way you will get their attention is to embrace where you came from. It is one of the reasons Dhareyin pushes himself away from you. He thinks you are ashamed of the tribe and that you only want to destroy it. He is proud of his people, even with all that is going on. His heritage means everything, even if it means losing you. He feels that if you don't love your tribe, then how can you be the best ruler for it? He cannot see himself with someone who doesn't want to be a part of something he is so proud of, even if he does love you deeply."*

"You are not telling me anything I had not considered. There is this stubbornness in me that will be shaken today at the execution—this I know. I know I love Dhareyin, but I feel this incredible connection with Daegorth that I cannot explain even to myself. There are parts of me that feel ashamed and disgusted that I enjoy having sex with him. I am hungry for him in a way I have never been hungry for another man. I feel like people would be disgusted with me if they knew I enjoyed having sex with the man-beast who brutalized me in such a way."

"You feel your power around him, and you no longer feel helpless. You know that if you unleashed on him, he could handle it. The connection is great between you two because of what you have been through together. This isn't for anyone else to feel something about. You must decide how you feel about it and embrace it. Sit with Gaia and talk it out. Only you can make peace with this. It is not for someone else to do it for you. Have Daegorth do an extra protection around that wee babe of yours. What you must do today will be exhausting and stressful. Freeing and terrifying. Liberating and transformative. We must make sure the wee one is kept safe."

"I am scared, but I am not. I feel like this human-trained mind is getting in the way."

"You don't have a human mind, but you grew up thinking you did, and that is what you keep forgetting. To continue to think you are human will take you away from fully transforming. You can keep your love and kindness. The empathy and compassion. The strength and determination and willingness to always move powerfully forward in your evolution. Those things learned from the human world will come in handy today and every day forward. Keep all those lessons you have learned, because they will help guide you when you least expect it. You have an incredible capacity to love, and even tough love can be transformative. Your mission is to see how you can best rule the tribe with all that you are. It is time that some of the old ways are reshaped to include the new. That is what you bring to the tribe; Aoroia is the NEW!"

"I have been thinking for a bit that there needs to be some change. How do I get them to see how important humans are? I am tired of hearing that humans are garbage. How do I change that?"

"You change it by being you. Show them a better way. Show them it is time for things to change. That is why they are so disgruntled. They are bored and tired of the old ways, but they will not tell you this. To them, you are an outsider and do not understand their ways. When you transform, you will be downloaded and upgraded to a cellular level. When this happens, all that is, was, and ever will

be will become one with you. Aoroia, you don't have to look or be like them to be them. You were never meant to be like them, and that is what Dhareyin has fallen in love with. Find the prophecy; you will see what it means for all of you. You already know you carry a forgotten piece on your body, and that is for you and the one you choose to be your mate. Dhareyin will love this child and teach him the ways of the shaman and the water dragon, but what you don't know will come when he is born. He is going to be more powerful than Dhareyin and Daegorth put together."

"I do feel this wholeness when we talk. It helps me to understand things so much better. Would it be wrong for me to choose Daegorth as my mate?"

"The choice has always been yours, Aoroia. Remember that Daegorth is your beast. The biggest part of his purpose is to serve you. As your mate, could he do his job effectively? Could he help you rule in a way that is most beneficial for your people? You also must ask the same questions of Dhareyin. Choose wisely, Goddess; you only get one shot at this."

I could hear a bunch of commotion going on with the collective. They sounded rushed and disturbed by whatever they were talking about.

"Goddess, you must wake up. They have decided to do the execution early. There have been way too many people objecting to the killing of a human. Dhareyin is included in those protesting Luna's decision. Go, and we will help in any way we can. There is a set of trees not too far from the wall. There will be a portal there for you to send Dr. Roxanne to us. You need to keep Daegorth with you; it is vital. Wake up, wake up, wake up!"

I came awake with nervous energy rushing through me. Daegorth was standing next to me with his hands on my arms, shaking me.

"Get ready. They are starting early. We have got to go and save my brother and Dr. Roxanne."

13

After I said my goodbyes to my family, Daegorth opened a portal to the wall. I didn't feel like I had accepted the tribe yet, so I didn't know if it would work or not. The trip through the portal was stirring up some excitement in my cells and buzzing through my whole energy system. Daegorth was holding my hand and keeping my feet on the ground. All the energy stirring was causing me to levitate. I felt light as a feather. I was no longer afraid, because I knew that I was finally in control of who I was always meant to be. I made a point of thinking about the time Dhareyin brought me down here. I was hoping that would be enough to gain entrance at the wall. Holding Daegorth's hand helped me to transfer the invisibility to him as well. When we stepped out of the portal, no one was aware of either one of us.

The whole tribe wasn't there but enough to make a crowd. There was a loud buzz of everyone talking at once. Some were there because they were being forced, and others because they believed in what Luna was doing. I reached out with my hand and snatched their nervous energy away. If they were making the choice to be here, then they would be here present in this moment knowing what they were willing to participate in. A hushed calm came over the crowd. Luna looked around with surprise on her face. I was not going to allow her to have the frenzied audience that she was looking for. I could see Dr. Roxanne chained up against the building waiting to be taken to the wall. The wall that was covered in the blood of beautiful beings was stirring the destroyer, for she could see that every death was done in hatred instead of justice being served. I could see Dhareyin lurking in the crowd determined to find a way to help the Doc.

"I need you to put extra protection around this wee babe of mine. A protection so strong that not even a stone wall could hurt him. When they grab me, let them, Daegorth. Your main job here today is to make sure that the Doc makes it to the portal stashed in those trees over there. You could tell that the energy around the trees looks slightly skewed. The Council of Magick will be waiting for her on the other side. Then you can help me out if I need it. Make sure Dhareyin is safe afterward."

"No, Aoroia, I won't let them take you. We can do this together."

"We were never meant to do this together. I am asking for your help with my baby and the Doc because they are both so important to me. What happens next was always meant to happen. It must happen this way. If I don't get myself out of this and I am crushed just clean up the pieces and chant my name—Aoroia."

The tears were flowing down his cheeks. He did as I asked and protected my baby. I changed into the clothes I wore as Star. I was going in as human as I possibly could. I walked forward and felt the eyes of the crowd upon me. I could see that my father and brothers had attended as well. A part of me was disappointed that they would take part in something so barbaric.

Luna turned to see what all the commotion was about. The look she sent my way was filled with gruesome, grotesque, and violent death. This ability to read minds was not always such a great thing to have. Dhareyin glanced in the direction Luna was staring. He had a look of surprise upon his face. I could also see the worry and concern — that hurt more than I realized. I know I shouldn't be bothered by the fact that he was concerned for me, but it made me feel like he didn't believe in me.

"Star, you cannot be here. Get out of here," I could hear him yelling at me as she commanded her warriors to take me into custody.

"You will die first, and it will be the slowest the wall has ever gone. I want you to think about how afraid the Doc will be and there is nothing that you can do about it."

"Luna you cannot do this. You cannot kill her. I love her."

"You would betray your tribe for a human; that is treason. Chain my father up," she commanded of her warriors.

She looked straight at me with cold, dead eyes. She had been entirely consumed by power. Where was Seth in all of this?

"You two will never be together. It is your fault he is dying here today. You have killed my father, Star."

She backed away from the wall. I could hear Dhareyin's heart screaming out for me. He had to see her for who she was. She was broken, and there was no way to go back. I could feel him reaching out to me to talk to him.

"I love you, Aoroia. I am so sorry I didn't try harder with you."

"Aw, my love, you did just fine. I hope you know that at some point in this little display, I will have to put your daughter down?"

"I know you will do what you think you have to do."

"Would you rather all four of us were crushed just to save your daughter? What I can see in her, Dhareyin is she does not have remorse. I don't know how she came to be this way, but she is. She will not stop."

"Four?"

"You have trespassed upon a sacred ritual only meant for members of the Heart of the Godz Tribe. For your trespasses, your sentence is death. I am not sure what they see that is so special in you that they are willing to die for you, but you will carry that knowledge through every lifetime you happen to come back to."

She walked up to me with this wild gleam in her eye. She got close enough to whisper in my ear, "I am going to enjoy watching you being crushed and splattered all over this wall."

"You will carry with you, Luna, the knowledge that you killed the only man who has been your father and ever loved you enough to see past you being one fucked-up psycho bitch."

"START THE WALL," she screamed at her warriors.

I could feel the wall slowly creeping my way. It sounded like heavy stone being dragged across other rocks, grating, and crunching its way along the surface. I could hear its powerful sounds of death and destruction as it came my way. I could hear Dhareyin trying to reach out to me, and I had to slam that door shut. I wasn't shaking, and I wasn't afraid. As the wall got to me, I knew what I had to do. I let it start to crush me. I could hear some of the tribe vomiting in the crowd. There were gasps and cries coming from where I saw my father and brothers. I could hear the Doc and Dhareyin crying and their tears hitting the ground. I could feel Daegorth's love for me, and I knew then that he would always be by my side.

I could feel the pressure of the wall on my skin and organs. My bones were cracking and crunching. My skull was starting to compress, and I could feel blood coming out of my eyes, ears, and nose. I was mourning for all the ones who had died upon this wall. I called to them and their ancestors and asked for their forgiveness. I healed their lineages and DNA to no longer carry such a traumatic experience with them. I released the hate and judgment against humankind. I forgave each one of the souls involved in such a torturous execution. I saw the parents who raised me. I forgave them for not being better at what they chose to become when they accepted the responsibility in adopting me. I could see James and Layla and how much they meant to me. I sent many blessings their way. The love that was filling my heart was creating an energy that was the color of an aurora borealis with bright neon pinks, purples, greens, and blues from the darker end of the color spectrum. It filled my inner landscape with such intensity that the wall went flying back into its proper position.

I spun around and levitated in the air. With the flick of my hand and wrist, the Doc and Dhareyin were free. I watched Daegorth dive in and grab both. The skewed energy in the trees disappeared. I knew my hellhound was waiting for me.

"This cannot be. Who are you?"

"Luna, you can call me Goddess."

There were many loud gasps from the crowd. I could see my

mother out of the corner of my eye, standing by my father. The tears running down her face were true sadness and pride.

"Where are my father and the Doctor? You cannot take this away from me; that is not your right. You do not belong here. Only tribe members can be here."

She ordered her warriors to take me down. They were throwing their spears directly at me. With each flick of my wrist and hand, I was able to deflect them and send them back to their owners. I slowly came to the ground and stood in front of Luna. She came at me with her sword. I held my ground. I dodged and jetted with each swing of her arm. I spun around and knocked the sword out of her hand. The force pushed her to the ground and laid her out cold. I stepped away from her and started walking out of the kill zone when I heard Ramsey command that they start the wall again. I could let the wall take out Luna which looked like that was Ramsey's plan or I could save her. The saying "WWJD" popped into my head. I started laughing so hard that I was grabbing at my stomach and doubling over. It made me think of what the Council had to say about the human experiences popping in when they needed to.

I let the wall get closer. Luna was waking up and screaming for someone to help her. In the process of knocking her down, she landed in such a way that she broke her arm and her leg. She simply could not help herself. I let the wall come closer and closer. At one point, I moved her just enough that her lower body was still in the path of the incoming wall. I knew Dhareyin would not be happy with what I was about to do. It was not his decision, but the decision of the Destroyer and healer.

I stepped completely out of the wall's path and allowed it to crush Luna's legs. My hopes were that she would have time to think about her life and what was important to her. Instead, she was screaming obscenities at me. She continued with her hate for humans. I could see now it was something that had been pushed on her when she was young. Was that from Daegorth and Dhareyin, or did she have some other influencer? Ramsey ran to her side and just watched. He didn't plead for her or anything. I was disgusted by the cold-heartedness emanating from him. Why wouldn't he want to save his daughter-in-law, and where the hell was Seth? Something was off here, and we needed some answers. When I felt like her legs were crushed entirely, I flung the wall so hard it shattered into a million pieces. I would see to it that it would never be rebuilt.

"How dare you destroy our wall of execution? You have no rights here, Goddess," Ramsey said as he came at me with a spear.

In a flash, Daegorth was in hellhound mode, ripping Ramsey's right arm out of its socket.

He was screaming, and no one in the crowd knew what to do.

"Carry them both to your dungeons, Daegorth. My work is not done here."

"Yes, Mistress!" He picked them both up and carried them to the place I was held for a month.

I stepped upon the stage where Luna demanded my death. I looked out over my people. I allowed that truth to sink into the entirety of who I was.

"Why have you come here at this time?" asked the one I knew as my father.

I thought long and hard before I answered. "The prophecy of your people spoke of my arrival. Why were you not ready for me?"

"We know of no such prophecy, Goddess. Perhaps you can enlighten us?"

I had no answer for them, because I had yet to see such a prophecy. Maybe it was time to show them who I really was. I slowly took my clothes off. The scars that I carry from Daegorth, I will always carry. They are mine and they are a part of my story of rebirth. They were lit up like a prism. With each piece of clothing, I could feel my body changing. For Aoroia of the Heart of the Godz Tribe was stepping forward in full form. It was then that I knew I had already accepted her. That was why I was let into the ritual. The hair, eyes, and color of my skin started to take shape. My small pointy ears, horns, and body followed suit. What I was coming to realize was that many of the traits that happened that night with Dhareyin had already started to take place. Like the hourglass shape, lean muscles, and slim body. I stepped down off the stage and started walking toward my family. The lines that Dhareyin had talked about, the ones that told of my family lineage, began to appear.

"How is this possible? My daughter is dead; you cannot be her?"

I allowed for silence to consume the crowd. Peace filled every part of my body and mind. I allowed myself to feel what it felt like to be in this incredible body, to be present and to know this was how I came into this world. I knew I was beyond beautiful, and I could shape-shift back and forth just like the rest. How could I answer his question without the prophecy? I had hoped it would give me some explanation for why my mother did what she did.

I looked up and saw Dhareyin standing there with an ancient scroll in his hands.

"Please read the prophecy out loud, Dhareyin!"

He unrolled it slowly, glancing at my form.

"For the prophecy reads:

A girl child born on the night of the aurora borealis with the mark of the Milky Way upon her skin will start in motion the coming forth of the goddess of destruction and renewal. For the goddess to step forward, the girl child will die at the hands of the flesh-eater when she becomes the age of an adult woman. Her death will be brutal enough to initiate the events that will bring forth the goddess. The one who brutally murders the woman child will then be in service to the goddess for an eternity. He shall become her hellhound.

The one that has the abilities of shaman and water dragon is promised to the goddess, but only when she has accepted her place within the Heart of the Godz Tribe.

The goddess will then make way for the return of the Goddess of all Magick. Before this can be fulfilled, she must help the Goddess of Premonition to awaken fully.

"I am sorry, that is all there is. There has always been a piece missing."

I knew exactly where that missing piece was, and for now I was keeping that to myself. I understood now why my mother did what she did. She knew of the brutality I would have to go through as an adult, and she wanted to prepare me for that by sending me out into the human world. I could also feel that had Daegorth and I remained connected, he could not have fulfilled the prophecy. I think on some level she thought I would literally die and be lost to her forever, and she could not do that to her baby girl.

"Where have you been all this time, Aoroia?"

"I have lived in the human world my whole life."

"So, does that mean we are going to lose you again so this goddess can step forward?"

"No, I am her and she is me. I am the destroyer and the healer. For I am Goddess Aoroia."

"I wish your mother were here to see all of this taking place. She died many years ago."

"I know; she has been to visit me. I have not been friendly with her."

"That is not possible. She went through the ritual with the flesh-eater."

"Well, he only partially did that. He wanted her to suffer for sending me away."

"What do you mean, she sent you away? You died in your sleep. We had a funeral for you and everything."

"Mother knew of the prophecy, and she handed me over to a human couple to adopt me. She wanted me to be with people who would smother my light. They tried to fulfill that wish of hers. When they were murdered by Daegorth when I was seventeen, it allowed me to spread my wings and fly."

"It sounds to me like Daegorth needs to visit that wall you just destroyed."

"No one will ever hurt Daegorth again. He will serve by my side for an eternity as my hellhound." As I finished my words, he appeared at my side with my hand resting on top of his head. "He is mine, and you will not touch him."

"Would you like to meet your brothers?"

One by one they stepped forward and introduced themselves. Unfortunately, there was no connection with any of them. I would give it time because we all deserved that.

Dhareyin stepped forward and handed me the prophecy. "I am so sorry it took me this long to show this to you. I figured if I did, it would accelerate this process, as you are standing here as one of our people, and I wasn't sure you were ready. I hope you can forgive me."

"Let's talk about this later. Right now, I want to talk to my mother."

The crowd dispersed. I think they were all in shock and needed time to process what was happening.

"Dhareyin, I am disturbed by something. Where is Seth?"

"I was wondering that myself. I have been trying to reach him telepathically, and I am not getting anything."

"Something is wrong here. I am going to talk to my mother. Take Daegorth and see if you can find Seth."

He walked away with his head held high and his shoulders back. I looked back at my father and brothers with a smile on my face. "Go get some rest; we will talk soon."

I turned to my mother. "It is time you and I talk. Let us find a beautiful space to sit with Gaia."

"I know the perfect place. Follow me."

She took me to an incredible place. It reminded me of a book I read and later watched on television; it looked just like *The Secret Garden*. I chose to sit on the ground. I loved my connection with Gaia, and I really needed her right now. I knew that what I was hiding from was all the pain of knowing that my real mother knowingly placed me in an unhealthy place to be raised.

We sat for the longest time not saying anything. I think we were both just absorbing the situation and what had happened back there. She came closer and sat next to me.

"I know the last time we talked, you wanted to kill me. That was not the reaction I was hoping for from you."

"What were you looking for? For me to get on bended knee and praise glory to you for what you did?"

"I would like some understanding and appreciation."

"Are you fucking kidding me right now? Appreciation for what? Putting me with people who neglected me, verbally and emotionally abused me? I was not wanted there. I grew up thinking I was nothing and worthless."

"That is why I sent you there. For them to snuff your light."

"For what purpose? I was assaulted when I was fifteen years old. Then I was brutalized by Daegorth, the one who was my watcher and protector. What did you do all of this for? Why would a mother allow her child to be tormented and abused in such a way?"

"When I hear and see what you went through, I question my motives as well. I can only answer for that time. I thought I was doing what was right to protect the parts of the prophecy from coming true. I thought maybe if your light was smothered, the prophecy would not come true. I also knew that Daegorth would not turn on you like that. What a horrible fate, to determine how beings will act. I never stopped to think what it would take to smother your light."

I could feel myself getting angry. I would love to snuff out her light. I knew those were my angry feelings, and that I wouldn't act upon them.

"I have nothing of you but your DNA. Daegorth stood up for me and he was angry with you. He tracked me and killed those people so I would have a better life."

"You want to rip me apart, but you speak fondly of him. I don't get it."

"It is not yours to get. What happened between Daegorth and me is between us. He and I have been through some very life-altering experiences together. You weren't part of that prophecy, and you decided to take it upon yourself to alter it."

"Well, I wish they were alive; I would kill them myself right now."

"You gave up any right to care about me when you dumped me off on them. I learned to be strong and independent despite them. Everything I have become is because of them. They twisted, tweaked, and broke those parts of me that taught me my strength at an early age."

"If you can talk so well about them, then where is our problem? Why can't you forgive me and let this go?"

"I guess I struggle because you think you can just bounce back into my life and everything will be all right. You won't ever be a part of my life. Once we are done here, you can go away."

"There is a way to revive me, and you are the one who can do it, with all your powers."

"So now you want me to have these powers so I can help undo what you asked Daegorth to do in the first place? You know what makes me sick? I was sent away because of some prophecy. The prophecy has brought me back into this world that I never knew about. Members of my tribe are trying their best to kill me because they know nothing about me. You made damn sure that people thought I was dead, including my father. Then when I am needed, I am just expected to come back like I owe you all something. I am angry and hurt that I was sent away. I am pissed off as hell that all of this has been pounced upon me when I should have grown up knowing about it. What fucking irks me more than anything is you and the part you play in all of this. I have feelings and they have been fucked with beyond what I can feel sometimes. I will have to think about your request. I don't want to talk to you anymore. Go away."

I felt no resolution within me. I had this incredible baby growing inside of me, and I couldn't fathom doing what she did. We would find a way to prepare him, not push him into a world he wasn't born into. I lay down upon Gaia and let her cover me. I needed her comfort more than anything right now.

"Aoroia, Aoroia!" I could hear Dhareyin calling for me.

I came back to the surface and waited for him to show up.

"What can I do for you, Dhareyin?"

"Where is my daughter?"

"In a cell just like the one you found me in."

"What are you going to do?"

"I don't even get a hello or thank you for saving you? How about it is great to see you, Aoroia? Maybe I should be as hospitable as you are being. You really do not want to mess with me right now, Dhareyin. Did you find out where Seth is?"

"No, we are still searching for him, and Roman seems to be missing as well."

"Ask his father-in-law what has been going on between him and your daughter. After their wedding, I didn't see them together. Luna seemed to be making all the decisions. Did you know that Ramsey didn't even try to help your daughter from the wall?"

"Was she in the way of the wall?"

"Yep, right where I put her. I was hoping something would shift within her, but it didn't. She and Ramsey both are in cells waiting for me."

"Dammit, Aoroia, I cannot believe you would hurt my daughter. I don't know if I can forgive you for this."

"I don't give a fuck, Dhareyin. I am not here for you. I am here for my tribe and to make sure that we are up to date when SHE returns."

"Your tribe? Since when?"

"Since the day I was conceived. I have always been coming back here; I just didn't know it until recently. You kept trying to confuse my feelings by making me feel unwanted and not worth your time. I don't need you, Dhareyin. The prophecy may state that you and I are meant to be together, but we will see."

"I am sorry I made you feel that way. I was pretty confused myself. When I saw you transform the night that I brought you here, I was worried about the rest of the prophecy, and then you became her in the trailer that night. I knew then we had read the prophecy wrong. You didn't seem to want to be a part of the tribe, and you were mega angry."

"I had so much to be angry about. I don't expect you to understand, because you can't. I have been through so much; there is no way to explain that to anyone. The only one who might understand would be Daegorth because he has been through similar transformations. I have something to tell you, but I am not sure how you are going to take it?"

"What is that?"

I walked over to him and looked into his beautiful eyes. "I love you so much. We butt heads so bad that I am not sure that we are fit for each other. We have had sex one time, and even though I wanted more, you went distant."

I took his hand and placed it on my belly. I waited for him to get my meaning.

"I thought you said you couldn't get pregnant. How is this even possible? We only had sex the one time."

His reaction was not what I was hoping for. I felt a pang of hurt inside.

"WOW, I responded to your news all wrong. Can we take a couple of steps back and start again? You are pregnant with my baby. I am beyond words and so excited."

"Well, it would have been nice like that the first time, but I will accept it. Apparently, when Daegorth and I were ripping each other apart some type of cellular healing took place inside of me. You can get pregnant even after one time. It is possible because he was meant to come to us at this time. He will be more powerful than you and Daegorth put together."

"Is there anything that I can do for you?"

"I just want to be held and told everything is going to be all right. I don't need you to fix anything, just listen. I am scared, Dhareyin, because if Luna doesn't shift somehow, then I don't know what I am going to do with her. I cannot set her or Ramsey free. There is someone else involved in all of this, and we have to get to the bottom of this before they start dumping toxic waste again and reach the Heart."

"Thank you for saving me and not killing my daughter."

"How could I do something like that? I know how important she is to you, but I don't think she can be trusted. What do you think, Dhareyin? Maybe we should start working together instead of separately."

"I would like to talk to her but without you there. Hear me out. She has an issue with you, and we are not going to get anywhere if she is trying to fight you. I do believe there are listening tubes that they used back in the day, and we have adapted them using some human technology. We have cameras to keep an eye on them. We will have to find a way to not only protect them but protect us from them."

"Daegorth has already taken care of the protection on both sides of things. Speaking of Daegorth there are things that you do not know about him. You should take the time to get to know the real him. You just might be pleasantly surprised."

"You two have gotten close. Is there anything that I need to know? Are you together? Have you had sex?"

"How about this? I know the baby is yours. That is all you need to know. We will always be together because he will be in service to me for an eternity. Daegorth and I have gone through things that create one hell of a bond. What we have shared is personal and private. I hope you understand."

"I get the impression that you have had sex with my brother. I am not sure how I feel about that. We weren't together or committed to each other, so there is nothing I can do about it. Do you plan on doing it with him again?"

"Those are some pretty personal questions for someone who cannot decide whether he wants me or not. I am a free agent, and so are you."

"I haven't been a free agent since I met you, Aoroia. You are right; I have a lot of thinking to do. In the meantime, let's go figure things out with Luna and Ramsey. Hopefully, Seth and Roman have been found and we can get some answers."

We walked side by side until we reached the entranceway to the dungeons. The stairway was narrow, and so we had to go single file. It had to be difficult for Daegorth when he carried Luna and Ramsey down these stairs. Maybe he took another route. The walls and floors were made of old cobblestones that were taken care of and in pristine shape.

I could hear the walls speaking to me of torture and pain. The voices of old telling me the tales of hopelessness and fear hung heavy in the air, clinging to the walls like a heavy soot begging me to wipe it clean. The energy in this entire place needed love, understanding, and clearing. Would the tribe be willing to do a cleansing on this grand of a scale? For now, it weighed heavily upon my heart, and I felt like I wanted to explode. The destroyer and healer both within me wanted to set fire to it all. There was no logic to any of these deaths.

It didn't matter if I was who I was; I could not keep the feelings at bay. The rage and anger inside of me was threatening to overcome this moment. I could feel the fire ignite in my hands and all around me. My heart was breaking on every level. I was about to consume every inch of this place with my wrath.

"It is overwhelming, isn't it?" Dhareyin said as he turned to see how I was doing.

I could see the look of terror on his face. He wasn't there the last time when I consumed everything with fire; he came in at the tail end. He really had no clue what I was capable of.

"I understand your anger, Aoroia, and we need to find a way to heal this place. This is not the way. There are people alive down here, and as much as they are guilty, it would not help to add to the pain so heavily ingrained in these walls. Please, my love, let me help you!"

I could hear his words of love--not just for me but for the people down here. He was keeping at bay the anger that had consumed him for a long time about this place. Realizing that we were on the same page, I snapped out of the trance I was in. I could feel myself calming down, and the fire within me was cooling for now.

"How long have you been able to do that?"

"Ever since the day I healed the Heart meadows. Can we talk about this later? Your daughter's agony is calling to me."

He hurried forward wanting to reach Luna. I followed closely behind. The love and concern that he was feeling were breathtaking. I found myself hugely attracted to his fatherly side. It calmed the mother inside of me that wanted to make sure that her child had a great father to teach him all the things she couldn't. I loved that he was my baby's father.

When we reached the corridor where Luna was being held, there was a strange energy coming from her cell. Dhareyin looked at me to see if I knew what was going on. I shrugged my shoulders in surprise. We walked slowly and quietly, sneaking up on her cell. There was a yellow energy, consuming her in a deliberate, slow torture.

"Stop," I whispered to Dhareyin. "Take two steps back and give me a moment."

He did what I asked him to do. I stood in place and centered myself. I tapped into Gaia and Source. Taking in a deep breath, I slowed my heartbeat and perked up not only my physical ears but my energetic ones. There was a disturbance in the energy fields coming from somewhere above, and Ramsey was being affected as well. I could not tell precisely where the energy was coming from.

The energy would not be hard to diffuse, but I had something better in mind. I knew how to place a protective bubble around Luna and Ramsey, keeping the destructive energy in place. I wanted the person responsible for this to come check on their work.

Walking up to her cell, I could tell she was being used. They had tapped so deeply into her grief over the loss of her parents that she was deeply unsettled and angry over their deaths. Just like Daegorth, their pain had been used against them to turn them into something they were never meant to be. I was starting to see a pattern here, and I didn't like it. I had a lot of work ahead of me, but right now I had to protect Luna and Ramsey and find out what was going on.

I didn't want to get close to the energy, in case there was a way for them to be able to pick up on me. I stayed outside the cell door and went to work. I could feel Luna's energy calming down. A strange thing was starting to take place that I did not expect. You could no longer read her energy at all outside of the bubble, which meant I had to get busy on Ramsey before the culprit decided to make an entrance.

After finishing with Ramsey, we slowly backed away. "Where would be a great place to hide down here, Dhareyin?"

He pointed down the hall, took my hand, and we headed that direction. We had no idea how long it would take for them to realize that there was no life force energy coming from Luna or Ramsey. He took me into a deep, dark old cell with no doors. There was a hard bench bed like the one I slept on for a month. The memories were terrible enough, but they would have been worse if I was awake the whole time. Even though the dungeon was in pristine shape, it had a musty mildew smell to it.

"I have been awful hard on you, haven't I? I never knew all the things that you were capable of doing and what turmoil it must bring on you. I wasn't a great listener, and I am sorry."

"No, I guess you haven't, but I haven't been with you, either. I should have kept you more informed. Do you know what it did to me to realize that Daegorth and I would be working together? It ripped me apart inside. I didn't want you anywhere near me. I just wanted to rip and shred away all the fear, anger, and hate. I did want to protect you, because I didn't know what I was becoming. When everything went down between Daegorth and myself, something powerful shifted within me. The loss of personal power I have felt most of my life living in the human realm is unexplainable. Then in one set of events, it was all coming back to me. I was hungry and consumed by it. For the first time in my life, I felt alive."

"I cannot say that I know where you are coming from, but I have seen incredible changes within you. It scared me because I felt like

I was losing the woman that I had fallen in love with. I saw you coming into such intense, raw power. I was afraid for you and us. You were so angry, and the idea of you unleashing that on your own people terrified me. I did not want to have to stop you, Aoroia, and now I know you cannot be stopped."

"Dhareyin, you never lost me. I was always right here in front of you. You kept pushing me away by being so nasty and controlling. I couldn't reach you, and it pushed us farther away from each other."

"I see that now. You were right here in front of me the whole time. I had the prophecy playing over and over in my head, and I thought I was going to have to watch you die. I was so blinded by it that I couldn't see that it never meant two separate women. It was one woman going through many terrors over and over that would fulfill the prophecy. I felt like I was drowning in my feelings for you. How could I love you and be expected to love the one they spoke about in the prophecy? As the shaman of our people, I am highly disappointed in myself that I did not see this sooner."

"Where do we stand now Dhareyin? I need to know if you are with me or against me? I know she is your daughter, and these are your people more than they have been mine. There are changes that must be made around here before SHE returns. We should start by figuring out who is behind the toxic spill. This is an inside job; I know this now, more than ever. What to do with Luna and Ramsey is at the forefront of my mind. I need to know if you are with me or against me."

"Aoroia, those are all difficult questions. It sounds like an either-or situation and I am not sure I like that. We are talking about my daughter."

"Yes, and she damn near killed your son and the person you say you love. Putting that to the side, she tried to kill a human. I know where Daegorth stands. What about you?"

"Daegorth is nothing more than your lap dog. Do not ever compare him to me. He should be put down like the dog that he is."

"I cannot believe you would talk about your brother that way.

Considering the things your daughter has done, I am surprised how judgmental you are toward your brother. Did you ever stop to think that maybe both of their minds have been fucked with by someone with an agenda?"

"What do you mean by that, Aoroia?"

"When I was putting the protective energy around Luna and Ramsey, there was something there that didn't belong. I could also see and feel who they really are. I had the same experience with Daegorth when he was slashing me apart for the second time. There is something going on here that is deceitful. It will tear apart this tribe if we do not do something about it. Somebody has been manipulating them to where they cannot see the deception."

"Do you have any idea who it is?"

"No, but we may just get some clues here before too long. We seem to fight so much, Dhareyin. I do not know if this is going to work between us. You are always so quick to jump to conclusions and judgment. Where is the shaman who protects his people and their rituals? Why have you heavily integrated yourself into the human world?"

"That really is none of your business, Aoroia."

"More secrets what a surprise! Well, you had better start spilling those secrets soon before I begin to realize that maybe it has been you all along that is mind-fucking people."

"If that is what you think, then you do not know me at all."

"How am I supposed to know you when you will not let your guard down? You don't trust me enough to know you or the truth. How can I be with the father of my child when I do not know him? You have put up this wall and you won't let me in. You fight me with every step I take. I am not less than you, Dhareyin."

"You sure as hell are not higher than me, either."

"I never said I was. I am trying to find some common ground with you so we can build a solid foundation together and you cannot seem to budge one inch in my direction. What do you want from me Dhareyin?"

"I want you to trust me. To know that I would tell you what I know if I could. Believe in me, my love, and stop second-guessing me. We both have roles we play here. There is one thing I can tell you. There is something going on here that could ruin magick for everyone, including humans."

"Trust goes both ways and it would be nice if you would believe in me as well. Someone is coming; I can smell them. They are in a fevered state of fear. I don't think they were supposed to kill Luna and Ramsey. They seem to be near panic. Let's go see who our yellow-energy culprit is."

We sauntered out of the old, dark, damp cell. I could feel a sense of completion with the whole situation. Who we found was not who I was expecting? Crumpled on the floor sobbing her eyes out was Ms. Moonpye. Dhareyin and I both looked at each other. How was it possible that she could be down here and be able to cast such a torturous energy field?

"Ms. Moonpye, what are you doing down here, and how did you find this place?"

She looked up at me with deep sorrow and sadness. She stood up and went directly into my arms. I held her until she no longer needed to release. "It wasn't supposed to kill them. I just wanted them to feel pain. I am so angry, and I could not control it."

"MoraKat, why would you want to make them feel pain?"

"They tried to kill my mother, Dr. Roxanne."

"Well, this is an interesting turn of events. How is it that you are human, and you have powers?"

"My father is from this tribe."

"Do you know his identity?"

"Star, his name is Raffen."

"You can call me Aoroia—or should I say, half-sister."

"Raffen is your father? I had no idea. He met my mother after she started working at the Bureau many years ago. They fell in love, but he told her they had to keep it a secret. When father found out that I had powers just like him, he chose to train me himself."

"Well, I haven't had a chance yet to have a full conversation with him but when I do, I will have to stress to him the importance of bringing you into the tribe. Did anyone else know of what you were going to do here or encourage you to do this?"

"No, Dhareyin, I acted on my own. I don't know how I am ever going to stop feeling guilty for their deaths. I am no better than they are."

I walked over to Luna's cell, disbanded the yellow energy, and released the protection bubble I had placed on her. I did the same thing for Ramsey.

"How did you do that? Father said no one could ever take away my magick or a spell I had placed."

"She isn't just someone, MoraKat, she is the one foretold of in the prophecy."

I could hear a pride in Dhareyin's voice that was not there before. Luna was starting to stir. When she awoke, she was completely healed. I didn't tell Dhareyin that I had put a healing blessing on both. She got up and ran to the cell door.

"Thank you for healing me, Father."

"You are thanking the wrong person, Luna. Aoroia healed you not me. It is she that you owe your gratitude to."

She turned and looked at me. I suppose Luna was sizing me up. I could tell that she could remember everything that she had done. I could see she was filled with confusion, guilt, regret, and remorse.

"You are welcome, Luna. We need to talk to you and Ramsey. For now, we will move you to more comfortable quarters under heavy sanction."

"I don't understand why you are letting us out of our cells, is that safe?"

"I am sure your father knows some guards he can trust." What I didn't tell them was that I had my own protective energy I could put around them to keep us all safe. "We have questions for you, and I hope you can provide us with some answers."

I pulled Dhareyin to the side. I had important things I wanted to say to him. He pulled me into his arms and kissed me passionately. Then he held me for the longest time. I could tell he was emotional and crying. "What is wrong, Dhareyin?"

"The compassion you have shown for Luna, MoraKat, and Ramsey astounds me. I learn something new about you all the time."

"It is all-encompassing for me. I may not be human, but I lived in the human world long enough. You learn how to deal with experiences there that none of you get here. It does no good to leave them in a place that is filled with such pain and hatred toward others. I think we need to put MoraKat in a protective room as well, until we check her story out."

"I agree with you, Aoroia. You asked me earlier if I was with you or against you. I am with you all the way, love."

I watched him say he was with me. I could feel his conviction was true. I think he thought Luna was the instigator of all of this, and he didn't want it to be true. Honestly, no parent would want to know their child was capable of the horror she was willing to inflict. We headed over to Ramsey to see how he was doing. You could tell he was confused about why he was in a cell.

"We have some questions for you, Ramsey. We have decided to move you to more comfortable quarters so we can get those answers. You seem like you are a little confused; just know that after a time, that will wear off and the highest truth will flood in."

"Dhareyin, I think we should start with MoraKat and then work our way to Luna and then Ramsey."

"Why do I have to go? I told you why I was here. Don't you believe me?"

"To be honest, no, we don't. After the shenanigans at the gym that day, I am hesitant to believe you completely. I just want to check your story with your mother and father. When we have those answers, we will set you free. In the meantime, I know you will love spending a bit of time with Dara and Fera." I gave Dhareyin a look, and we just grinned at each other.

14

I was quite curious to know who was causing all the problems in this village of mine. We got everyone adequately situated, and now it was time to go meet my dad and brothers. I felt nervous not knowing what they would think of me. It was interesting how housing was set up in this place. There were no separate homes, just big living quarters that spread on for days. Everyone was connected, much like the roots of trees connecting all over the place. The ceilings were all tall, and each room was spacious. Each living space had small kitchens because they ate together as a tribe. Big spacious windows and open courtyards allowed the fresh air to cool the homes. It reminded me of one gigantic adobe mansion that had a fortress of giant trees and fences holding everyone in and everything else out. It was a true underworld paradise, with wild animals and waterfalls. I wouldn't mind having a place of my own, but I also loved my cabin I purchased. Maybe I could have lodgings closer to my property. Who says I need to live here? If I am their leader, I suppose I would have to.

Walking down the corridor deep in thought, I failed to pick up on someone following close behind me. I knew I had nothing to worry about, but still, I should know better than to be distracted like I was, especially after my incident with Luna. Turning to face my follower, I was struck by the mere nastiness of energy coming off this being. The bitterness and angst were nauseating.

I turned and faced the energy. What I saw was not okay or right.

Hard to explain, I suppose it would be better to describe. The eyes were huge and hollowed, almost drawn out beyond proportions. Bones barely covered with paper-thin skin. Its eyes were a transparent chartreuse-green color. Dark and light gray hung heavy in the air, mixed with a weird smoky-green color. The energy had a putrid smell to it and looked like it was dripping on the floor. It gave off this soul-sucking vibe. This being was neither light nor dark, it just was. I wanted to know its purpose here and why it was following me.

"Mistress slowly step away," I heard behind me. I turned to look over my shoulder and Daegorth was in full hellhound form. "Do as I say, NOW!"

I slowly backed away, never taking my eyes off the apparition in front of me. It remained where it was, hanging in the air, eyeing me and then my hellhound. I reached Daegorth, and he came to stand in front of me. He turned and looked at me.

"My beautiful Mistress, what were you thinking? You could have been destroyed."

"What do you mean, I could have been destroyed? We know better than that."

"It was sent to see if you are worthy of fulfilling the prophecy. Someone must have contested either your rights or abilities to become who you are."

"I am already me, so how could there be any question? Do you know who it is?"

As the last word left my mouth, the air in the hallway became heavy and dense. I could feel pressure building in my ears, head, and body. My hellhound pulled me into the protection of his body. In a raspy voice, the entity began to speak.

"You have protected Aoroia well, Daegorth. Your part of the prophecy has been fulfilled. Even though Aoroia seeks and accepts your protection, there has been another who has come forward to claim her rights according to the prophecy. The Council of Magick does not believe she has a claim, but we have to make sure."

With every word it spoke, it sounded like chain going across gravel. It was almost deafening to the ears and blinding to the eyes. I felt incredibly sick to my stomach and was on the verge of vomiting. I could feel myself slipping into an alternate reality.

"She does not have a true claim to the throne. You must watch your back, for she will deceive you at every turn. Do not do what she asks of you. She has been gathering power and talismans these last few years and somehow has figured out a way to dupe some members of the Council. She is cloaking herself from us so we cannot get a clear read on who she really is."

"Who are you?"

"I am the truth-seeker and I have come to set matters straight."

"I don't understand why you look and smell like that."

"There are many ways truth can be seen and heard. I find I can pick up subtle truths when I look like this. Normally, I look like this," and before me, she transformed into the guardian that came to me before Daegorth got a hold of me the first time.

"Aseret Nwad, is that you?"

"Yes, my dear girl. I am so sorry for the things that you and Daegorth had to go through to get you to where you are now. No one will take this crown from you. It was made for you since before you came here to this planet and dimension. Just watch your back and be careful who you trust."

"Why do I struggle to trust Dhareyin and not Daegorth?"

"You and Daegorth made a pact before you even came here to this realm. It may all seem so strange to you, considering you lived so long with the humans, but this was always meant to play out this way. You struggle with Dhareyin because you both cannot yet see what you mean to each other or how much this tribe needs you both. You are both strong-minded and you struggle to see the other person in their entirety. You have been so busy figuring you out that you haven't seen what Dhareyin is about. Remember him when you first met him and go from there."

"Can I trust him?"

"You can trust him and Daegorth. Be careful of everyone else.

It is time you got reacquainted with your father and brothers. Have Daegorth take you and stand guard. I think Dhareyin would like to go with you. If you will let him."

"What do I do about my mother? I am so angry with her, and nothing comes out civil when I talk to her. She wants me to undo what Daegorth did to her, but I am just not sure."

"Don't worry about your mother right now. Go visit with the rest of your family. There is nothing you can do to help her until you take the throne, so don't worry about that one too much. Don't forget to tell your father that you know about MoraKat Moonpye and her mother. That way there are no secrets between you. Go now! Dhareyin is not too far away. Talk to Daegorth and let him know what I have told you and keep him close."

Coming out of this alternate reality was not for the faint-hearted. I felt woozy, and it was hard to open my eyes. Daegorth was lying on the floor next to me, cradling me in his paws.

"What is going on here?" I could hear coming from down the corridor.

I couldn't quite pull myself out of it and I waited for Dhareyin to reach us both. In her truth-seeker form, Aseret Nwad was powerful and robust.

"Aoroia, is everything okay? How about the baby? Is something wrong?"

"Give her a moment, will you? She just had a run-in with the truth-seeker. She took her under, and she is just coming to."

"Why would the truth-seeker be after Aoroia?"

"You two are loud. Give me a moment, and I will tell you everything. Right now, I am on the verge of throwing up. I need something to calm down the queasiness. I want to lie on my side—can you help me, Dae?"

He slowly tipped me toward him with his paws. He pulled me in close and sang the most beautiful song to me with his heartbeat and the strange chuff sound he makes. I was starting to calm down when Dhareyin tapped me on the shoulder. "Here you go, my love," he said as he handed me a piece of papaya-like fruit. "This will help calm down your system. The truth-seeker can be quite powerful and overwhelming to the body. I would suggest you eat some protein as soon as you can."

I slowly ate the fruit as Dae sang to me. I could feel something changing in me slowly. My baby was healthy and happy. He seemed to be growing a little quicker than he should be. I was struck with such an incredible pain in my lower abdomen that it caused me to suck in a breath sharply. I could feel myself go instantly into the fetal position.

"Something is wrong, Dhareyin. You had better look at her. Do me a favor and open a portal to somewhere she would feel safe. Take her to James and Layla."

"What is going on, Daegorth?"

"Something is hurting her inside, and the baby is growing too fast for her body. Open a portal--now!"

I could feel Dhareyin hesitating. "Please, my love, help me. We cannot lose our son."

I must have said the right thing, because he opened a portal to the cottage by the lake and we were well on our way to James and Layla. I was petrified that I would lose my baby before I even got a chance to meet him. Suddenly a euphoria came over me and I went under.

"Don't worry, Mama. This is the right time for me to come forward. I need to know if you still want me the way I am."

"Oh, my beautiful boy, what could ever possibly make me not want you?"

He appeared before me in his natural form. I was shocked—no, maybe it was more that I was surprised by his shape. I couldn't let go of this feeling of such deep love and adoration for this child before me and what I knew he was meant to become.

"Of course, my darling boy, I want you. Never let that thought cross your beautiful mind again. Is everything okay with you?"

He just smiled a toothy grin at me, and I could feel myself surfacing again. I knew now what the tattoos and wording meant on my body.

I awoke with a smile on my face. I couldn't help but feel a deep connection with Dhareyin. There was a part of me that thought he would be surprised when our baby was born.

"What are you smiling at, beautiful?"

"Our son is ready to be born. He is beautiful and wonderful. Just you wait until you meet him." The pride and joy inside of me were bubbling over.

The cottage was empty, which I had expected. There was no point in making all of them put their lives on hold. Daegorth had done a fantastic job placing protection up around them. Daegorth took me to the room where we shared a night of passion. It was all cleaned up and tidy. He had erased all traces of our being there together. He laid me down on the bed with such gentleness it soothed my heart. I knew he would be a great uncle to our son.

"Does anyone know how to deliver a baby?"

"Aoroia, do you really think the baby is coming now? You haven't been pregnant long enough."

"I think something has changed since I started spending more time in my goddess form and being down with the tribe. When the truth-seeker took me under, it changed something in my chemistry. The baby took off like we fed him Miracle-Gro. He has told me he is okay and ready to be born. Daegorth, why don't you go see if you can get Layla to come down, and James too, if he is available."

Dhareyin helped me undress and get under the sheet. He went and found some towels and the other instruments we would need to deliver this baby in a healthy, sterile environment although giving birth while lying upon Gaia would have served us perfectly.

"No one is home, Aoroia. Do you want me to see if I can call them here?"

"That is okay, Dae. Are they okay?"

"Yes, they are playing at the park with their little ones. I have them fully protected, Mistress."

"We cannot wait for them to show. You both will have to help me out."

I could feel the contractions slamming through me, one after the other. They were incredibly painful but worth the agony. I grabbed hold of Dae's hand and squeezed hard when the next contraction ripped through my abdomen. I could feel it through my entire body. "It is time to push, Layla," Dhareyin said as he looked up at me with a smile.

After several pushes with all my strength, I pushed one last time. The contractions were far more painful than the actual delivery of our son. I felt like he was a little bitty thing.

"He is absolutely perfect, Aoroia. He has all his fingers and toes. Everything looks properly developed. I am so surprised, for how short a time you carried him."

"Let me see him, Dhareyin."

Dhareyin handed our son to Daegorth and then to me. He was so beautiful, healthy, and tiny. He had black hair all over his head and back. His eyes were electric blue and his lashes were long and black. I could swear they almost glowed. He had two small dimples on both cheeks. I could feel my heart swell with so much love. What happened next shook me to my core. He started turning a blue color and then red. When I looked at his face, he seemed to be playing with me. "Dhareyin, do you see what our son is doing?"

Dhareyin looked at me with big eyes and an open mouth. Our son was flashing red and blue energy. He seemed to be shapeshifting into something else. He looked like a miniature dragon boy about the size of Dhareyin's hand. He had little tiny wings, tail, hands, and feet. Before we could digest what was happening, he was back to a little boy again.

"Now I know why he asked me if I could accept him the way he was."

"When did this happen, Mistress?"

"He came to me as we were coming through the portal. He asked me if I would accept him the way he was, and I said yes. How about you, Dhareyin? Can you accept our son?"

Dhareyin came to sit on the edge of the bed. Our son crawled out of my hands and nuzzled into my neck. I placed my hand upon his little body and held him lightly in place. He snuggled deeper and deeper until he became a part of my body. This was getting interesting. "Where did he go?" Dhareyin asked, confused.

He was completely a part of my upper chest like a big removable tattoo. He wiggled around and sat up to meet his daddy.

"Well, what in the green hell is this?"

"Daegorth, I don't know. Interesting, isn't he? I just love him so. What do you think of our son, Dhareyin?"

He just watched his little boy sitting there staring at him with gorgeous firelit blue eyes. Dhareyin held out his hand to encourage his son to come to him. He stood up wobbly and slowly walked into his father's hands. He snuggled into the palm of Dhareyin's hand and cooed. He looked at me with tears in his eyes. "Will he always be this little?"

"No, one day he will be bigger than you could ever imagine. I told you once that he will be more powerful than you and Daegorth put together. Trust in that, my love!"

"I don't understand what he is or why he is this way."

"I can answer those questions later, but right now we have to keep quiet about his birth. No one is to know that he was born. Not even the Council of Magick!"

Dhareyin laid our son gently upon my chest, where he once again became a part of me. We would have to come up with a name soon, but right now we needed to clean everything up and head back underground.

"Why are you looking at me like that, Daegorth?"

"You are glowing, Mistress, and sparkly all over. You have this renewed energy about you that is shining like a prism."

I just smiled, for I knew why I was glowing and sparkly. I had just become a mother and understood why I had been brought here and why all of this had to happen the way it did. Maybe one day when the time was right, I would tell them what I knew, but for now, it was mine to keep close to my heart. We tidied up and left through the portal Dhareyin created. He insisted on carrying me back. I was healing quite rapidly, but he wanted me close. We came out in his quarters. What I saw next took me by surprise. He had his place set up as if a family were going to live there. I loved it and at the same time cringed, because he just assumed. Sometimes this independence thing was a real pain in the ass. I was going to take it for what it was, and that was a leap of faith. Dhareyin laid me down in a room that was not his. All I could think was how interesting this beautiful man was turning out to be. I was grateful for the rest, but I had to go meet my family and check on Luna, MoraKat, and Ramsey. Daegorth followed us into my room, sniffed around, and left.

"I am not sure how I feel about Daegorth being close to our child, Aoroia."

"He is mine and will always be by my side, no matter how you feel about that, Dhareyin. Before you fly off the handle about what I just said, keep in mind that he only tends to come around when I am in danger."

"I don't want him in this room alone with you. Is that understood?"

There it was! The controlling asshat that always showed up when things were not going his way. I sat up and swung my legs over the side of the bed. I took a deep breath and stood up. I knew it was time to set some boundaries with Dhareyin.

"It is you that I have to set boundaries with. You have no right to tell me who I can or cannot bring into my room—which, by the way, I never asked for in the first place. You know I have my property and cabin that is all mine."

He just stood looking at me. I could tell that he was trying to figure out how to reply to me. Apparently, he didn't, because he shook his head and walked out. I was about to sit down when he rushed back in.

"You are such a hardheaded female. I wanted you close to me with no pressure. I thought we had plenty of time to court and get to know each other better before our son was born. I want you with me, Aoroia, in my life and in my heart. Is that too much to ask?"

I walked over to him, wrapped my arms around his waist, and held him for the longest time.

"Aoroia, why is my shirt wet?"

I stepped back realizing that I was leaking. "I think it is time to feed our son. I don't have any clothes here; do you think you could find me some?"

"I brought some of your clothes here earlier because I wanted you to stay a few days with me. You should have everything you require in the cabinet in the corner."

"Could you get a message to Layla for me?"

"I will have Daegorth do it; they seem to know him better. What do you need?"

"I need some breast pads to stop the colostrum and milk from leaking through more of my shirts, and I need diapers for the baby unless you have a better idea?"

"I am trying to remember what we used for Luna when she was little. Make a list, and I will have Daegorth get what you need as soon as possible."

"Thank you. I am going to go change and feed the baby. We do need to come up with a name for him, though. Do you have anything special that you would want to use?"

"Let me get this taken care of for you, and then we will talk about it. Do you want anything to drink or eat while I am out?"

"I will just take some water for now. I am supposed to go see my father and brothers, and I would rather go on an empty stomach. Will you do me a favor, love?"

"What is that?"

"Will you kiss me and hold me for a moment longer?"

He took two steps and was right in front of me. He lifted my chin up with his fingers and slowly grazed his lips across mine. He pulled me in close as he dipped me back and took full advantage of my mouth. His tongue played delightfully with mine. It was a good thing I could heal my body quickly. I was feeling quite playful. He helped me to stand back up straight. I just stood there in a euphoric state.

"Ow, ow, ow!"

"What is going on, Aoroia?"

"I think our son decided to get his own breakfast. I am not ready for this."

I opened my shirt and sure enough, he was busy suckling. I looked up and Dhareyin was watching with lust in his eyes. "Hey, my eyes are up here, big guy. We will talk about that look in your eyes after we have taken care of everything."

I watched him walk away full of pride. Truth be told, I loved to watch him walk. He had the sexiest ass and the longest legs. It was conjuring up some delicious images in my mind. I was clenching and reacting in places that were not ready.

It didn't take much time before the baby was fed and I had my clothes changed. Dhareyin seemed to be taking longer than I expected. I was about to doze off when he blasted into the room.

"What is going on? And don't wake the baby."

"Somehow the tribe found out that MoraKat tried to kill Luna and Ramsey. They say that your father is a traitor for mating with a human. They are looking for Dr. Roxanne to bring her here. They want to punish MoraKat for her crimes. She is part human; we cannot allow this to happen. What do we do, Aoroia?"

"I destroyed the wall, so they cannot use that. What else would they try to use?"

"They are erecting a whipping pole in the center of the village. They will strap her to that and give her one hundred whacks with the cat-o'-nine-tails."

"What is that? I have never heard of it."

"It is pretty bad and can cause intense pain. The way it is made and used, it can cut the skin as well. It is brutal, Aoroia, and I don't know if her human body can withstand that type of brutality."

"Are they going to charge my father as well? What about Dr.

Roxanne? Did they not learn their lesson?"

"I don't know. Right now, they are after MoraKat. Somebody has gotten them all riled up."

"Can you take our son and burp him so I can go use the restroom?"

I handed little man to his daddy. He crawled up on Dhareyin's shoulder and allowed his daddy to burp him.

"Aoroia, come check this out," he said with a chuckle.

I walked back out and Dhareyin was pointing at his chest. Our son had found a spot to rest on his chest. He became a part of him just like he did with me. A significant relief came over me. It made my decision that much more straightforward, now that I knew that Dhareyin could protect him as well.

15

I could watch Dhareyin with his son all day long but right now saving my sister was my top priority.

"Let's go see what is going on, and hopefully we can do something about it."

We walked out into the courtyard at the center of the village. My sister was stripped naked and chained to a pole in the center of town. I could feel her humiliation and fear. She was so scared you could see that she had peed down her legs and it was dribbling on the ground.

"Stay here with our son. If I don't come back, you know how to take care of him. You have done it once, and you can do it again. Watch over him, because he is something special."

"What are you talking about?" he said as he reached to bring me back. I stopped turned around and looked deeply into his eyes.

"I love you, Dhareyin, and please don't forget to tell our son about me," I said as I walked away with my shoulders held high.

I walked straight to MoraKat. I put my forehead to hers. "It will be fine, dear sister. I will not let anyone hurt you." I started to undo her chains when I was stopped by the guards. With one flick of my hand, they were flung up against the stone wall behind me. I undid the chains and held her in my arms.

"How dare you go against our rules?"

"I dare because they are outdated laws and rules. If one is to be punished here, it should be my father. He knew better. Why should

MoraKat be punished for her parents' mistakes?"

"Well, give us her mother, and we will punish the mother."

"What about my father?"

"No, we will not punish him."

"Then you will not punish the mother, either."

"If we do not get the mother, then the girl must answer for her parents' crimes."

"If that is how you feel, then I will take her place."

"Aoroia, NO!" I could hear Dhareyin yelling at me.

I was hoping that my father would step forward and take his punishment. That did not happen as they stripped and chained me to the pole. I knew if I could withstand Daegorth ripping me apart, then I could handle this. It would be brutal, but I would take it to prove the laws of this tribe had been broken. I was meant to show that to them. I made sure that I was present and aware. I chose to be here taking this punishment for another. I wasn't sure why this was important, but I knew deep down this had to happen for what came next.

I settled my eyes on Dhareyin, and it helped me to focus. When the first strike hit my back, it took my breath away. Each hit after brought a new intensity that shook me to my core. I could feel blood running down my back. They didn't just aim for my back; they hit my buttocks and my legs. I was starting to believe that my tribe of people enjoyed inflicting pain. I might have to do something about that.

I refused to cry out as the tails were ripping my flesh apart. I would not give them the satisfaction. Between each strike, I would take a deep breath and anchor into Gaia even deeper. I could feel Dhareyin crying, and the anger he was carrying was terrifying.

One hundred lashes from this thing seemed a bit much. They had no intention of her surviving this beating. I would have to remember that when they were done.

"Mistress, I am right here. Let me rip them apart," Daegorth whispered in my ear.

"No, Daegorth. Something needs to change, and I plan to do just that. I could get free at any time. I am not some helpless female."

"I know this, Mistress. I am sorry if that is what you thought I was saying. I want you to know I am here if you need me."

What came next, I did not expect. A mighty dragon swooped in and stood guard over me. He proceeded to blow flames all the way around me, protecting me from the guards' next lash. His roar was so mighty that it cracked the sound barrier. I could feel this excruciating pain coming from him. I watched as Dhareyin walked up and undid my chains. He held me in his arms, and I could feel his tears dripping on my naked shoulders. "Not too tight, love; it is pretty sore back there."

He turned me around and looked at what they had done. I could see the anger and revenge in his eyes. "I need to address the tribe. Let me go for a moment, and then we will go somewhere together. I am not sure I want anything to do with my father after this."

I walked up to the dragon and put my hand upon him and leaned against him. "Thank you, my dear friend," I whispered to him.

"Do you not know me, Mother?" He looked me straight in the eyes, and what I saw was pure love and protection.

I looked back at Dhareyin and pointed to his eyes. The look of shock and surprise on his face was understandable. How was it possible that our baby, born a few hours ago, was the biggest dragon I had ever seen?

I stood before the crowd of people who had decided to take matters into their own hands.

"What has transpired here today will not ever happen again. I am ordering that all means of punishment be banned until further notice. You are taking justice into your own hands without council from your leaders. We do not work alone. We work together and with the Council of Magick."

"Who are you to even be addressing us? Some human hybrid who is a busy body trying to do her good work."

My son looked at me with confusion. "I haven't had time to take care of anything. There has been way too much going on," I whispered to him.

"I was born to this tribe. I am Aoroia, daughter of Raffen and Dominya. I was given to the humans to live by my mother." I allowed myself to transform into my natural form. "You all know this. You were all here when Luna was trying to kill Dr. Roxanne. Why do you refuse to believe what is right in front of you?"

"You speak blasphemy. You died when you were younger and your mother soon after. She died of a broken heart. How dare you bring a dragon? They have been extinct, and we will make this one as well."

My son opened his mouth and spewed ice and buried them with it. The only thing that stood out was their heads. "I am Jaren, the Dragon King. Aoroia is my mother and you will treat her with the respect that she is owed. The time has come for HER to return, and we must put our time to good use cleaning up our magickal world."

He took me by the hand and brought me around to face him. "Oh, my beautiful boy, I didn't get much time with you, did I? How is it possible that you have evolved this much in such a short span of time?"

"No, we didn't get much time together. As far as being born a few hours ago means nothing in the magickal world. Anything is possible with magick. Besides, we all have our purpose here, and it is urgent that I start fulfilling mine. HER return is coming faster than we realized and we must be ready. I have been waiting for you to accept your purpose so I could be created and born. I love you, Mother. It is time you accept your throne and your crown."

He pulled a crystalline seed the size of a golf ball out of his cheek. He said a few words to Gaia, and she opened for him. He gave Gaia the seed and blew fire upon it so it could sprout. Gaia closed over it as soon as the sprout sprang forth.

"Father, we could use your help here."

Dhareyin walked forward and stood before our son. "How can I help?"

"You are a water dragon, and I need you to produce water for this precious and priceless seed I have planted. Will you accept this honor, Father?"

Dhareyin started to water the ground where the seed was. What came forth was magnificent. At first, it looked like a tree. It was so much more than that. A crystalline throne big enough for two was being born right in front of us. It did not stop at the throne. It created a massive interconnecting floor and walls, ceilings, and a roof. A mansion fit for a goddess was being designed right in front of us.

It encapsulated the whole village and town with the throne right in the center of our home. The tree became the lifeblood of the entire place. It was as if you could see the walls breathing. I was watching the members of the tribe, and they were confused.

"You have been waiting a long time for the prophecy to be fulfilled. What I built here is for my Mother Goddess and Father Shaman and Chieftain. As you can see, there will no longer be those in charge of their clans. Later we will set up a governing board that consists of tribal members from each clan and the Council of Magick. For now, know that your homes are within this mansion. They have all been updated, and you will all continue to live together as one big happy family. It is time to crown my mother and father. Please take a seat on the ground." He waited for everyone to be seated.

"Mother, please step forward. On this day I crown thee Aoroia, goddess of destruction and renewal. Father, please step forward. Today I crown thee Dhareyin, God shaman and chieftain of the Heart Tribe. Mother, you will rule this tribe with all the compassion and empathy you have learned from the humans and all the strength and conviction you have learned through your many experiences. Father, you will rule alongside Mother. You will not only see to the spiritual needs of our people, but you are chieftain now. You and Mother must rule together with balance and harmony, for your alignment was created in the stars long before you came here."

I could feel something strange happening to my body. I could feel all the tattoos showing up on my skin. My transformation was taking place, and I was not looking like the tribe anymore. The crown was forming on my head. I knew it would be one that could not be taken off.

"Please, both of you, sit upon your thrones."

We both sat down, and the crowns took full form. Out of the top of our heads came a crystalline cellular structure that looked like a mix of big tree branches, leaves, and antlers. The crystal was a rainbow prism, and it contained all colors from the light end to the dark end of the color spectrum. They were a part of our heads. We could call them forth or allow them to return to the tattoos on our bodies. They were the biggest ones we had.

There seemed to be a strange commotion at the back of the room. "NO! You cannot do this. The crown and all of this is mine and was always mine. You cannot give this to her she does not belong here."

I could not help but feel so many things when I realized who was screaming from the back of the room. I didn't know how she was doing what she was doing, but I was completely taken back by her words. Everything that she had ever said and done was making more sense to me now. I could feel my heart shattering and coming back together over and over, fusing together with liquid crystalline rainbow. I maintained my outer composure, but my inner equilibrium was a mess. I knew that what was taking place within me was supposed to happen, but that did not make the hurt go away. Her words continued to fester inside of me like a thorn under the skin. I knew at some point this thorn was going to surface, and the damage it could cause concerned me. I noticed Dhareyin was watching me, and I could see why. The fire in me was surfacing, and the walls of the mansion were beginning to crack.

I looked straight at her. My father and brothers were all standing there with their mouths wide open.

"If you believe this throne is yours, then you must come forward and claim it," I said uneasily as I watched her saunter her way forward.

"Mother, you do not have to do this, the throne has always been yours. That is why my process had to be stepped up. It was time for you to claim it, and you have done so beautifully. You cannot give this away."

"Jaren, my love. I know this to be true, but she believes it is hers to claim. What comes after is the consequences of her choices. I am neutral in this decision, but it is one that has to be made."

He took a step to the side and watched puzzled. She was getting stronger with every step she took toward me. I was not afraid of what might happen when she reached me. I knew that no matter what took place, I would always have myself and the child I bore.

"You are a stupid girl. Do you know what you have done? When I claim my crown and throne, I will destroy you and everyone you have ever loved. I will take away everything you have earned in agony and destroy you never to exist again."

"If only you knew me better, Mother, you would know that your threats do not frighten me. Step forward to claim your throne and crown."

She stepped forward with arrogance fed by her lust for power.

"Kneel before me."

"NEVER!"

"I cannot give you your crown if you are not willing to bow before me. It is your choice."

She slowly dropped to her knees and bowed before me. I removed the crown from my head. I stood next to her ready to place it upon her head. I held it high above my head and looked out to the people, and I spoke.

"She has chosen to step forward to claim a throne and crown believed to be hers. Who am I to get in the way of another's legacy? I place this crown upon her head, and we will let the crown decide who is the rightful heir. Dominya, do you accept that the crown will choose its rightful heir?"

"Yes. It has always been mine. That is why I got rid of you. People would be blinded by the little things that stood out in you that I didn't have. I have known I was the one to fulfill the prophecy since I was a small girl and Dhareyin's father showed me the scroll.

Yes, Dhareyin, your father knew I was the one that was spoken about in the prophecy. He made Aoroia's death as a child look real."

I placed the crown upon her head, and she started to change in front of me. I was a bit surprised as she took shape and the crown seemed to be accepting her. It was filling her even more with power lust.

"Every one of you is a fool. I have been working on you all from the other realms to turn you against humans. I was shown by your father, Daegorth, how to make your process slip up so that I could be more powerful on the other side. You thought you had tricked me, but I always maintained the upper hand. I put a blinding spell on Daegorth so he couldn't find you or remember you. I turned Daegorth against himself and his nature. I put a curse on him to make him believe that he enjoyed killing and that he had done it many times, when in fact he didn't. Ramsey and Luna were so easy to turn. I have been working on her since she was a little girl. I reached out to everyone in your life and turned them against you or helped them to leave you, Aoroia. I have always hated that name," she whispered under her breath.

"The child borne from my husband's loins with a human was easy to manipulate. When I take control, I will see to it that MoraKat will be flayed over and over until she no longer exists, and her human mother with her. Can you not feel my power? Reaching into the human realm was so delicious. Manipulating greedy humans to dump toxic waste in the forest was easy. Then to find out that my daughter was the one over toxic removal was the cherry on top of the cake. We hide under the ground in other dimensions when we should be ruling humans." She looked at me defiantly. "It gave me great pleasure in turning you over to people who would destroy you. I never wanted you and I have hated you since you were born. Your father forced me to keep you, and the first chance I got, I threw you away like the piece of worthless trash that you are. I have hated you since the day you were born."

Dhareyin reached out to take my hand and reassure me that he was there for me. I could tell that he wasn't sure what was going to happen. Did this mean he would have to rule next to her?

"The great part of all of this was watching you two fall in love with each other. I put so much doubt in his mind that you could never really touch base. The one time you copulated and brought this monstrosity forth was out of irritation and anger. I found it interesting that I could never put doubt in your mind, Aoroia. So, I put more in his, and it worked wonderfully. The delicious part of all was turning Daegorth and the gory things he did to you, and then to watch you accept him by your side after all of that was deliciously hideous. You, my daughter, are a monster. You are ugly, and there is something seriously wrong with you. I will enjoy taking Dhareyin to my bed and showing him what a real female can do to a man-beast. I will rule over him like I will over all of you. I may just keep you alive long enough to watch it all. It will give me great pleasure knowing you will never have each other. I will bear the children meant for you both and I will take great care in turning them against humans. When I fully take the throne, we will rise above and rule over them. They will become our servants. We will do what we want with them. I will start with your two lady friends, Ginger and Liz. Next will come your ex-husband Rex. Mark, Matt, Matilda, and Griff will all rue the day they decided to help you. They will know what true pain really is just for knowing you. The yummiest part of all will be Daegorth. It was not hard to turn his mind before, and I can do it again."

I could see the power surging through her, and she was enjoying herself deeply. There was so much anger and hatred inside of her toward humans that she had no qualms about using her own people. I was not afraid for myself or my child. I knew he could take care of himself. I realized that no matter what Daegorth was turned into, I could handle it. I had before, and I was better for it.

A sadness was creeping into my bones about Dhareyin. I knew he loved me, and yet I felt like he was pushing me away—and now I understand why. There was something in me that wanted to see where it would take us, no matter the result. It enraged me that she used her powers in such a manner. After all the things I had experienced in my life, I recognized that we were all guilty of manipulating people because we were hurting. Sometimes we do not realize what we are doing until it blows up in our faces. I know there have been plenty of times since I came into my power where it rode me for a while. No matter what would happen to me, I was grateful for everything that I had been through and where it had brought me. My most significant accomplishment was my child!

I was disgusted and hurt by the idea that I gave her the reins to unleash hell on humans. If the crown chose her, what would be the outcome of all this hatred and anger? What would happen when HER return was upon us?

"Can you not all see that I was meant to rule? I can feel the power surging through me. The crown and the throne have accepted me. It is coursing through my entire being. Do you have anything to say, Daughter, before I take your place?"

I thought long and hard about what I wanted to say—what I always wanted to tell her but never felt right in saying it.

"For whatever reason, I was brought back into your life, Mother, I am happy. I feel blessed that we have had an opportunity several times to chat and get to know each other. Whatever it is that you think you must do to me, I accept. I know that even though you could torture the ones I love and me, I am grateful you gave birth to me. I am even thankful that you threw me away."

"What is this? You are so weak; I don't know how you thought the crown and throne would accept you. I don't know why I ever thought you could be in competition with me?"

"Most importantly, Mother, I want you to know that I love you!"
"WEAKNESS!"

Her voice was getting louder and stronger. "This power is breathtaking. I should have embraced it years ago."

You could hear the energy snapping in the air. It was crackling and everyone's hair was standing on end. You could see it coursing through her body and it was becoming transparent.

"YES, YES, YES!" she exclaimed with such intensity. "NO, NO, NO," were her last words as she exploded into a million pieces. Fragments of her went everywhere. Her particles were like fine dust and they were airborne. The only smell that hung in the air was brought on by all the electricity and power. You could see little tiny sparks floating midair.

I was so wrapped up in what was happening around me that I wasn't paying attention to the heaviness upon my head. I reached up, and the crown sat firm and stable upon my head.

Jaren stood up and blew his icy breath across the air, causing all the particles to freeze and fall to the ground. He gathered her up and waited to give her remains to Daegorth for safekeeping. There was no reason anyone else had to breathe in my mother ever again. I must ask myself if I knew what would happen to my mother, and I cannot answer that at this moment. Daegorth appeared at my side as my hellhound who would always, from this day forward, transform back and forth. My Jaren would rule his own kingdom as the Dragon King who was man and beast. Dhareyin would rule by my side for an eternity because we were immortal. I imagined there would be many more children to come.

As my inner dialogue was coming to an end, I became a witness to a miracle. Instead of my people retaking their seats, they all went to their knees in front of Dhareyin and me. I stood before them, humbled that they had finally accepted me.

"Please take your seats. What we have witnessed here today was a true tragedy for us all. The emergence of the prophecy fulfillment has been a long time in the making. I apologize to you all for the misunderstandings and harm that have resulted in its fruition. I wish to speak to you today from my heart. I never knew my mother, and that saddens me. The hatred and disgust she carried for me I feel to my core. Even though my time was short getting to know my own son, I could not imagine feeling such things for my child. I hope that we have all learned a powerful lesson here today about hatred and anger for another species and those within our tribe." I took a deep breath as I stepped out into the crowd.

"If there is one thing that I have learned from the humans, it is that LOVE is the most powerful thing we can feel—love for ourselves and for others. I hope that we can all forgive my mother for her offenses against us all. In this realm and the human realm, I have seen what we can do to each other. None of us are without offense against another. We are done here today. Dhareyin and I would love to meet with all the clan leaders in the next few days. Please go spend time with your loved ones. There will be no communal feast tonight. Enjoy your time with your families and reflect on how lucky we all are. Just know I love you all, and I look forward to meeting each one of you."

I looked at all the love around me, and my heart was filled. Dhareyin was holding my hand, and Daegorth was at my side. Jaren was staring at me with wonder in his eyes.

"Mother, I love you. Thank you for who you are," he proclaimed as he transformed into the most handsome man I have seen. He looked like a mix of Dhareyin, Daegorth and my father. He was tall, burly, masculine, and stable. He had dark hair almost the color of a raven. His eyes were that beautiful electric blue, and they had depth to them. "If you ever need me, call for me, and I will be there. I must go for now, but we are always connected by our hearts. Keep your cabin in the woods special for Father and yourself. Daegorth and I have things that we need to chat about. I will leave you both for now."

As he transformed back into the beautiful dragon, my heart was full of love. Daegorth stepped forward and stood in front of me. "Mistress, I must go for now. I am always at your beck and call and a portal away. I will be watching you and your special family. Here are your mother's remains. I have placed them in a protective box so she cannot escape. My suggestion would be to delete her completely. I know that decision is yours to make, but I need you to understand she can come back. There is some form of black magick attached to her particles, and you are all protected from that, but BEWARE."

He handed the box to me and left with Jaren. I turned to Dhareyin and without words, he took my hand, opened a portal, and we were gone to places unknown. There was something new flowing within him, and his energies were open like they were the night we met for the first time. We came out at my home in the forest. He led me down the path illuminated by fireflies and pixies. They all bowed before us. He brought me into the open meadow by my pond. It was all lit up. So many incredible colors were cascading over all surfaces, and the delicious smells in the air lightly kissed the senses.

He stood still, let go of my hand, and stepped forward two steps. "Close your eyes, my love."

I could hear him doing something and I was intrigued. "You can open your eyes, Star."

I opened my eyes and what I saw before me sent tears tumbling down my cheeks. There was a place on the ground that was made into an enormous bed. I could tell that it was not an actual mattress, but Gaia fluffed up and her comfort laid out before me. On the table next to the makeshift bed was a picnic basket and the tribe's specialty alcohol he had told me about. I could feel the tears dripping slowly off my chin. I was so happy and joyful inside. This was the Dhareyin that I knew was under all that doubt. I knew that he was mine and I was his and that our LOVE would be grand. When we both accepted our crowns and the throne, we were instantly married to each other for an eternity.

"Why are you crying, Star?"

"Why do you keep calling me Star, when that was only a disguise to hide from Daegorth?"

"I know when we met you told me your name was Dabney. Later, I found out you were going under the name Star. Then when I took you down below, I knew that your true name was Aoroia. For me, the name Star stood out because of how brightly you shine, my love. You shimmered your light right into my heart. I was full of doubt and I didn't know why. That light of yours was as bright as a magnificent star, and I couldn't get enough of you. Even when you kept coming at me from your dark place, you were all bright and shiny to me. If you want, I can call you Aoroia, but in my heart you will always be STAR to me!"

I ran to him and jumped into his arms. I wrapped my legs around his waist and started kissing him all over his face. "I have never felt so loved and cherished in my life, except for the day that you placed our son upon my chest. I have waited for you to share your heart with me. Your words astound my heart and make it pound with giddiness."

He took me over to the bed and laid me down gently. He removed my shoes and then my clothes. I was lying there exposed to the world. I watched him slowly take his clothes off, and what I could remember from the first time we were together there was something that had changed in his demeanor and body. He had many new tattoos and writing on his body. It looked like different signs and symbols from runes to many forms of tribal. He was standing there erect and waiting. "Do I have your attention, Aoroia, my bright Star?" he asked me with lust in his eyes.

"You do now," I said with a purr in my voice.

He came down on top of me. He made it a point to go slow with me this time. He kissed me all over, inspecting every inch of my body. It was like he was memorizing it. He rolled me over slowly kissing the side of my neck, breast, and sides all the way down my hips and legs. He rolled me onto my back, and there was not a place that was not touched by his lips. Once he was done with my back, he turned me onto my other side and kissed me up and down until I was so hot and bothered, I thought I would melt into a puddle.

There was something about using Gaia as a bed. I could feel my energy being renewed over and over. I knew that I was in for an eventful night with Dhareyin. He slowed his roll and for just a moment he held me cocooned into his side. He was kissing my back and neck and fondling all my lovely bits.

"You are more beautiful than I ever knew anyone could be," he whispered softly in my ear. "You take my breath away, Star."

I rolled onto my side facing him. Our legs were intertwined, and we just stared into each other's eyes. He rubbed his thumb lightly across my lower lip. "Your face is so tiny, compared to my hands. Do you know how much I love you?"

"I have a pretty good idea, but why don't you tell me in your own words."

"You know how big the universe is? I love you a quadrillion times, more than that. I have never felt such LOVE in my life. It feels so exhilarating and yet terrifying all in one. I think I understand now why she could instill such doubt in me."

"Why is that?"

"There was already doubt there about you. I have been around some incredible beings of light, but you, my love, outshine them all. The love that you were sending my way, I couldn't even fathom. I didn't know how to accept it let alone invite it in. Thank heavens our hearts don't listen to us because I started to develop these feelings for you that I did not understand. My question is—how could you love me so quickly when you knew nothing about me?"

"I have had many experiences with love. It was one of the benefits of living among humans. When I first met you, my heart saw something in you that it could not forget. It wasn't always easy when you would say judgmental things to me. I couldn't deny my heart any longer. I hoped beyond measure that you would finally see me and what I had to offer you. I cannot even put into words what I feel about you. Your smell drives me wild, and your body makes me think naughty thoughts. Sometimes when you are around, it is hard to catch my breath or even focus."

He brought his lips to mine. He started out slow and gentle, increasing the intensity with every movement. Before long, our tongues were intertwined in this pleasurable erotic dance. He had one hand on my buttocks, grinding against me slow, then fast. I lifted my knee and opened myself to him. He slowly plunged inside of me, rolling onto his back, bringing me on top of him. I sat up with a wicked grin on my face. We were rising and falling in motion with each other. At first, he put his hands behind his neck and let me do all the work. He watched me intensely. I leaned forward and nibbled his bottom lip, kissing him slowly and reaching up and biting his ear lobe. I sat back slowly, taking him in, and just when I could feel him about to thrust forward, I would sit up again. He got this wicked lusty grin on his face as he reached over and placed both of his hands high up on my thighs. He reached over with his thumb and found my delicate sweet spot. He rubbed slowly and then fast, and he kept doing this until my movements were matching his.

"OMG, OMG," I screamed as my release shattered through me, soaking us both and filling his belly button with my release. I lay down on his chest, stretching my legs out alongside his. I started rocking back and forth slowly. I sat up on my hands as my movements became more deliberate, allowing my hips to take him in. He looked at me with mystery in his eyes. His orgasm was getting ready to rock through him when his eyes rolled back in his head and he hollered out in unison with his release. I lay back down on his chest and couldn't help but bask in the glow. I shifted to my side and put my head in the crook of his arm.

"Where did you learn to do that?"

"I have my secrets, handsome."

He let out a hearty laugh. We held each other for the longest time in silence, feeling our way through the moment we shared.

"Can I ask you something, my love?"

"Ask me anything you want, Dhareyin. I am an open book!"

"I have had something on my mind since earlier today."

"What is that?"

"When will you let Ramsey and Luna out?" he asked carefully.

"We are ruling our tribe together, and I wanted to discuss this with you. How do you feel since my mother isn't controlling you anymore?"

"I suppose I feel better. There is some lingering doubt there, but not as much as before. It is not that I doubt you, it is doubt itself!"

"With her being in the box, I think we should be careful about how we reach out to them. I don't want to erase from their minds what they did. I want them to remember and to understand what they are capable of. I feel like we must make sure that there is not some form of residue left over that could be easily ignited if she escaped. That means checking out you and Daegorth as well. We must find my old boss and all the people at the Bureau. I don't think it would hurt to check everyone. What do you think, Dhareyin, my love?"

"I think you will be a wise ruler of our people. What you say makes sense and I don't ever want to be under her control again. Do you still hate my daughter?"

"I never hated her, Dhareyin. My heart was hurt due to her treatment of me. I now know that she was under some form of influence, but there had to be a small piece of her that struggles with humans for her to be turned into what she was. I don't know if I will ever be able to trust her again, but we will see what happens when she is not under the influence of others. I love her not just because of the friendship we developed, but because she is yours."

"I can understand that. How do you trust Daegorth after what he put you through?"

"When he started ripping me apart the second time, I got to see something in him that changed something within me. It wasn't just what had been done to him but who he really was at his core. There was something more there that was not being allowed to shine. When I flayed him wide open and feasted upon him, something changed within me. I realized what I was capable of, and it was so freeing. Do you want to know what the biggest thing for me was? When he protected my special family without my asking him to do so. He was protecting them for me because he knew that would make me happy and allow me to do the job I needed to do."

"Did you enjoy making love to him?"

"Are you sure you want to know?" I asked as he shook his head, pensive about what I would say. "What is between Daegorth and me is hard to explain. I have yet to understand it completely. When you do something to someone else that is so primal, it brings something animalistic out in you. What Daegorth and I shared was mind-blowing and free. I love him and I will always protect him because he has always been mine. To be honest, had you continued down your path and kept pushing me away, I would have taken him as my lover. There is something that gets sparked between the two of us that allows me to be my true self without judgment."

"I have been pretty judgmental of you, and I am sorry. It does smart some that you would take him for a lover, but I get it. What the two of you shared was raw and intense. The night the destroyer came out and you slashed me, I had a hard time keeping my animal at peace. I wanted us to consume each other, but I was not ready. A passion so strong fills both of us, and it would be incredible to unleash that and experience it with each other."

"I love how you think, Dhareyin. Open a portal and take me to galaxies far away. Make love to me on the moon and let me bask in the heat and brightness of the sun. I will travel to different worlds and universes with you. Until then, we have many things that we have to take care of before HER arrival."

"I will take you anywhere. Right now, we need to figure out what the spiral wording means that just showed up around your belly button."

We both looked at the writing:

She is air, water, earth, and fire. Her dreams can be catastrophic and metamorphic. She is next to awaken. Send help her way, or all will be lost!

"What do you suppose that means, Dhareyin?"

"I don't know, but it looks like we are headed for our next adventure," he said as he picked me up and dove into the water, along the way transforming into his water dragon and taking me to depths and worlds unknown!

Also by
BELLA RAYNE

Darkest Betrayals

I had never felt such a dark presence before in my life, but there was one here tonight. I stepped toward her to see who it was; my curiosity got the best of me. Even though I wasn't sure what she meant to do, I knew she meant to do me some sort of harm. The hair on the back of my neck was at attention, and I was covered in cold sweat and goosebumps; my primal instincts flaring wildly. She charged at me like a crazed animal, and as we struggled, my bracelet broke into many pieces. I could hear them bouncing like little hard balls across the wooden floor. As the struggle got more physical and enraged, I felt an intense pain in my left side below my rib cage. I felt an increasing dampness where the pain came from. I looked down in horror as I saw blood soaking through my gown. I heard a scream that sounded surreal and realized I was the one making that noise! I could smell blood and I could taste it. I was choking on my blood with every scream. I realized she was tugging at me, and I wasn't coherent enough to register just exactly what it was that she had done! Then she was gone like a ghost in the night. I could hear footsteps and hollers in the corridor, responding to my screaming. I knew I had to hold on, so I could tell someone what happened to me. I knew that I didn't have much time to say goodbye to my dad and my love. "Hold on, Aeryana, hold on!" I could hear someone saying to me, as I left my body! As I snapped out of this vision like dream state in a cold sweat terrified at what I just observed, the panic seemed hell bent on consuming me. What the hell did I just witness and who is Aeryana?" Layla asked herself as the panic took over.

Learn more at:
www.outskirtspress.com/darkestbetrayals

CPSIA information can be obtained
at www.ICGtesting.com
Printed in the USA
LVHW040754100520
655288LV00001B/63